CONTUSION

OFELIA MARTINEZ

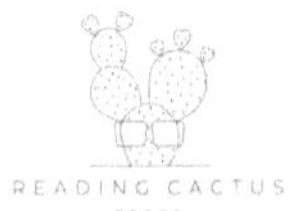
READING CACTUS
PRESS

READING CACTUS
PRESS

Library of Congress Control Number: 2021911212

First Edition

ISBN 978-1-954906-07-5 (hardcover)

ISBN 978-1-954906-03-7 (paperback)

ISBN 978-1-954906-08-2 (eBook)

CONTUSION

To Rob, for always going out of your way to make me laugh.
Thank you for setting the bar so high for all my fictional leading men.

AUTHOR'S NOTE

This is a love story between Valentina and Rory. This is not a story about cancer. Specific treatment and symptom details have been omitted because I want the reader to focus on the love story.

Every cancer patient's journey is different. I am not an expert, and Valentina's specific case and the clinical trial depicted in this novel are entirely fictional.

In the United States, the National Breast and Cervical Cancer Early Detection Program assists uninsured women with free cancer screening services. You can learn more about eligibility at www.cdc.gov/cancer/nbccedp/.

CHAPTER 1

It's either the machine or me. *You are going down,* I telepathically warn the vending contraption holding my Pop-Tart hostage. I've never had a Pop-Tart in my life, but I haven't eaten all day, and *hangry* Valentina Almonte . . . well, let's just say even inanimate objects wouldn't want to meet her. "I train with two-hundred-and-fifty-pound men, so you better give it soon," I mutter under my breath as I think about my coach, Chema. Chema, who didn't know where I was and was probably worried. Two-hundred-and-fifty-pound Chema, who I have only been able to wrestle to the ground once. I should call him today, but not until I eat. Chema isn't fond of hangry Valentina either. I shake the vending machine as discreetly as possible.

I'm getting ready to start kicking the thing when someone clears their throat nearby to grab my attention. I turn and am faced with a red-headed, freckled man who has about four inches on my five-foot-five frame. I stare with surprise at the handsome stranger with piercing green eyes. His nose and cheekbones are chiseled like a Roman marble statue. I've never seen a red-headed person this close before, and I've always been a sucker for bearded smart guys. He wears glasses, so he has to be smart. That's the rule, right? Yet there is something manly about him, starting with his short beard and solidifying with a surprisingly deep voice considering his slender frame.

"Here," he says, extending two dollar bills my way.

"Um, it's okay," I say, self-conscious about the last remnants of my Spanish accent that I was never quite able to shake off.

"Please," he insists. "I'm afraid for its life." He points to the vending machine and smirks as he extends the bills my way again.

I cock my head to the side, unsure I should accept—my brain misfiring at what to say to this handsome stranger—when he sweeps past me to insert the bills into the machine. His arm brushes mine, and I jump back like I am dodging a strike from my opponent.

"What was it?" he asks and smiles broadly.

I point to the lopsided pastry package dangling from a corner caught on the claw of the feeding coil. "The Pop-Tart," I say. This is so embarrassing. I finally meet someone in the U.S., someone handsome, and he is buying out my hostage snack.

When the snack drops, he bends down to grab my prize, and I don't check out his ass. Not one little bit. But if I had, which I didn't, I'd have to admit it is quite a fine ass in that light-colored denim.

"Are you waiting for family?" he asks, handing me the Pop-Tart.

I look around nervously at the nearly empty waiting area. I'm not ready to tell anyone, even a stranger, so I shrug and change the subject instead. "Thanks, um—what's your name?"

"You betcha. I'm Rory," he says, and his smile extends to his eyes. He offers his hand, and I take it in mine.

"Valentina. Nice to meet you."

He adjusts the backpack strap over his shoulder, and I wonder if he is a college student because he has to be in his early twenties. "Valentina," he tries out the name in his mouth. "That's pretty. I don't think I know any Valentinas."

Except for the salsa, I think. "It's Mexican," I say abruptly.

"Is that where you're from? Mexico?"

I nod. "Well, thanks again for the snack. I appreciate it."

I'm walking toward my spot in the waiting room when he calls out after me. "Anytime. And take it easy on the equipment, tiger."

Sitting in my chair, I track the fiery-haired Rory as he leaves the waiting area. I slump back in my seat and open the silvery package—my stomach groans at the sound, and my mouth waters. I had seen Pop-Tarts on American television many times, but by the time I was old enough to travel north, I was already in training.

My rigorous training included a strict food plan that was gluten-free, sugar-free, dairy-free, and all the other trendy '-frees' that coach Chema could throw my way. I had fought it at the time, but he'd refused to train me if I wouldn't agree to follow his rules to a T.

Chema is a coveted mixed martial arts coach, and I wasn't about to pass up the opportunity to train with him, so I promised I would stay on the food plan if he would train me. He has coached me since I was sixteen, and after eight years of training, he's more like an older brother than a coach.

If he could see me now, about to eat a gluten-full, sugar-full, dairy-full atomic snack, I'd be doing push-ups for days in punishment. I smile and take a healthy bite. My face contorts, and my nose scrunches up. Maybe I should have taken baby steps with the sugar after eight years without.

Yes. Eight years with no sugar. It wasn't a sacrifice. Well, it had been at first, but it was one I was more than willing to make if it meant I could one day get to the UFC.

I only manage to eat half of one Pop-Tart before I have to throw it out, completely *empalagada,* and I wonder what the

English word is for that sickening over-sugared nauseous sensation. The search engine on my phone has no answers, and I let it go.

"Valentina Almonte," a young woman calls out, and I follow her through two sets of doors until we settle in a small office.

"Please take a seat," she says with a warm smile.

This woman has to be close to my age, and I find myself relaxing a little at the familiarity.

"I'm Amanda. You can call me Mandy. We spoke on the phone."

"Yes. I remember. You did the eligibility questionnaire when I first signed up for the clinical trial."

"Exactly. I'm Dr. Ramirez's research assistant." She smiles again and splits her attention between my face and her computer screen as she reads my medical chart.

"I have to confirm information you have already given."

"Okay," I say. I squeeze my hands into fists and relax them, repeating the motion several times. I follow my calming technique with deep breaths as I prepare for what's next.

"Please state your full name."

"Valentina Almonte."

"Age?"

"Twenty-four."

"City of Residence."

"Well, it was Mexico City, but it will be Kansas City for the duration of the treatment as well as six months of follow-up care."

"Any changes in symptoms?"

"No symptoms other than the slight back pain I already reported."

"Has the frequency or intensity of the back pain changed in any way?"

"No. It's the same."

"I know when we spoke on the phone, you hadn't received any treatment, but have you received any treatment since?"

"No cancer treatment. No. I only take over-the-counter pain medication sometimes for my back, but not every day."

"Thank you," Mandy says. "I know it's weird because you gave all the information already, but I want to prepare you. Many doctors, nurses, and even hospital staff will have you confirm a lot of the same information over and over. Please be patient with us. It's hospital policy."

I smile reassuringly at her. "Sure," I say. "No worries."

"I do have a few concerns about your eligibility," Mandy says, and my stomach drops.

No. She can't turn me away now. This is my best shot. The only one I want to take. I can't be kicked off the clinical trial before I've even started. My mouth dries up as I try to focus on her words. I picked this trial—and Dr. Ramirez—because it is the most aggressive cervical cancer treatment anywhere, and I want to be as aggressive as possible.

"You're a very special case, and Dr. Ramirez agreed to make some exceptions for you, but I want to reiterate that this process will be very difficult. Are you sure there isn't any support system you can count on? A friend, perhaps? You'll need someone to care for you after hospitalizations and drive you when you are too sedated after appointments."

"I'll be able to hire help as needed. That sounded really stuck-up. That's the American expression, yes? Stuck-up?" Mandy nods. "I just mean I have family in Mexico who is paying for my treatment and resources while I'm here. I'll be able to hire nurses and drivers as needed, and besides, my apartment is only two blocks from here. I wouldn't compromise my eligibility into the trial. If it's money you are worried about, I understand none of my treatment is covered under the trial. Since I don't have medical insurance, I've given deposits already, but if you want, I'm happy to pay in full in advance."

Mandy's eyes soften, but I don't mind it as much as I would anyone else's sympathy. I couldn't stand Mom or Dad looking at me like that. I definitely couldn't stand Chema or my sister Pilar looking at me like that, so I keep it all to myself.

"It's more than that," Mandy says. "You'll want some emotional support."

"I don't want anyone to know. Not unless they absolutely have to—if the treatment fails."

"Okay. I'm following protocol, making sure you are going to have all the support you will need. But I'll take your word for it that you have it figured out."

"Thank you. I appreciate that. And I do. Really," I reassure her.

"Okay, then. Are you ready to meet Dr. Ramirez?"

I nod, and Mandy walks me to an exam room. I wait, shivering in the hospital gown Mandy provided before she left, until Dr. Ramirez announces her presence with a knock at the door.

"Come in," I say.

In walks a stunningly beautiful Amazon of a woman. I press my lips together to avoid gawking at her. She is tall and has muscular legs I would kill for—I can tell even through her scrub bottoms. I'm only a flyweight at one-hundred-and-twenty-five pounds, but I bet she is a bantamweight, or maybe even a featherweight, if she were a fighter. She wears a white coat over her blue scrubs. Her hair is up in a ponytail of straight dark-brown tresses that almost hit her waist, and she has the most expressive eyebrows I have ever seen on a woman.

"*Hola Valentina. Soy la doctora Ramirez. ¿Prefieres español?*"

"English is fine."

Dr. Ramirez smiles with what seems like relief. "Good. I'm Dr. Carolina Ramirez. It's a pleasure to meet you," she says. Her amber eyes hold my gaze, and I can't help but smile back. I'm already at ease.

Dr. Ramirez grabs the chair in the corner and rolls it over to sit in front of me. "I've gone over your chart, and it sounds like your case is an excellent fit for the trial," she says.

I let out a breath, feeling more reassured that I have done the right thing by coming here and seeking her out.

She finishes my physical exam and pelvic exam, and I sit up to close the gown once again. I wrap myself in the flimsy cloth that does nothing to warm my skin.

"We're retaking some images. So long as there is no change, we will be able to start treatment this week as part of the trial."

What she means by 'change' is if the cancer has progressed further. There's still a chance this could go the other way, but I nod because Dr. Ramirez's presence is somehow reassuring, and I'm feeling calmer than I thought I would.

"It's part of the trial protocol, but I have to ask again," she says. "Are you sure you understand the trial treatment is more aggressive than the standard of care, which is still an option for you at this point? This trial will take a toll on you."

"I know, doctor. I want to be as aggressive as humanly possible."

"There's one last concern I have," she says. "I'm sorry, I must insist, you are so young and with no children. You understand the radiation will more than likely render you unable to conceive naturally?"

"Yes. Mandy went over all my pre-trial plan options."

"I'm willing to wait a few weeks if you want to freeze your eggs."

"Won't we risk the cancer spreading further?"

"That is a risk. Yes. But if having children at some point is important to you, I want to make sure I'm also advocating for what you'll need to have a happy life."

I smile. She wants to make sure that if she saves my life, she's not leaving me with a miserable one. "Look," I say. "I've never given any thought to children. I may one day want children, but I don't need that child to be biological. There are many children in the world in need of good parents." I don't say that I have chosen family I love more than bloodline family. "I'll be very happy with adoption if children ever become important."

"Okay, then. Let's do this."

Four hours of waiting and several scans later, I finally get to leave the hospital. It was all cold metal, shivering, and waiting in exam rooms, but it's not my first rodeo. I already went through all of this in Mexico when I first received my diagnosis.

I stand in front of the hospital, unsure of my next steps. Less than twenty-four hours in Kansas City, and for what is probably the first time in my adult life, I don't have a schedule to keep.

Pulling out my phone, I call a car with my car service app. I ask the driver to take me to any street with multiple car dealerships, and he drops me off in front of a Ford dealership. I look down the busy boulevard, flanked by dealerships, feeling daunted at all the options. I shrug. *When in Rome . . . or in this case, America.* I walk into the Ford dealership, and a nice old man hooks me up with a used but reliable Ford sedan. I could probably afford new, but I don't want to take advantage.

I had ordered furniture to be delivered to my apartment, but it won't show up until tomorrow. Realizing I need essentials, I pull up the navigation app on my phone and roll away in my new pre-owned car. The salesman was adamant it isn't 'used.'

After shopping, it takes three trips to get all of my supplies into my new barren apartment. I was shocked at how expensive rent is in the U.S., but being close to the hospital was a priority. I opted for a two-bedroom, thinking if it came to it, I could rent out one of the rooms to offset some of my expenses. I could only ask my sister for so much money before she got suspicious. Not that she wouldn't give it in a heartbeat if I told her what was going on, but I'm not ready to tell her.

I plop on the cream duvet over the white carpet, not sure I will be able to sleep on the floor—first time for everything, I guess. Once chemo and radiation start, wine will be off-limits, so I went to town at the grocery store's liquor section.

Uncorking the bottle of merlot, I sip straight from the bottle as I sit in my dark apartment. On the second floor, the apartment faces the busier side of the street. Two restaurants and a small used bookshop sit directly below, and I wonder if they call the books 'pre-owned' too.

The coolness of the glass in the floor-to-ceiling windows soothes my skin as I press my arm against it to look down the street. There are a few bars, and it's late enough that people are starting to go inside with broad smiles and flirty looks.

It's a beautiful city, and I wish I had come here under different circumstances. Now all I will have as souvenirs will be the bitter memories of cancer treatment.

I take a long pull from the bottle of wine, not caring when some of it spills from the corners of my mouth and down my chin, splattering over the white duvet. I'll get a new one tomorrow. I press my forehead to the glass and hug the bottle to my body while I look at the lights of the city night.

My phone is on silent mode, so I don't hear it when it rings, but the bright glow in the dark apartment signals the incoming call. I block the light with one hand as I grab the phone with the other. *Pili* is displayed on the screen—my nickname for my older sister Pilar. I've called her Pili since I was four-years-old, and she's hated it ever since.

"Tini?" I hear on the other end when I pick up. I hate her nickname for me as much as she hates mine for her. We would both benefit from a truce, but we are both too stubborn.

I roll my eyes. "Hi, Pili. How are you?"

"You promised you would call me when you landed yesterday, and I never heard from you," Pilar whines.

"I'm sorry. Been busy with training and all. I was actually about to call you—"

"Sure you were," she huffs. "Well?"

"Well, what?"

"How's it going? Are you settled in? How's the new coach? Give me an update!"

I suppose as my benefactor, she deserves information. "I just got here, but yes, everything's fine," I lie. "I got my apartment keys yesterday, furniture comes tomorrow, and I've been training all day."

"Furniture tomorrow?" She yells, appalled, and I pull the phone away from my ear for a second after her shriek. "You should have stayed in a hotel until then. Do you need more money?" she asks.

"No. You've given me more than enough. Don't worry." A million dollars should cover treatment and living expenses in the U.S., shouldn't it? I couldn't ask her for more. I just couldn't, not even knowing she could spare five times that amount without batting an eye.

"You sound tired."

"Yeah, training right after a long day of flying can really take it out of you, you know?" I never lied to my sister before my diagnosis, and I am surprised at how easily it all rolls off my tongue.

"And when are you going to tell Chema?"

I wince. "Soon. I need to find the right time to—"

"The right time was when you were here. *In person*. I hate to tell you this, Tini, but you are a little shit for not being upfront with him. He deserves to know you got an agent and a new coach. You basically just ghosted him."

She isn't saying anything that isn't true about me being a shit, though nothing about the agent or coach is true—that's my cover. I rub my temples. "I know. Trust me. I know. I'll tell him soon."

"I miss you," she says.

"Me too." Guilt washes over me for leaving her alone. My brother-in-law doesn't allow her to go out with her friends, and

I'm one of the few people he does let visit her. I've left her more isolated than ever. He wouldn't have allowed her to come with me for treatment. Of that much, I was sure. Not unless he could come too, and if there is a last person in the world I wouldn't want to see, it is Felipe Conde, followed closely by Dad. "I'll call more often," I promise.

"Good night."

"Night, Pili."

Half of the bottle of wine is gone, and I pour the rest down the sink before bedtime. I lay down on my makeshift sleeping bag next to the window and stare at the smooth ceiling. Taking deep breaths, I repeat my intentions over and over into the echoes of the empty apartment, exactly as I would do before any fight.

"Get back to fighting."

"Beat the shit out of cancer."

"Get back to fighting."

"Live."

CHAPTER 2

Nothing appetizing takes up space in my fridge. After extensive research, I bought groceries to pack on the pounds. My one-hundred-and-twenty-five pounds are all muscle, and I know I'll lose weight once chemo and radiation start. I need to gain some weight before I start treatment. I'll have a hell of a time fattening up after an entire adulthood of balancing food to keep muscle up and fat down. I bought all the things the internet suggested, all high in calories, proteins, and fat, but low in volume. I look at the eggs, olives, butter, peanut butter—why are there so many butters?—avocados, and whole milk. None of it seems to go together, so I close the fridge and hit the shower to go out to breakfast instead.

The furniture delivery service won't arrive until after ten, so I have time to explore the neighborhood and grab a bite. I hardly slept a wink as I thought about my web of lies, but I didn't want to waste any more of my precious time sleeping.

Kansas City is flat. At least compared to the tall buildings of my home city. None of the structures in this neighborhood are taller than a few stories, except for the hospital that reaches a whopping seven floors and sticks out above everything else on this street. Also, unlike my home city, greenery flanks almost every road.

I'm surprised when I find a gym not too far from my apartment. I look through the window, itching to go in, but what's the point? I can't get a membership. It's not a fighting gym of any kind, but it would be better than nothing. I watch men and women go in, and I get a few friendly hellos. Maybe I could get a week's membership and just come to lift weights until the treatment starts? I'm getting ready to open the door when I hear a voice behind me.

"Don't even think about it." I turn like the kid caught with my hands in the *masa* to find Dr. Ramirez and Mandy staring at me. Dr. Ramirez's arms are crossed over her chest, and one of her brows is arched in warning. Mandy is pressing her lips together, suppressing laughter at this exchange.

"I-um, I wasn't going to go—"

"Yes, you were," says Dr. Ramirez.

I hang my head with shame. "Yeah, you're right."

"You're supposed to be softening up and trying to gain as much weight as possible this week."

"I know. I know. I just don't know how to not do what I was born to do." I smile lamely at the women, and we all ignore my eyes misting over.

"We're just going for breakfast," Mandy steps in just in time to avoid my tears spilling over. "You're coming with us." She isn't asking. She grabs my arm and laces hers through mine, tugging me away from the first place that has looked like home since I got here.

∽

"Are you going to work today?" I ask as I sit in front of the two women looking at their menus.

"Yes," Mandy says. "We grab breakfast together Monday mornings. You're welcome to join us."

"Thank you, I might do that," I say, relieved to have someone to talk to besides a bottle of wine.

"So, are you really a UFC fighter?" Mandy asks with interest and much too loudly.

"Mandy," Dr. Ramirez scolds. "I don't think Valentina wants to talk about that."

I look between the two women who couldn't be more different. Mandy is short and has unruly wavy hair in a chocolaty dark brown shade. It's almost witchy as the tresses stir with her movements. Her skin is a smooth, cool-toned light brown. Her rectangular face meets in a square jaw, and she has one of the widest smiles I have ever seen. She is almost my height and definitely much shorter than Dr. Ramirez.

It's not just their physicality that is polar-opposite either. Dr. Ramirez moves with grace and sits with impeccable posture, while Mandy looks a bit frumpy and slouches in her seat, making her seem that much shorter. But what she lacks in physical height, Mandy makes up for in volume. Mandy is *loud*. So loud it's almost embarrassing, and I can't help but look at the other diners when she speaks.

I take a deep breath and answer Mandy. "No. I wasn't a UFC fighter *yet*. I was starting to get close—before—well, before everything happened."

"I'm sorry, *amiga*," she says and reaches across the table to grab my hand.

I smile at her choice of words and hope she is sincere because, lord help me, I'm going to need a friend.

When the waiter comes to our table, Dr. Ramirez snatches the menu from my hands, and my brows knit together.

"I'll be ordering for her," says Dr. Ramirez. "She'll have two fried eggs over-medium. Hash-browns, Texas toast with butter, two slices of bacon, and one biscuit on the side with gravy, if you have it."

"And for you, ma'am?" the waiter asks Dr. Ramirez.

"I'll have the spinach-egg white omelet with avocado slices and half a grapefruit," says Dr. Ramirez.

I blink at her, and Mandy throws her head back with a roar of laughter so magnified, several rows of tables turn to stare at us. I sink in my chair.

The heaping plate of food set before me doesn't look even a little appealing. I tug the plate, and the mountain of food jiggles. "Do I really have to eat this?" I ask.

"As much as you can, within reason," says Dr. Ramirez.

I turn my attention to a glob of something white that seems to have bits of sausage in it. "What is *that*?" I ask. It looks revolting, and despite my hunger, my stomach churns at the sight of it.

Mandy laughs again. "That's biscuits and gravy," she says with a bright, toothy smile. "Welcome to America."

"There's no way I'm eating that," I say.

"Fine," says Dr. Ramirez. "But eat as much as you can of the rest. Have a milkshake later, if you can, for a snack. When you find it hard to eat in volume, you'll be glad you can drink some calories."

"It's true," Mandy adds. "A few weeks from now, you'll be sending me on an errand to get you this very breakfast, and you won't be able to keep it down."

I take the fork and knife, one in each hand. *You can do this, Vale.* I pep myself, and Mandy roars with laughter again. My glare rises to her, and she presses her lips together.

"It's not so bad," says Mandy. "You'll see."

And it really isn't. It's greasy, and I'm not used to it, but I stop when I'm comfortable, and Dr. Ramirez nods with approval at the amount I manage to devour.

"Well, ladies," she says. "I have to get to work. Mandy, why don't you take the morning off? You haven't used any vacation time in a while."

"Thanks, boss," Mandy says, between mouthfuls of the pancakes she ordered, before Dr. Ramirez leaves us alone.

When we ask for our checks, the waiter informs us that both our tabs have been taken care of.

"Dr. Ramirez is generous like that," says Mandy. "Sometimes too generous. People tend to want to walk over her."

"Don't take advantage. Noted."

As we make our way outside, I ask Mandy something that crossed my mind during breakfast. "Hey, is it okay for us to socialize outside the hospital?"

"Not with Dr. R. Today was fine, but she won't be hanging out with us on the regular. She needs to keep a line drawn between her personal life and her patients. But I'm cool."

"You won't get in trouble?"

"No. I don't handle patient care or anything like that. The hospital won't have a problem if we're friends, if that's what you're worried about."

We are on the sidewalk, and Mandy stands in front of me. "So, what would you like to do? Seems I'm free this morning."

I shrug. "I was just planning on exploring the neighborhood a bit."

"That's great." Mandy starts to rattle off suggestions on which direction we should take when I see the glint of red hair walking in our direction. The man in front of him walks into a shop, and I can clearly make out Rory—the guy who saved my Pop-Tart. He is looking at his phone and hasn't seen us yet, and for some reason, I don't want him to.

"Let's go there," I quip and grab her arm as I haul her across the street and into the used-book store. I look out the window as Rory passes by, swallowed in a crowd of people.

When we are safely inside the bookshop, Mandy flashes me a funny look. "Okay, weirdo. What was that?"

"Just this guy I met the other day—"

"Oooh, a guy? Which one is it?" She cranes her neck after the group of people crossing the street. "Is he cute?"

"Doesn't matter. I can't really date now, can I?"

"No, but enjoy your sex-drive while you can. Trust me. It's going to take a bit of a vacation once you start treatment. Everyone handles it differently, but your body will change a lot. Sex will be the last thing on your mind."

I'm so stunned at her directness, I change the subject. "Well, I have to get back. I have furniture deliveries today."

"Oh, I'll come with. I can help move things around."

"You really don't have to."

"I want to." And just like that, Mandy invites herself over.

As we walk to my apartment, it dawns on me I don't know her full name. "What's your last name?"

"In case you have to give the cops a description?"

"What? No!" I laugh. "I just—I like to know my friend's names."

"Gomez. Amanda Gomez."

When she walks into my apartment, Mandy whistles. "This is nice," she bellows but stretches the word 'nice' into two sylla-bles. "I knew you were rich, but this is . . . I think only surgeons live in this building."

I stiffen. She already knows the trial requires patient insur-ance or upfront out-of-pocket deposits for treatment and hospital stays. This shouldn't be a surprise to her.

"I'm sorry," she hastens to apologize. "I'm working on my filter. It's not very good yet."

"How old are you?" I ask.

"Twenty-eight."

"Twenty-eight? You don't look it." It's hard to believe she is older than me. I laugh nervously. "And no worries about the filter, but no, I'm not rich. My sister is. She's bankrolling my treatment." *Without her knowledge*, I think, but don't offer Mandy that information.

"Oh yeah? What does she do?" Mandy walks around the apartment on a self-led tour as we talk. She grins when she sees the kitchen with its marble island and brand new appliances. The white subway tile backsplash particularly catches her eye. Then she walks from room to room, making sounds of appreciation at each one.

"Nothing. That sounds bad. I don't mean 'nothing.' She's a homemaker."

"Nothing wrong with that," Mandy says with a wide, toothy smile that is growing on me. She pops a piece of gum in her mouth and talks through the chewing. "My mom is too. She's amazing. So your sister, she married money or something?"

"Sort of. I mean, she did. Her husband owns a company in Mexico, but she has her own money."

"From what?" Mandy asks.

Geesh. She wasn't kidding about the filter. Is it common for Americans to talk about money like this? "From her dowry," I say like it's the most natural thing in the world, but I know it isn't.

"Her *dowry?*" Mandy's jaw drops, flashing me the pink bubblegum in her mouth. "Like Jane Austen and shit?"

I laugh. "Yeah, Mexico had colonizers too. They brought their dowry ideas with them."

"No shit?" she says and plops herself on the floor as she leans on the wall for a back-rest.

"No shit," I say.

"Will you get one too?" she asks.

"What?"

"A dowry."

My nose crinkles, and I shake my head. "Nope. Don't think so. There's a clause Dad has to approve of my husband-to-be, and to Dad, it means he gets to pick him out."

"So your Dad has money?"

I side-eye her. "Yeah. He does," I say with resignation.

"So I was right before. You're a rich girl."

"I'm really not. I was starting to get sponsors and handle my own money that *I earned* before I got sick."

"Hey, I didn't mean anything by it. I'm honestly just curious. I don't give a shit one way or the other."

"You say 'shit' a lot."

"Yeah. I like to cuss when I'm not at work or at home because it's the only time I can."

"Why can't you cuss at home?" I ask.

"I have a thirteen-year-old baby brother."

She lives at home? At twenty-eight? That can't be right, but I'm not comfortable asking such personal questions. "You know he's probably cussing already."

"Oh yeah, he says shit way worse than me. But my parents still think he's a sweet little innocent angel."

"Got it."

"Where'd you go?" Mandy snaps her fingers in front of my face when I stay quiet too long.

I'm now sitting next to her on the floor, and I know I checked out of the conversation. "Sorry. Just thinking about what's ahead."

"Hey, don't worry. Dr. Ramirez is amazing. You are going to be fine."

"How do you know so much? I mean, you mentioned about the food and drinking calories and then the sex drive thing. Do research assistants usually know so much about the trials?"

"Yeah. I also keep the database of adverse events. If any trial participants experience side effects, they call me, and I add them to the database. Expected side effects are par for the course, but if they are unexpected, we have to monitor those closely."

"I see."

"Can I ask you something?"

I side-eye her. "I have a feeling you will even if I don't say yes."

Her toothy grin spreads, but then her face turns serious. "How come you didn't tell any of your family or friends?"

I think about that for a moment, trying to find the right words. "I don't want this to define me. I was a rising star in my field, as *fresa* as that sounds. Everyone in my life has a perception of me as the strong one. I can't now be the sick one."

The doorbell rings, ending our conversation, and I'm glad I don't have to keep explaining something I'm in the process of trying to understand myself. I make my way to the intercom, and a man's voice fills the living room. "I have a delivery for Valentina Almonte."

"That's me." I buzz them up.

Three muscular men trickle in and out of the apartment as they bring in all the furniture I could possibly need. I even ordered a second bed for the guest bedroom. When I'd shopped online, I'd opted to buy entire showcase rooms from the website because I've never been good at putting together home decor. Pilar would have loved to help, but the less she knew, the better. I didn't want to slip up and have her get suspicious.

Feeling more in the way than helpful, Mandy and I press our backs against the living room window. A few of the pieces of furniture require assembly. One man goes into the bedroom to start on that while a second crouches in front of us, putting together the sectional.

"I'm so glad I came," Mandy says. I look at her to find a twinkle in her eye. It's amusing until her intentions become clear. "Go talk to him," she says in a hushed tone.

"What? No!"

"Remember what I said about the sex drive? He is so hot. Do it."

I panic because even though we are whispering and the living room is large, he is right there, and I'm sure he can probably hear us.

"Fine. You're too slow. I'm calling dibs."

"What? Mandy!" I warn, but she only puts her hand on her hip and tussles her hair over one shoulder.

"Hey," she calls toward the man. "What's your name?"

The tall, dark, and handsome man looks up at us with a bright smile. He had introduced himself to me when I opened the door for them, but Mandy was at the other end of the room. "Chris, ma'am," he says.

Mandy walks toward him. "None of that 'ma'am' business. I'm Mandy." Chris stands to stretch out his hand, and their hand-shake connection lingers for a beat too long.

Chris is much taller than Mandy, allowing me a view of the amusement in his eyes from her flirting. She finally lets go of his hand and starts rummaging through her purse. I see the corner of a piece of paper that she pulls out and hands to him. "I have a solo art show soon. You should check it out." She gives him what I assume is a flyer. "Hold that," she says and keeps rummaging through her purse.

Chris smooths out the flyer in front of him and looks at it. His mouth forms up into a smile. "An artist, huh?"

"Yeah, I'm a painter. Landscapes and portraits mostly. Here." She stretches her hand out so he'll give the flyer back, and she starts writing something on it. "My number," she hands back the flyer to Chris. "You know, if you want a sneak peek before the show." Mandy turns and starts walking back to me. She continues to ogle Chris as he works and brings more furniture in, both of them smiling like fools the entire time it takes the three men to get my apartment furnished.

"Ma'am," the man who seems to be in charge calls after me, a clipboard in his hands. "Could you please sign here that you received everything you ordered?"

"Sure." I sign, and the men leave. Mandy looks out onto the street as she watches them go.

"You are shameless," I say to her jokingly.

She turns and winks at me. "I'm so tapping that ass," she says, and I laugh.

There's not much moving around I want to do, so Mandy and I try out the sectional.

"So, you're an artist?" I ask.

"Yeah. I'm an RA, and I work the information desk at the hospital so I can have health insurance, but one day I'll make a living just from my painting," she says as she stares dreamily into space.

"I'd love to go to your show too."

"Well, duh, you are going," she says and rolls her eyes. "I have to go. Still have half a shift I have to cover."

"Thanks for everything, Mandy. It's nice to know someone here."

Mandy smiles at me. "I'll see you soon, okay? And hey, think about what I said," she says while turning the doorknob.

"About what?"

"Have a sexathon tonight, then let your body rest the last two days before treatment starts."

I throw one of the sofa cushions at her, but it only hits the door after she is on the other side.

After she leaves, I try to remember when was the last time I got some. I've been so numb and in shock since my diagnosis. Sex has been the last thing on my mind. I'm lucky not to have some of the more embarrassing symptoms many women in my situation have. Maybe a night of reckless abandon will help me feel alive again. *I'm not dead yet*, I remind myself. And the furthest thing from the act of dying is the act of lovemaking.

I've never had a serious long-term relationship. I mostly

lived at the gym. Luckily, Chema's gym is full of hot men to pick from, and I have a deep bench of booty-call friends I call on when I need to scratch the itch or just relax after hefty training.

I sigh because I have to admit it has been too long, and that bench is oh so very far away in Mexico City. Maybe I could offer to pay for one of them to come here?

No. Not only was that too desperate, but I would lose a day or two before they could get here, and treatment starts in three days. Not to mention a disrespectful use of my sister's money when she thinks she is sponsoring a future UFC titleholder. Looks like the bar it is.

IN THE EVENING, I SHOWER AND THROW ON A PAIR OF FAUX-leather leggings with a navy-blue silk camisole. My breasts are on the small side, so I feel comfortable skipping a bra and showing a bit of cleavage. I hate wearing high-heels and instead opt for black moto boots that I leave untied and slouchy.

The one girly thing I do enjoy is makeup. I don't get to wear it often because I'm always training, but now seems like the perfect opportunity to wear it.

I opt for a smokey eye with charcoal-black eyeliner. For the lips, I wear a kissable nude shade just a few shades darker than my tanned natural color to give my face some life.

Standing in front of the mirror, I look at my full figure. Taking in those slim, toned muscles I worked so hard to perfect sends me into an emotional state I wasn't expecting. I look great, and I know I won't look this way again for a long time, or maybe even ever. I can't even begin to imagine the many ways in which my body will change and am so grateful Mandy suggested this so I could enjoy my body—this version of it—one last time. I blink away the tears before they get the chance to ruin my makeup.

Not wanting to take a purse with me, I place my ID and credit card in my back pocket. I secure my apartment key into my boot laces, and I head outside.

I have several options to choose from as I walk down my street. For some inexplicable reason, I walk toward the hospital instead of away from it. I hadn't noticed the bar precisely across from the emergency room entrance. *Smart location*, I think.

The door's sign is in a simple font with white LED lights that reads *La Oficina*. Looks like I found my bar.

CHAPTER 3

*I*t's early, and the bar isn't even at quarter capacity. It's easy to find a space at the bar, and I pull out my credit card to open up my tab.

A bartender so beautiful I find it hard to formulate words comes over to take my order. She has the body of a model, and I can't tell what race she is. She has an other-worldly face, fair skin, and a perfect black bob hairstyle. Her beautiful full lips move again, and I replay what she just said in my head. *What can I get you?*

"Um—sorry. Whiskey sour, please."

She takes my credit card and comes back with my drink a few minutes later.

"Here," she says. "I like your accent."

"Thanks." My face grows hot, and it's not the whiskey.

"*¿Hablas español?*"

My head snaps up to her in surprise. Her Spanish is impeccable. "*Sí,*" I say. We switch back to English after that. "Where are you from?" I ask.

"I'm Chicana. Mom's Mexican, and dad's Chinese. It throws

people off. I know." She laughs easily as she says this. "I haven't seen you around here. You work at the hospital?"

"No. New in town," I say.

"I'm Sofia," the bartender says and stretches her hand out to me. "I own the place."

I shake her hand and smile. "Valentina. Nice to meet you."

"Welcome to KC. Let me know when you want another one, okay?"

"Thanks."

Sofia walks away to flirt with two customers a few seats down the bar. Poor suckers don't know she is playing them so that they buy more drinks. I smile. I like this woman.

Sipping on my cocktail, I scan the room for a potential one-night-stand. Someone muscular and handsome who won't need to ask for my phone number after. Someone alone, and more importantly, someone single. Nothing on the menu is appetizing yet, so I order a second drink and nurse it as I wait for the place to fill up.

A few guys come up to hit on me, but they aren't my type. I don't feel any attraction physically, and if Mandy is right and this is my last hurrah for a while, then I want something yummy. I mean, someone yummy. Fuck it. Men objectify women all the time, so I have exactly zero qualms about objectifying them just this once. They would be doing a humanitarian service, I decide. Would they go for it if I sold it as some sort of make-a-wish-for-adults service? No. That would probably kill the mood.

A third man walks over to hit on me, clearly inebriated. I resist the urge to roll my eyes. Could he even get it up, as drunk as he seems to be? Probably not. I smile and do my best to be nice to him—though I hate that's my impulse.

He sways a bit, but it's enough for me to notice. His black hair is slicked back with gel, like this is the nineties or something. "Can I buy you a drink?" he asks.

I point to my glass, showing it's half full. "Got one. Thanks, though." I smile curtly and divert my eyes from him, hoping he takes the hint.

"Oh, I like your accent. Where are you from, *señorita?*" he asks.

I do roll my eyes this time and take a sip of my drink. "I'm from Mexico. Where are you from?" I ask pointedly, though I probably shouldn't engage him any further.

Sofia looks at me with a question in her eyes. I roll my eyes and shake my head as if to say *I got it, thanks.* She tips her chin, and I know she'll throw his ass out if he gets rowdy. Hopefully, I can get him to back away without having to make a scene. I am here to catch a big fish, after all. I won't have a bite if I come across as drama before the night even starts.

"I'm from this here, the U.S. of A." He grins, and it feels eerily like he is about to pound his chest with his fists like a Neanderthal. He is somewhat handsome, tall, black hair, blue eyes. If he wasn't that far drunk, and he hadn't opened his mouth, I may have considered him as my boy-toy for the night. "I'm Doctor Keach," he adds. When he says *doctor*, I take it I'm supposed to be impressed.

"I'm actually waiting for someone, so if you don't mind . . ." I trail off, hoping he gets the hint this time.

"Oh, come on. You look so exotic, like a spicy Latina." He says Latina with a mocking accent that I can only assume is meant to mimic my own. My nostrils flare, and I count to ten.

This idiot doesn't realize I could have him on the ground and begging for his mommy in less than ten seconds flat. *Don't use your power on civilians, Valentina.* I remind myself of Chema's anger management lessons. Leave it for the cage. *Never out in everyday life.*

"We can have a good time, honey," he slurs.

"Sorry, buddy, she's with me." A voice much too deep for the body it came out of turns both our attention. I do a double-take when I see Rory, who is in the process of placing his hand on the small of my back. He doesn't make contact with me, though, and instead lets his hand hover over my backside. He wants drunky here to believe it, and he is selling it good.

"Like I said," I tell Dr. Keach, "I was waiting for someone."

"All right, all right. No harm done." He raises his hands in surrender as he walks backward, stumbling on a few people before he turns to face the opposite direction.

"Thanks," I say to Rory.

"No problem. It didn't look like you were having fun."

"I wasn't, but I had it under control."

"I don't doubt it," says Rory. "But I thought maybe I could save you some time."

My gaze sweeps his body from face to shoes. He is wearing jeans and a grey t-shirt, but the outfit is polished. His short, reddish beard is expertly kept, and he looks fresh like he just got out of a shower. This will do nicely. Very nicely indeed.

"That's the second time you saved me this week," I say.

"I thought you looked familiar."

"The vending machine?" I remind him. "You bought me a Pop-Tart."

"That's right. That was you." His eyes squint like he is trying to place my face in that scenario.

"In your defense," I offer, "I look much better tonight."

He smirks, accepting my awkward flirting. God, I'm so bad at this. My booty-call bench is so much easier. All I have to do is text one of them, at random, so no one's feelings get hurt, and ask: Free to fuck tonight? Somehow I don't think that methodology will go over well with Rory. "Can I buy you a drink?" I ask.

"Um—" he looks toward a group of men sitting at a table in the corner of the bar.

"Hey, don't worry about it." My heart sinks a little, but I keep smiling. "I just wanted to thank you for the Pop-Tart and for coming to my rescue tonight. Let me buy you the drink—no strings. You can take it over and enjoy it with your friends."

"No, that's not what I—um, just, let me go say bye to them, and I'll be right back."

My heart flutters, and I don't understand this new sensation. It must be the whiskey. "Sure. I can order in the meantime. What's your poison?"

"A beer?"

"You got it."

I order his beer, and Sofia has it ready for him before he gets back. I swivel in my barstool to look at him standing near the table with his buddies. They roar with laughter, and one of them pats him in the back. His fair complexion makes the reddening of his neck glaringly obvious, and I smile. He palms the back of his neck as if he can feel the heat there. It's cute, really.

Rory is nerdy and slim and oh so very handsome. I hope he'll let me take him home tonight. If this fails, I have to make a mental note to hit the nearest adult toy store first thing in the morning.

He grins as he takes the barstool next to mine. "Thanks," he says as he grabs his beer and takes a long pull. He is nervous and buying time. It's adorable.

"It's the least I could do," I say, opening up the conversation for him. He seems lost for what to say next, so I speak again. "Are you from Kansas City?" I ask, starting with a safe topic I hope will engage him.

"No," he says. "I'm from Minnesota." His entire face brightens when he thinks of home, and I know I've chosen the right topic. "Here for work. I've been here a few years now."

"I'd love some advice on what to check out. It's only my second night in Kansas City. Sofia?" I call her attention, and she looks over right away. She smiles knowingly as she looks between Rory and me, and I point to my empty drink.

"Oh, KC is great. You'll really love it," says Rory.

I start on my third drink, and Rory falls silent. His brows crease like he is thinking of something and he is unsure if he should say it. "Well?" he asks finally. "What are we waiting for? Let's go."

"Go where?" I ask.

"I'm going to show you Kansas City."

"*Tonight?*" I set my drink down and wipe my mouth with a napkin.

"No time like the present."

I cock my head to the side. Is this man serious? *No time like the present?*

"Come on. You are wearing walking shoes. Let's do this."

"Can I at least finish my drink?" I ask.

"Yeah. Sure. The night is young."

I almost spit my drink. Does he only speak in clichés? "Did you just say that?"

"What?"

"*The night is young?* That's such a cliché," I inform him.

"It's going to take a lot to impress you, isn't it, Miss Valentina, um—what's your last name?"

"Almonte. And are you trying to impress me, Rory . . . ?"

"Dennis," he says. "And, yes. Maybe I am trying to impress you."

I bite my lip as I lock eyes with him, and his jade-green eyes darken. The third drink is plunging me into tipsy territory, and I push it away. As I stare deep into his eyes, I realize even his eyes have freckles.

"What are you looking at?" he asks.

"Your eyes have freckles. These little flecks of brown swimming in the green."

"Ah, that." He takes another swig of his beer. "Yeah, my mom used to tell me it was poop."

"What?" I almost yell as I ask, my eyes wide with surprise.

"Yeah, when I was a kid, she had me convinced the little pieces of brown were tiny flecks of poop floating around my irises. Said it was because I was so full of shit." He smirks and drinks from his beer bottle again.

I throw my head back with laughter. This man is funny. "Your mom sounds like a badass," I say.

"She really is."

We are both laughing and relaxed. I don't remember feeling this way with anyone on a first date. "I don't think I'll be finishing my drink after all," I say. We both stand, and I press my hand to his chest. It's firm, and my body heats at the feel of it. "Rory," I say with a breathy voice.

"Yeah?"

"If we go out tonight, I hope you understand I intend to take you to bed before the date is over. Don't leave with me if you are not interested in that."

His eyebrow arches, and he pushes his glasses further up his nose so he can better look at me. His jaw slackens, and I know his brain is misfiring. I walk out of the bar without looking back but hope he is right behind me.

I step into the warm night and take a deep breath of air. Not even three seconds pass before Rory is at my side.

"Sorry," he says. "You kind of caught me off guard there."

"You're here, so I take it you are interested?"

He nods. "You're very forward, aren't you?"

"Not really, but I don't have any time to waste," I say plainly because it is the absolute truth.

CHAPTER 4

ory orders a car, and I frown when we arrive at our first stop. "A gas station?" I ask.

Rory nods.

Not only is it a gas station but a somewhat shabby one at that. We get out of the car, and as we round the corner, we have to walk past a long line of people waiting to go inside.

"Pro-tip," Rory says, "whenever you travel anywhere new, find long lines. Nine times out of ten, that's where the good food is."

"What could there be that's so good at a gas station?" I scoff.

"Barbecue. The best in the states, dontchaknow."

"Barbecue?"

He nods as we take our place in line. I frown. This line will take an hour before we can go inside, then another hour to wait for the food and the eat it. Maybe I should have gone with Dr. Keach instead of Rory. He was ready to go right then and there.

As if sensing my turning mood, Rory nudges me. "Don't worry. The line will move fast, and you'll see, the wait will be more than worth it."

He is right. We get through the line and have our food in

front of us in less than thirty minutes. The dining area is small and crowded. People don't linger and talk, so other diners can have a table.

"This is huge," I say, looking at the brisket sandwich Rory recommended as the only thing worth having. Piles of brisket on a bun with melted cheese and onion rings tower on my plate. Adjusting to the portions in Kansas City will take time but serve my weight-gain goals well. I close the sandwich with the top bun and take a bite. My eyes draw closed. The meat is tender and smoky and so delicious.

"You didn't put any barbecue sauce on it," he says, and hands me a bottle.

I try the sauce first and wrinkle my nose. "Too sweet," I say.

He then hands me a second sauce that is spicier and less sweet. I add only a little of that to appease him.

"So?" He asks.

"It's delicious," I say and mean it. "Except for the fries."

"What's wrong with the fries?" Rory looks down at the tray with the fry mountain.

"They have sugar. Who the hell puts sugar on fries? It's like everything here has sugar. It's really annoying. Sugar is for desserts—that's it. Maybe sweet and sour at Chinese. But that's really it."

Rory blinks at me, then shakes his head. "The fries don't have sugar."

"Are you serious?"

"What?"

"They are like candied fries; they have so much sugar! You really can't taste it?"

He shakes his head. "You're crazy," he says.

I only eat half of my sandwich, even though it's so good I could probably stuff it in. I want to avoid what saucy Chema christened 'TFF' or 'Too Full to Fuck.' I heed all of Chema's warnings.

Our second stop on my tour of the city lands us at a plaza that I have to admit is stunning. The architecture reminds me of the Spanish-style haciendas typical in Mexico. We walk for an hour past restaurants, bars, and shops, never once going inside. Rory talks about his love of traveling and how he wishes he could do it more and asks me questions about Mexico, but we don't go too deep. I won't let it, even with the ample invitations he opens up.

"How's your English so good? I mean, you know a lot of colloquialisms . . . I wouldn't expect you to. I'm sorry, maybe that's a rude question," says Rory as he cups the back of his neck like he did at the bar.

I laugh. "Not at all. A lot of middle—and upper—class kids in Mexico love American culture. English is so cool when you're a teenager in Mexico. We pay attention to all the music, movies, everything that's popular here. And I did a year in a Swiss boarding school when I was fifteen."

Rory stops in his tracks to look at me. "Fancy," he says and resumes his walk.

I scoff. "Yeah. That's one word for it. I think Dad was hoping I'd come back a lady," I say wryly.

"Did you?"

I shake my head. "No. It backfired. I've always wanted to be the furthest thing from a lady that I could. But anyway, the school was mostly for Americans—though I was never quite able to completely shake off the accent—"

"You shouldn't be ashamed of it," says Rory. "You speak multiple languages, and it's easy to understand you. Not to mention, it's very sexy."

"It is?" I ask, my cheek heating up. He nods. "Rory? Are you trying to avoid going to my place? If you didn't want to—"

"No," he says and grabs my hand in his. "I just want to make sure that when we are together, we are both completely sober."

"Oh," I say, unsure how to respond to that. "I'm sober." I'll admit the food helped, and I'm starting to realize nothing Rory does is by accident.

He smiles. "Good. But I also do want you to see a little of this city before you leave—one last stop. I promise, then we'll head back to your place. No way in hell I'm backing out."

We get to the last stop of my tour at nearly one in the morning. Our driver warns us we are probably not allowed at the park this late, but I let Rory lead the way. I smile when he insists on opening my door. Men like this just don't exist anymore. Or so I thought.

"This is Liberty Memorial. The building is a World War I museum, and that is the Liberty Memorial Tower." He points to an obnoxious structure.

We walk through the park toward the tower, and I compress my lips together.

"What?" asks Rory.

My shoulders shake with my suppressed laugh. I can't hold the laughter any longer, so I let it out. "Sorry, it's just . . ."

"Spit it out, Almonte."

"The tower. Isn't it a bit . . ." I trail off and point to the tower because he has to see it. How could he not see it?

Rory cocks his head to the side as he studies the tower. His face scrunches up, and he scratches his head. "What? What are you saying?"

"It's rather *phallic*. Don't you think?"

He tosses his head back with laughter and then nudges my arm. "You are a one-track-mind kind of gal, aren't you?"

"Sure you don't want to just go straight to my apartment?" I ask and wiggle my eyebrows.

Rory shakes his head and takes my hand in his. Our fingers lace together, and I stare at our hands where we join as we walk. I blink. I've never held hands with a man before, and the intimacy of it has me regretting that I've selected Rory for this job. He needed some sort of 'date' before he could go to bed with me. He is boyfriend material, and I am not girlfriend material. This is such a bad idea. But his hand is warm and inviting, and the gesture brings us closer together so I can take his scent in again like I had at the bar. It's a mix of sandalwood and suede and so refreshing mixed with the park's cut grass.

We walk to the edge of the building until we come to a short wall where I rest my elbows on the ledge and look down at a Kansas City starting to come alive with nightlife. The lazy pulse of light traffic in the veins of the city streets flows below us. It's dark, and the lights are bright. Straight ahead, a beautiful building that reminds me of the Met in New York displays fountains on its front lawn.

"What's that?" I ask, pointing at the building.

"That's Union Station," he says.

"Like an actual train station?"

"Yeah."

"It's beautiful," I say dreamily. Would I ever get the chance to ride a train? I was so dedicated to my sport, I barely experienced life at all. You always think there is more time, *later*—to do all the things you ever dreamed of. But time is not a guarantee, and it is not owed to anyone. Too bad I learned this lesson at the expense of my life.

You are not dead yet, Valentina, I remind myself. There's still a chance.

"The inside is great too," Rory says, oblivious in the dark to the prickling tears in my eyes.

"Yeah?"

"Yeah. There's a coffee shop and a restaurant. They have all sorts of science exhibits. Maybe you'll let me take you on a date? We can go there. This weekend? Are you free?"

This weekend I'll be puking my guts out. "Rory, I don't want to give you the wrong idea. I—"

"I know what this is," he says. "I'm not asking you to be my girlfriend or my wife. You were at that bar looking for something, and I'm just the lucky bastard who caught your eye. But I'm not going to stand here and lie to you. I can't tell you I don't want to see you again after tonight."

"The thing is, I'm not sure I'll be here much longer." I mean *life*, but Rory, I know, hears *Kansas City*.

"Can we just enjoy the time we do have, then?" He ducks his head to hold my gaze, and I suddenly am not sick Valentina. I'm not cancer-patient Valentina. In his eyes, I'm hot and sexy Valentina. The girl with the Spanish accent who bought him a drink. "Please?" he nudges.

"Okay," I say, unsure how the hell I'm going to get out of this. The thing is, spending what little time I have before treatment with him sounds lovely. I can always make an excuse later if I'm not feeling up to going out on the weekend.

He leads me by the hand as we make our way back through the trees and lays down on the grass. He pats the spot next to him. "You gonna join me?"

"This is the weirdest hookup of my life," I tell him, attempting to joke, but he doesn't laugh. His beard shifts lightly with the movement of his clenching jaw.

We are nestled between two trees, looking up at the black sky through the leaves. There are no stars out tonight. I'm completely sober now, and a gust of wind makes me shiver. I press my naked arms to his body as I curl up to his side.

"Hold on." Rory shifts. "Lift your head a bit." I do as I'm told, and he slides his arm under my head so that I nestle next to him and lay my head on his shoulder. He wraps his other arm around me and rubs my arm a few times to warm me up. "Better?"

"Yeah," I say. "I get cold easily."

"That's great because I'm always running way too hot." And it's true. His warm skin soothes me, and I bet my cool skin refreshes him. I fit next to his body perfectly and can only imagine what it will be like to have him fully.

A short gust of wind rattles the leaves into the most soothing sound.

"Valentina?"

"Mmm?" I moan, too relaxed to form words.

"Why did you pick me?"

I shrug. "You're handsome. And . . ." I bite the inside of my lip.

"And what?"

What the hell. *Pa' luego es tarde*, as Chema would say. "When you were getting the Pop-Tart from the vending machine, I *may* have checked out your ass."

"You checked out my ass?"

I lift my head so I can read his expression, and he chuckles. "Yeah. I checked out your ass. Sue me. It's a cute little bubble butt."

"Oh, Valentina—"

"What?"

"I was checking out your ass the entire time you were threatening the machine."

"You were?"

"Yeah."

I laugh, and a moment of silence follows. I'm thinking about the train station and all the places I want to go one day. "Rory?"

"Mmm?"

"If you could go anywhere in the world, where would you go?"

"Easy. India."

"That's unexpected."

"I'd eat my way through India until I got sick of it."

I laugh. "Really? You chose your dream destination based on the food?"

"What else is there?"

"I don't know. People? Places?"

"Well, yeah, India has both those too."

"Smartass," I say, and he chuckles. "So, you like Indian food?"

"Don't you?"

"Don't know. I kind of live on protein shakes, broccoli, and chicken breasts. Slight exaggeration, but it's not far off from the truth."

"A picky eater, huh?"

"No. It's for work."

"Work?"

"Yeah. I'm an athlete." Or was an athlete, I think. "So my eating habits are controlled, to put it mildly."

"Well, if you can ever have a cheat day, I'd love to take you out for Indian food."

I blink slowly, then smile when he doesn't judge my eating regimen like most people do. Everyone not in the sport always assumes I'm exaggerating and should be able to cheat my diet more than I do. But Rory accepts it without question, and it's so strange to me. He also doesn't ask what kind of athlete. He wants me to open up to him because I want to.

"Maybe one day," I tell him finally.

He nods, and we both fall silent for a long stretch of time. So much so that when I wake up, I have no idea how long we've been out because next to me, Rory is letting out the cutest little snore. I poke his ribs gently, and he stirs. "Rory," I whisper.

"Mmmh," he groans but doesn't open his eyes.

"Rory." I shiver. The night got significantly cooler. What the hell time is it? I pull out my phone from my back pocket, and my eyes widen with horror. Five in the morning. We slept *all night*. What the hell are cops doing that they didn't notice us? Not only did we miss our booty call, but I slept like I had never slept in my life. "Rory," I hiss, louder this time. "Wake up. We have to go."

He stirs and wipes a bit of drool from the corner of his mouth. His eyes dart around his surroundings, trying to place where he is. "What . . ." He sits up and looks around. He starts grasping around for his glasses that must have fallen from his face in the middle of the night and puts them on once he finds them. He looks around, and what he does next, I would have never in a million years have guessed would be his reaction.

He rolls onto his back with laughter so intense, he wraps his arms around his middle to clutch his stomach. "We fell asleep!" He cries between guffaws.

"It's not funny, Rory," I say, gritting my teeth.

"It's pretty funny."

"Rory, it's five a.m."

He laughs harder. "Really?"

I stand to shake any dirt from my outfit and try to straighten my hair. I use my phone as my mirror, and I turn away from him at record speed. My mascara is running, and I look like a raccoon. My hair is knotted and has blades of grass stuck in it.

Rory stands to look at me, and I pull my face away, horrified.

"Come here," he says. He grabs my chin, so I face him. "You look adorable," he says.

"No, I don't," I whine, and I slap his torso playfully. My hands can't help but linger over his hard oblique muscles. I'm only holding on to him for balance, of course, while he pulls out blade after blade of grass from my hair.

"Here, let me get that." His finger is reaching for my eye next, and I rear back.

"What are you doing?"

He laughs as he tries to approach me again. "You have an eye booger."

"Oh my god!" I turn away from him and start walking in the opposite direction while I clear out the corners of my eyes.

"Hold on," he calls after me. "It's no big deal," he says. He continues to laugh, and I'm trying to be annoyed like I should be, but it's getting harder to suppress my own laughter.

"This was supposed to be a sexy night. I'm not going to let you clean my eye-boogers."

"I'm sorry if you're upset," he says. "But I'm not."

"You're not?"

"No. That's the best night's sleep I've had in a long time."

"Me too," I admit.

"See? It wasn't a total waste. But I am sorry we missed our night together. I'm sorry for falling asleep. Not that it's an excuse, but I had a long shift at work yesterday."

"It's on me too. I can't just blame you. Even if I wanted to," I say.

"I don't have work today," he says. "Do you?"

I shake my head. "Do you still want to . . . ?"

His expression changes from that playful-young-boy demeanor of his into a dark one full of hunger. It's like he has two personalities, my very own personal Jekyll and Hyde. He draws me to him and kisses me with greed I have never known before. He crushes his lips to mine and nibbles at my lower lip when he comes up for air. Then he plunges in again to play, his tongue on mine. His beard grazes my skin, and I whimper into his mouth. A groan comes from deep within his throat in response, and I bunch up the fabric of his shirt in my hands.

I push him away, and we are both panting. I touch my lips that now feel bruised. I can't believe I slept with him in the literal sense of the word and hadn't so much as kissed him. "We need to get a car," I say. He nods and pulls out his phone.

"Your place or mine?" he asks. "I have roommates. They'll be up soon."

"My place is fine. I live alone."

We ride in the back seat together and can't help giggling as we look at each other conspiratorially. He tries grabbing my hand, but I pull it away. He chuckles, and I can't help smiling around him. I should be mad. So mad. And with any other guy, I would be fuming if this had happened, but sleeping with him didn't seem like a waste of time—not even with the precious few days I might have left.

"Valentina?"

"What?" I try to snap but fail.

"How do you say eye booger in Spanish?"

"Oh my god. Why do you want to know?" I look over at our driver, who doesn't seem to care about our odd conversation.

Rory shrugs. "I think I'd like to learn Spanish."

"And you think the best place to start is with 'eye booger?'"

He presses his hand to his heart. "The word has sentimental value to me." He chuckles as he says this, and soon I follow with my own laugh. Have I ever laughed this much? Rory radiates a warmth that makes it hard to be mad at him and instead has me smiling and laughing like I wasn't already walking on death row.

"*Lagaña*," I say.

"*Lagaña*," he repeats.

"Excellent pronunciation," I say, a bit proud. "But next time, let's teach you something more useful."

"I don't know. It would have been useful today," he jokes, and I smack his arm as we turn onto my street.

Dawn breaks as we enter my apartment, and Rory stares into my living room with an expression not unlike Mandy's when she first saw it. *Here we go again*, I think, but unlike Mandy, he doesn't comment on how nice it is.

I'm locking the door when he comes up behind me. He wraps his arms around me, tucking his thumb under the hem of my blouse. It lingers there as he kisses my neck, his beard tickling a trail after his lips.

"Mmm, Valentina." He groans into my ear, and my skin breaks into goosebumps, forcing my hand to move of its own accord. I take his hand currently over my lower midriff and help him into my legging's waist-band. I turn to face him, and his lips crush mine once again like they had at the park. He's about to tuck my pants off when I stop him. "Wait," I say.

His hands break free of me, and he looks into my eyes. His

brows knit together, and I see concern there. "No, that's not what I—I still want to. We *are* going to. I just need a minute in the restroom. Freshen up and all that."

"Oh, okay," he says with a breathy voice.

"Make yourself at home. There's a guest bathroom if you need it. First door on the left." I smile and hasten to my bedroom.

I had to pee, but I wasn't about to tell him that. Then I wince when I look in the mirror. Rory had picked out most of the grass but missed many still lingering in the depths of my thick hair. I finish the job, take off my ghastly makeup, and run a brush through my hair. I can't waste time and shower, and I also don't want him to feel bad that he hasn't showered himself, so I run some water under my armpits and between my legs and hope that will do. I brush my teeth and use some hand lotion with a gentle flowery scent that will hopefully mask any odors from the night outdoors. I smirk, remembering our mishap last night.

I kick off my boots and find him in the living room.

"You took forever," he says.

"I'm sorry. I'm all yours now."

CHAPTER 5

$\mathcal{I}$ take my camisole off as I walk to him, and his eyes widen at my brazen exposure of my breasts. I'm about to start taking his shirt off when he grasps my wrists holding me in place. Crap. Did I miss my window? I'm suddenly vulnerable in my topless state. "What's wrong?" I ask.

He cups the back of his neck in a gesture exactly like what he did at the bar when his buddies were giving him a hard time about leaving with a woman.

"Rory?" I ask in as soothing a tone as I'm capable of. My arms wrap in front of my chest so I can cover my nipples. "Do you want to keep your shirt on? It's okay if you do." *I might cry*, I think, but don't share that last bit. I also can't imagine what he would be self-conscious about. I had felt the hard muscles of his abdomen through his shirt several times already.

Rory shifts his weight from one leg to the other, and his eyes can't meet mine. "No. It's okay. I just need to prepare you . . ." He trails off. Whatever he needs to prepare me for is difficult for him to say.

"What for?"

"I'll tell you about it later. Don't ask the story behind what you're about to see right now. Okay?"

"You're scaring me a little, Rory."

He chuckles, but it's nervous. "It's nothing bad. I promise."

"Okay?"

"I have a scar."

I laugh. "I don't have any problems with scars." I drop my arms, exposing my naked breasts again.

"It's pretty big."

I purse my lips because now I'm concerned about *why* he has this scar, but he asked me not to ask questions, and I intend to make him comfortable too. My eyes freeze over his chest for a second before I look at him again. His beautiful green eyes are frozen to the carpet.

"You never asked me what kind of athlete I am," I say.

His head snaps up, and he is looking into my eyes again, a question in his.

"Ask me what I do."

"Um, okay . . . what do you do, Valentina?"

"I'm a mixed martial arts fighter."

"Oh." He looks confused, and I know he doesn't understand where I'm going with this.

"Fighters tend to find scars sexy as fuck," I explain, and I know he can see the hunger in my gaze. I lick my lips in a blatant display of desire. He charges for me and picks me up in his arms like newlyweds in all the romantic comedies my sister likes to watch. I squeal as he lifts me. "Rory!"

He takes me to my bedroom and tosses me onto the bed somewhat forcefully. "You're fucking perfect," he declares. I sit up and then kneel on the bed so I can help him out of his clothes, *finally*.

I race to take his shirt off and lean back to admire his body. A shirtless Rory still in his jeans is a sight to behold. His fair torso is slim but well-defined. You wouldn't think it to look at him with clothes on, but this man has a six-pack with a trail of reddish hair leading to his waistband over the ripples of his muscles.

His chest hair in matching red covers a lengthy scar that starts at the top of his chest and spans down the length of his sternum. I know his chest has been cracked open, but no questions right now. I raise my hands to his chest, hovering over the scar, and search his eyes. He nods, giving me permission to touch, so I trace the scar from top to bottom. And in a move I have no idea where it came from, I dip my head to lick the length of it. His grip tightens a bit around my shoulders, but he doesn't push me away.

I reach to touch the muscles of his six-pack, and he stills but lets me explore where I want. I follow the trail of my hands with my mouth as I kiss and lick the granite muscles leading up to his scar. When I get to it, I lick it all the way to its start. I find his neck and nibble at it while my hands work his jeans open.

Underneath, I find boxer briefs with that mushroom tip poking out of the waistband. I lift the glistening droplet of his precum with my index finger and bring it to my mouth. I look him in the eye as I lick my finger and revel in the taste of him. The saltiness of it sends a shiver down my spine my eyes close with pleasure. I open them again to find a stunned Rory gaping at me. He shakes his head to snap out of it and hurries out of his underwear.

His cock springs forward, and my eyes widen. I gulp. I'm not sure I'll be able to fit him in. His length is intimidating, but my mouth waters all the same. "It's so . . ." I trail off.

"So what?" he asks.

"So pink."

He smiles sexily and peels off my leggings and underwear next, then steps back to ogle me as I had him. Fair is fair. His jaw tightens, and his Adam's apple bobs as he swallows hard. With that look of hunger on his face, I'm not the slightest bit self-conscious. Being naked in front of Rory is nothing but freedom and delight.

He leans over me and finds my mouth. This is our first kiss without the morning breath, and it is glorious. I purr into his mouth, and he matches it with a deep groan that has my legs locking around him.

His hand draws down so he can play with the folds of my entrance. I shamelessly grind against the feel of his hand, finding his rhythm. His thumb presses my clit while he dips a finger in me. He doesn't stop kissing me, though, and it's hard to stay put and not roll my head back at all the sensations he evokes.

When he sinks a second and then a third finger inside to stretch me, I can't contain it any longer. I pull away from his mouth and scream his name.

"Does that feel good?" he asks in that husky voice of his.

"Yes!" I scream and clench around his fingers. His fingers respond by curling upward. "So good. Oh, Rory! Don't stop!"

He brings his mouth to my nipple and circles his tongue gently around it, sending me over the edge. I'm moaning and writhing under his touch as my orgasm hits, and he isn't even inside me yet. Rory is a selfless lover. I'm so smart for picking him out of everyone in the bar.

His fingers withdraw from me, and he gives my nipple a peck with his lips. "Condoms?" he asks.

"Nightstand. I'll get them."

He pulls away from me, and I rummage through the drawer and sit up so I can put it on him. His abdominal muscles clench as I roll the condom down his length.

He grabs a handful of my ass as he groans. "I love this ass," he says.

I raise an eyebrow. "Is that right, Rory Dennis?" I ask. He nods, and I reward him by facing away from him and scooting back to offer him a better view of it. After years of working my body into a machine, I am very proud of all my muscles—ass included. If one more person gets to admire it, who am I to argue?

The bed moves as Rory stands, and I scoot further back until my entrance feels the tip of his cock. I grind against him, begging for him to enter me. I am so wet from my first orgasm and so glad he took that care given his size. Both his hands wrap around my waist to hold me in place as he starts to slowly slide in. His fingers were blissful, but this, nothing could compare to the stretch of me with him inside.

"Valentina, fuck," he gurgles out, and I reward the sounds by rocking back and forth to match his gentle stroke. He stops moving for a long moment, giving me time to adjust to his size. I grab a pillow so I can rest my chest to the bed, and my ass raises higher. I want him to enjoy this view almost as much as I want to chase my next orgasm with him inside me.

He plunges into me and freezes deep inside. I clench experimentally around him, and he growls before he starts pounding into me. The grip he has on my waist tightens, his fingers digging into my skin, but the pain mixes with the pleasure, and I can't tell him to stop. I can only ask him to keep going. "Yes, Rory! Yes! Right there!"

Rory is listening because next follow a series of pumps so forceful, he is slowly scooting me further up the bed. I bite into the pillow under me as I let out a scream that gets muffled. My orgasm comes in waves this time, and he keeps driving into me, rolling me into a second climax and then a third. My legs start to shake when he sinks into me as his body clenches with his own release. I'm now regretting this position because I can't see him as he climaxes. I pant into the pillow and come up for air.

Rory kisses my back gently and withdraws from me. He steps into the restroom, probably to toss the condom before he comes back to bed and lies next to me. I curl to his side like I had done last night. "No falling asleep this time," I joke.

He laughs. "No falling asleep. Though, I don't think I could even if I wanted to. I feel well-rested."

"Oh really?" I wiggle my eyebrows at him.

"Are you trying to kill me, woman?" He chuckles. "I at least need sustenance, then maybe after that, and a bit of a rest, I will make you come five more times."

My thighs tighten at his words. His lips lock with mine again, but this time it's sweeter and with less urgency. "I'm going to hold you to that," I joke.

"First, I must get food."

"I have food, but you'll be sorry if I cook. Would you like to go out?"

"No. I prefer to spend the morning with you naked. I'll cook."

"You can cook?" I ask with surprise.

"I know my way a bit around the kitchen."

"Would you cook naked?" I ask.

He chuckles. "Can I at least wear my boxer-briefs? A naked cooking incident wouldn't be pretty."

"Fine," I say with resignation.

"You, on the other hand, I insist you remain naked while you watch me cook."

"I can manage that."

We get up and make our way to the kitchen. Rory leans toward the fridge and scratches his jaw through his beard. "You don't have much," he says. "But I think I can whip up some egg sandwiches. How does that sound?"

"Great," I say. And it does. I'm starting to love real bread with actual gluten. I don't know how I'll ever go back to my pre-cancer diet. I purse my lips because this is the first time I've caught myself making plans for the future, and I have the sickening sensation in my stomach that this new outlook has everything to do with the redhead with the broken sternum.

Which reminds me of his scar. Is it okay to ask now? I

understood he didn't want to say before. I thought maybe he didn't want to ruin the moment, but *when* would it be okay to ask?

He's a one-night-stand, so maybe it's better to not ask at all. *Don't get personal, Valentina. This is just for today.*

Rory places several items from the fridge on the counter, and I watch him from my spot at the bar. I'm sitting with my arms propped on the bar top so he can have a view of my breasts as he works. My breasts swell over my forearms, and I smile at him.

He looks up at me, and the corner of his mouth quirks up into a sexy smile. "Fuck breakfast. I'm eating you instead," he says and walks around the bar to me. He takes me by surprise and lifts me to reposition me on the barstool, so I face away from the counter. Kneeling, his face is at the level of my sex. My entire body blushes, and I almost want to close my legs. What the hell? I'm not shy.

"No." He grabs my knees and pushes them wide to expose me fully to his face. "Don't close your legs." He slides his fingers down the length of my folds. "You're beautiful," he says in a husky voice. I found Rory's deep voice sexy to begin with, but when it deepens further with his arousal, that sexiness reaches an entirely different level.

My chest expands with each labored breath, and I nod. He plays with the black curls of my pubic hair and presses a finger to my clit, sending my head back with pleasure. I'm so sensitive from our time together in bed, and the sensation is so extreme, my face twists into a grimace he can't see. I feel his tongue on me next, and my head snaps down to look at him. His tongue is circling my clit, but not touching it in a teasing motion. His head moves between my legs as he teases at my entrance with his tongue, and the view of his red mane between my legs is the most erotic thing I have ever seen in my life.

My fingers find their way to his hair and tug on it lightly. I keep his head in place where I want him, and a moan escapes him. "Rory," I purr his name. "That feels amazing." He rewards my praise by pressing his tongue to my swollen clit, and my legs start to quiver. His hands are keeping my legs apart, his grip tightening over my inner thighs. I'm so sensitive, that familiar coil starts building in my core almost instantly. His lips enclose around my clit so he can suck on it gently, and I can't take it anymore. My hands fist his hair, and my abdomen convulses as I climax onto his tongue. He doesn't stop, and the orgasm keeps going. I had no idea an orgasm could stretch out that long. Rory Dennis has a magic tongue.

I can't take the maddening ongoing release anymore, and I start to beg. "Rory, please, Rory, stop!"

He encircles his tongue around my clit one last time and finally comes up for air. My legs shake as he trails kisses up my lower abdomen, licks a circle around my belly button, and trails his tongue to my neck. He stops to nibble at my jaw and finishes with a sensual kiss that lets me taste myself on his lips. He parts from my mouth to study my face, and his smirk is cocky, like he is so damn proud of himself.

"That was yummy," I say, coming down from my fuck-drunk state.

"Indeed." Rory chuckles.

I look down, and he is starting to harden again, though he isn't at his full size yet. I reach for the waistband of his boxer-briefs, but he grabs my wrist with a shake of his head. "No. That was just for you."

"Rory—" I protest because I want my turn, but he kisses me into silence.

"One down," he says when his mouth leaves mine.

"What?"

"I told you I was going to make you come five more times before I leave today. Four more to go."

I blink slowly at him. This man can't be serious. I don't know if I can handle four more.

"I'm a man of my word, Valentina. You'll see." He pulls away from me and goes back to his work in the kitchen.

I blink after him, too stunned for words. It was odd how this day started, with him shy about his chest, but the moment I licked his scar, Rory came out of his shell. I smile at him, glad he could open up to me, even if only sexually.

I go to the restroom to clean up a bit, and when I get back, he winks at me, starts chopping onions, and tosses them into butter on a hot pan. He moves quickly, like he knows this kitchen. Before I know it, the smell of butter and eggs has my stomach grumbling.

"Here." He places the egg sandwich in front of me before coming around the counter to sit next to me.

"Thanks," I say, and we both dig in. "This is great," I offer after the first bite. He smiles and keeps chewing but squeezes my thigh.

"Valentina, how do you say 'sandwich' in Spanish?" he asks between bites.

I laugh. "How do you say 'taco' in English?"

Rory turns to me slowly, a large bite bulging his right cheek, and he blinks. He starts laughing and trying to swallow at the same time, which makes him cough. He takes a sip of water, and when he successfully swallows, he faces me again. "I don't think our Spanish lessons are going very well so far. Maybe I should give up?"

I laugh. "No, don't give up. Spanish is a beautiful language. And in your defense, there is a word for sandwich, but it's not really used. A lot of people wouldn't even know what it is. At least in Mexico."

"So you just call it sandwich, then?"

I nod. "But you have to pronounce it in Spanish."

Rory scratches his head. "What do you mean?"

"You say it like, '*sanguish*' with a soft 'g.'"

"That's weird."

"Or brilliant," I counter.

When we finish eating, I wrinkle my nose. "Don't take this the wrong way, but I can smell myself. I need a shower bad. You want to join me?"

"It would be an honor to shower with you." He stands and offers me his hand as he bows. His wavy bed-head is adorable, and even his beard is a bit messed up from our intense fucking. I smile and take his hand.

I lead him to the shower and let him adjust the water temperature to his liking. "This okay?" he asks. It's a little on the hot side for me, but I don't mind it much.

His skin reddens a bit with the heat as the water glides down his body. I bite my lip.

"Again?" he rolls his eyes. "Fine. But you're really taking advantage of my body, miss Almonte." He grabs a handful of my ass and squeezes.

I laugh. "No. Let's clean up a bit. I really need the shower."

"Okay." He grabs my loofah and the washcloth I brought for him, and I pour body wash liberally on both. We soap up and giggle as we get clean. I feel naughty, like a little kid who ate too many sweets before dinner. I wash my hair and am surprised when he shampoos his beard.

He chuckles at my expression. "It takes a lot of work to keep this beard."

"I like it," I say.

"Oh?"

"It's a great feeling when it tickles my inner thighs."

"Only for you, Valentina, I promise never to shave it off."

We are both rinsed off, and he grabs me by the waist, so my body is flush with his. His lips crush mine as he plays with his tongue on mine. He cups the back of my head as the water falls down both our faces, keeping my eyes shut tight. As we devour the others' mouths, his erection hardens against my abdomen. The water rolling down my body, his tight grip on me, and the erection twitching between us are all too much. When the hell did I become so damn insatiable that I want him again?

I break away from him and kneel on the shower floor much too quickly to give him a chance to protest. Wrapping my hand around his shaft, I pump once, then twice, while I squeeze gently. Rory groans, and his hands fist at his sides. He leans his head back on the tile, and the water now hits his chest and six-pack. I look up at his body and lick my lips. His gaze is glued to my face with hooded eyes.

Bringing my grip to the base of his shaft, I lick the head of his cock.

"Fuck, Valentina," he groans. His breathing quickens, and I take the head into my mouth, sucking on it gently before letting him out of my mouth again.

I look up. The water bounces off those six-pack muscles, making me squint. "Is this okay?" I ask as I pump with my hand once again.

"Fuck, yes," he all but screams, and I take him into my mouth again.

This time I take him deeper into my throat as I continue to stroke his base with my hand. He grips my hair in his fist and starts guiding me to the rhythm he wants, and I let him. Rory tastes divine, and seeing his body wet like this has my own wetness gliding down my thighs all over again. My pussy clenches at the sight of him with his eyes shut tight and the veins in his neck straining with the pleasure of my mouth.

"Stop," he growls and pulls me away by my hair.

"No," I whine. "More. Please."

"Fuck. It's hard to deny you, but I don't want to come in your mouth."

"I want you to come in my mouth." I reach for him with my tongue, but his grip on my hair is too tight.

"No," he shakes his head, though I know his resolve wavers. "I'm not wasting this on your mouth. Not today." He bends and places his hands under my armpits so he can lift me to my feet. He lands a wet kiss on my lips and pants when he breaks away.

"I'm about to impress the hell out of you," I tell him, and his eyebrow arches. I'm leaning against the cool tile of the shower wall, and I bring my right leg all the way up to rest against his shoulder, effectively doing the splits while standing.

"You are going to be the end of me," he groans. He presses his erection to my entrance, and I grind my clit up and down the shaft. I could come from just this friction alone.

I hear a wrapper, and my eyes fling open. "When did you get a condom?"

Rory chuckles. "I have many talents, Valentina."

He withdraws his hips away from me so he can roll on the condom, but I keep my leg over his shoulder as he does this. Taking his cock in hand, he positions it at my entrance, parting me slowly. I wince a bit, and he stills. "Are you okay?" he says. I nod. "We can stop if it's painful."

"No!" I all but scream out. "It hurts so good," I say.

With a sexy smile, he gives me another inch of him slowly, so slowly, my head leans back. In this stretched position, my tightening around him is extreme.

"Fuuuck," Rory draws out. "You feel so tight like this."

I can tell he is holding himself back with the slow, lazy strokes by the strained muscles of his arms encasing me. He keeps one hand on the wall behind me and takes the other away from the wall to cup my chin, and brings his lips to mine. I plunge my tongue into his mouth, and his pace quickens a bit.

He releases my mouth and leans back to bring his free hand between us and presses his thumb to my overly-sensitive and swollen clit.

I scream, and my leg muscles tighten over his shoulder as I come yet again for the who-the-fuck-knows-how-many times today. He drives into me so forcefully now, he is almost lifting me off the ground by his cock until he stills, effectively impaling me. His eyes tighten, and he groans out his release. I'm so glad we are facing each other now so I can see his face when he climaxes.

We both pant, and he presses his forehead to mine. "Thank you," he says.

"Are you thanking me for making you come?"

He chuckles. "Yeah. Guess I am." He leaves me, and I unwrap my leg from him, bringing it down to the ground. We rinse again, then dry off.

Rory is drying out his hair with a towel when he looks at me with a devilish grin. "Only three more to go."

Oh, for fuck's sake. "You really don't have to deliver on that. You've more than proved your sex-god status."

"Oh, but I want to deliver," he says with a teasing smile.

"Can I at least have a break?"

"Of course. So long as you remain naked the rest of the morning."

"Fine, but I'm wearing underwear at least. It's more comfortable."

"Agreed."

We both put on underwear before going to lounge on the sofa. Rory sits, and I lay my head on his lap. "What a fucking glorious morning," I say.

Rory pinches my nipple playfully. "You got that right."

I giggle.

Rory's head rests back as he looks at the ceiling and I look at him. We are both basking in the luxury of this lazy morning where all we've done is fuck and eat. A lump lodges in my throat because I want more of this. Preferably with Rory if he is up to it, but the bottom line is, I want more of life. I've hardly lived, and now I have found someone who has given me so many firsts that I'm thinking there are a hell of a lot more firsts

I haven't even begun to imagine. My eyes prickle with tears. I need to live. I need to survive.

I want more time.

Suddenly I'm reminded that I'm Valentina Fucking Almonte. A new fan-favorite MMA fighter in Mexico and shortlisted for the UFC. I have never backed down from a fight; why the hell was I about to start now? I sought Dr. Carolina Ramirez like I sought Chema—I wanted the best on my team, and I got her. Like there was never an option to lose a fight, there isn't an option to die. Not yet. Not for a long time.

"Are you okay?" Rory asks, his brows creased together.

Fuck. He's looking at me with puppy eyes. "Yeah. Just a little homesick. Wish I could show you around Mexico City."

"You mean like I showed you around Kansas City?"

I laugh. "Yeah. Exactly like that. Except for the falling asleep at the park bit."

"Let me make up for that. Saturday. I'll really show you around a few more places."

I shake my head. "Rory," I choke on my words. "I haven't changed my mind. This is a one-night-stand, or rather, a one-day-stand, but we aren't seeing each other again."

"I thought we agreed we would spend together whatever time we do have?"

Dammit. "Yeah. Okay, but let's not put pressure on this, okay? I can't really handle serious right now."

"Okay. We can take it slow."

"Thank you. I can't promise we can hang out Saturday, but if you like, you can stay over tonight." It's my last night to have him, I think.

"I can't," he says. "I have a shift at the hospital tonight. I start at four."

My eyes widen with horror, and I spring up to a sitting position like a Jack-In-The-Box toy. "What did you say?"

"I work tonight." His head cocks to the side as he tries to figure out what's wrong.

"Yeah, but you said 'at the hospital.'"

"That's right. Where we met." He smiles. "I'm a doctor."

No. No. No. This can't be happening. Then all the pieces fall into place. How could I have been so stupid? It was so obvious. I met him in the waiting area at Heartland Metro Hospital, never thinking he could be a doctor. I just assumed he was a student. He knew that Doctor Keach from the bar, which is why he backed off so easily. He was at the bar across the street from the hospital. I clear my throat. "So you work at Heartland Metro?"

"Now you want to get to know me?" He is teasing me, and I try to smile. I don't want him to know, so I have to play this off even though I already acted like a freak.

I shrug. "Just curious."

Crap.

"Why do you look like that?" he asks.

"Like what?"

"All green, like you are going to vomit."

"Just a little hot in here, don't you think?"

"I'm fine, but if you want to kick up your AC, go for it."

I walk to the hallway with the thermostat pretending to adjust it and use the time to take a deep breath and calm my racing heart. Let's think about this logically. Heartland Metro is almost a small city with lots of buildings. It would be improbable for us to bump into each other again. The likelihood of him being in the oncology department is slim. I mean, what would be the chances? And what's the worst that could happen if he finds out I am a patient there? It's not like we are a couple; it shouldn't be a big deal. He couldn't get mad because why would I tell a one-night-stand my medical history? It's not like he told me about his scar. Calmer, I walk back to the couch and lie down again.

"Better?" He asks.

"Yeah. Thanks."

I want to change the subject, so I think. I look down his slim but muscular legs. "Are you a runner?" I ask.

"Yeah. Don't usually skip a morning run, but I figure you have provided me with quite a bit of cardio for today." He smirks, and I laugh. "Why do you ask?"

"Your legs. Well, really, your build. You have a deceivingly muscular body."

"Hey, what's that supposed to mean?"

"Nothing. I like your athletic build, but you don't really show it off much with your loose clothes."

"Some things are best left to the imagination."

I DOZE OFF AFTER A SHORT WHILE AND AWAKEN AT A SENSATION between my legs. I have no clue how long Rory has been fingering me, but his gaze is locked on my face like he is studying.

"Mmmm," I moan. "That feels good."

My head is on his lap, but he is leaning slightly so he can reach my center. He works me until I come again, and within the next twenty minutes, he delivers on his promise with the remaining two orgasms.

We lay in my bed for a few hours, Rory asking me how to say different words in Spanish. We keep the conversation light, and I'm grateful he can read my mood so well.

"I have to go," Rory says, and I look at the clock on my night-stand. It's noon, and our morning is officially over.

He smiles. "Sex and eggs," he says.

"What?"

"Sex and eggs. I could get used to this." I smack him playfully on the arm, and he gets up to start dressing. "I hope we can do this again soon," he says.

"We'll see."

"Can I get your number?" When he sees my hesitation, he adds, "I know where you live. Would you rather I stop by?"

"Fine." I enter my number in his phone. He calls it like he is not sure I gave him the right number, but it rings in my room, and he gives me one last kiss before he leaves.

Chema used to tell me I should promise myself rewards to keep up with my training and stay motivated, so I follow his advice now. I'm going to beat this thing, so I can have Rory once more before I go home, I promise myself.

Because I haven't had nearly enough of him yet.

CHAPTER 6

With Rory gone, there is nothing else to do in the apartment except eat. I didn't want to go explore because somehow, that is something I now want to do with him. I heavily smother my fourth piece of toast with butter as I think of what to do with my time.

In another first in my week of 'firsts,' as I now fondly think of it, I have free time. I would have to thank Mandy for prescribing the sex-athon because it had been a while, and it will be longer after treatment.

Going back to the bar to pick out another hookup doesn't appeal. Plus, I doubt anyone would measure up to Rory and his enthusiastic fucking. And if that wasn't enough of a deterrent, I couldn't go to the same bar without risking bringing home another doctor from the hospital where my treatment will take place.

Mandy calls at three in the afternoon, and I am glad for the distraction from my boredom.

"I'm having drinks at a friend's tonight, and you are coming with," she says before so much as a 'hello.'

"Hi Mandy, I'm fine, thanks for asking. Sure, thanks for inviting me."

"Sarcasm doesn't look as good on you as it does on me," she says dryly.

"What time? And where do I meet you?"

Mandy sighs into the phone. "Do you even have a car?"

"I didn't really have to drive in the City, so . . ."

"Oh, my, god. Don't tell me you don't know how to drive!"

I laugh. "I'm joking. I have a car."

"Forget it. I'll pick you up at seven," she says and hangs up.

I'm ready by seven, but Mandy doesn't show up until seven forty-five. I'm sitting on the stoop in front of my building when she shows up in an old, beat-up clunker of a car. When she rolls down her window, a litany of apologies trail out.

"It's really okay," I tell her once I'm in the passenger side. "Honestly, I wanted to enjoy the nice night out."

"Okay," she bites her lip, looking guilty as she drives. "I have a hard time getting to places on time."

"No worries. So? We're going to a friend's house?"

"Yeah. They work at the hospital with me, but don't worry, they're discreet, and you don't have to tell them anything you don't want to. I know I could use a girls' night, and I figured you might as well."

"I don't know," I say. "I don't really have any girlfriends," I admit, and I'm not sure why that makes me feel embarrassed.

"Not even one?"

"Does my sister count?"

Mandy shakes her head, and her laughter fills the car. "No. Your sister definitely doesn't count."

I shrug, unsure what else to say to that.

"Don't tell me you are one of those girls who is too cool for other girls? You only hang out with men because you 'identify' better with them?"

I laugh. "No. When you're trying to be a pro athlete, it's hard to have time for friends at all. I didn't really go anywhere, so it was hard to meet people, and yeah, fighting gyms are filled ninety-nine percent with men. I mostly have male friends because of convenience, not because I think I'm superior to other women or anything."

"Okay, girl. I get you. I get you."

"Also, my resting bitch face doesn't help."

Mandy laughs again. "Yeah, you do have one of those, though I would never have pointed it out."

"It's helpful in the fighting cage, but I think people find it hard to approach me in everyday life. Except for you. You are kind of fearless, aren't you?"

Mandy shrugs. "I don't know. I think I pick people. I find someone who I think, 'this person is worth my time,' and it's not always the obvious choice, but I always have my reasons."

My cheeks raise a few degrees when she mentions picking me to be in her life. It seems like an intimate statement I'm not used to having in friendships. "What was your reason for picking me?" I ask.

Mandy thinks for a moment, then says softly, "You're like the calm in the eye of the storm. You'll learn this about me, but I'm a fucking mess. It's all chaos when it comes to Amanda Gomez. I'm guessing opposites attracted when it came to you. I was impressed at how you have kept your shit together through the clinical trial process. Usually, it's a lot of crying and emotion. I'm not saying you are emotionless; I know inside shit is going on in your head, but you keep your cool. I'm guessing it's the fighter in you."

"Huh," I take in her assessment and examine it in my mind. "I think, for the most part, people think I'm hard to get to know, that I don't let anyone in, and maybe that's partially true, but I'd like to change that."

Mandy smiles at me with encouragement, and I get the

feeling this woman is going to be an important part of my life—
because she has already declared me a part of hers.

A young woman who has to be much younger than Mandy
or me opens the door. Mandy introduces her as Izel. She takes
me by surprise with a hug and steps aside to let us in. Izel's face
is round, and she has short, light-brown hair with curtain
bangs. She is wearing yoga pants and a slouchy sweater that falls
off one shoulder. Her body is on the plumper side, but those
curves could kill.

"Wine?" Izel offers.

"Sure," Mandy and I both say.

"Take a seat, *estás en tu casa*," she yells from the kitchen as she
gets our drinks. When she comes back, Izel is clumsily clutching
three wine glasses much too full with red wine. "How was that?"
she asks, looking at Mandy.

"Perfect pronunciation," Mandy says, and we both take a
glass each.

"You don't speak Spanish?" I ask Izel.

"No. My mom is super Chicana, and so is her sister, so they
gave their daughters the most Mexican names they could think
of. I kind of rebelled when I was younger and rejected everything about our language and culture. I regret it now, but at the
time, my own personal revolt against my parents was the most
important thing."

"When you were young?" I say pointedly. "Are you even old
enough to drink?"

Mandy is so close to me on the couch, her laughter startles
me. "Izel is older than you," she says. "She just has a baby face,"
Mandy says with a baby voice and pinches Izel's cheek. Izel
swats her hand away, annoyed. "Where's Tlali?" Mandy
asks her.

"She was just taking a shower. She had to stay overtime today and got home not that long ago."

"Tlali?" I ask, thinking. "Izel and Tlali, those are Nahuatl names, right?"

Izel blinks at me. "Man, my mom, and Tlali's mom would love you. I bet you speak like proper Spanish, huh?"

I don't have a chance to answer before Mandy does. "Yeah. The real shit. This girl here comes from old Spanish money," Mandy says and grins at me.

Geesh. I'm annoyed she continues to find it a novelty that my family has money. "To be clear," I say. "My family has money, not me."

We hear someone clamoring down the stairs excitedly. "Did I hear the door?"

A woman joins us in the living room and pulls Mandy into a hug. She is tall and slender, with beautiful tanned skin much darker than Izel's, so it's hard to believe they are related. Her hair is wet, but I can see the thick mass of curls that hit just below her shoulders. "Nice to meet you," she says and kisses my cheek. "I'm Tlali."

"Hi. Nice to meet you too."

The four of us claim our wine glasses and relax into the evening. I'm surprised at how quickly I become comfortable with this small group of women, but it's natural, like so many things have been in Kansas City.

"I can't believe you two are related," I say, looking between Tlali and Izel. "You don't look anything alike."

"Well," Tlali explains, "our moms are half-sisters, and my dad is Afro-Mexican."

"And my mom," Mandy interjects, "is not related to their moms by blood, but they consider her a sister as well, so we are basically cousins."

"So you have all been in Kansas City for several generations?"

They all nod.

"Wow," I say. "I didn't know there were so many Latinx here."

"Oh yeah," Tlali says. "There's even a small town several hours away that is a meat-packing town, and it is a minority-majority town."

"What does that mean?" I ask.

"More than half of the population is Mexican or Mexican-American. Sometimes Izel and I take long weekend vacations just to go there. It's like being in Mexico. Amazing food and all that."

"I'd like to go there sometime," I say, feeling homesick for real now.

"You planning on moving here or something?" Mandy asks.

I shrug. "I don't know what my plan is now. It kind of took a detour."

Mandy smiles with understanding, and I love her intuitiveness more than ever because she changes the subject.

"So, I met this guy," Mandy says as she tosses her hair over one shoulder as she did when she was flirting with my furniture delivery guy.

Tlali and Izel both lean in with interest. "Do tell," says Izel.

"And thank the stars, I hope this means you're over that other *pendejo*," adds Tlali.

Mandy rolls her eyes and ignores those comments about whoever her ex was. "His name is Chris. I actually met him at Valentina's."

The two cousins glance over at me. "He was my furniture delivery guy," I explain.

"Oh, my god, there were three of them, and they were all so hot. I almost want to have furniture delivered and send it back so they can come back again to pick it up," Mandy says.

Tlali raises her glass to Mandy in cheers of approval, and they clink glasses. "How'd you pick?" Tlali asks.

"It was so hard, guys. Seriously. It was like I was a kid at a candy store."

"She was drooling like one too," I say, and Izel snorts with her laughter.

Mandy rolls her eyes again. "In the end, Chris had the thickest arms."

"And you do love you some thick arms," Izel says.

"That I do. Anyway, there he is in the living room, and Valentina and I are watching him put together her sofa. And he is sweating and looking hot as hell; I couldn't help it. I ask him for his name, and I invite him to my art show. Then I give him my number."

"And he calls?" I ask.

"No," Mandy says. "Well, not fast enough. So I call the furniture company, I got the name from the truck when they left, and I give them your address. I tell them I was impressed with the delivery service—which isn't a lie—and that I'd like to thank them personally. They give me their numbers, and I call Chris."

"Stalker much?" Tlali asks.

"Shut up. I call him up, and he sounds glad I called."

"What do you say to him?" I ask, thoroughly impressed by her *cojones*.

"I tell him he took too long to call, and his window was closing. He claims he lost the flyer and was glad I called—not sure I buy it, but I give him the benefit of the doubt. He asks me out for drinks, and I take him to the studio for a nightcap."

"So, how was it?" Izel asks.

"Amazing," Mandy says. "I'm surprised I'm walking today."

I almost spit my wine out but manage to keep it in. It goes down the wrong pipe, and I start coughing. Is this what women talk about? What girlfriends talk about? I mean, it's no worse than the locker room talk at the gym, but I've never heard bluntness like this from women before.

Izel sighs and stares off into space. "I need to get some. It's been too long," she says.

"Amen, sister," Tlali joins in, and they clink glasses.

"How long?" Mandy asks them.

"Three months," Tlali says.

"Two weeks," says Izel.

"Two weeks is too long for you?" I ask.

Izel nods and sips her wine. "Yeah. Isn't it for you?"

I shake my head. "No. I'd say months would be long, but not just a few weeks."

"Speak for yourself," Mandy says. "I'm with Izel on this one. Can't go that long. Why? How long has it been for you?"

I feel the heat creeping up my neck, and I stare into my glass like it's the most exciting thing in the world, so it's hard to look back at Mandy's face, but I do.

Mandy narrows her eyes. "You little slut," she says in a playful tone. "You did it, didn't you? You listened to me?"

I look up at the cousins, hoping they'll help, but they blink at each other.

"We're lost," Tlali says.

"I told Valentina to have a sex-athon, and I think she did."

"Fine," I say. If this is what it's like to have girlfriends, then I should go all in. "Yes. I picked up a guy at a bar yesterday, and we spent all morning together until he had to go at noon today. That's all the details you're getting."

"No," Mandy whines. "We need details. Who's the guy? Is he hot? You can't leave us hanging like this."

Izel jumps into my rescue. "Come on, Mandy. Leave her alone. She's clearly not a *cochina* like you. Not everyone shares as much as we do."

I try to communicate a telepathic 'thank you' to Izel, and she tips her chin at me. If there is a chance Mandy knows Rory, I can't give out any further details.

"You said there were *three* hot delivery guys?" Tlali asks.

"Yeah," Mandy says.

"And you have all three cell numbers?" Izel asks with interest.

I can almost see the moment when the matching floating light bulbs over the cousin's heads light up.

"I do!" Mandy rummages through her purse, producing a yellow Post-It note. She crosses off something, presumably Chris's name and number, and hands the piece of paper to Tlali.

"I'm going to go put this on the fridge door before we spill wine on it," Tlali says.

"So," Izel turns to me. "Let's get to know you. What do you do? What brings you to Kansas City?"

Mandy smiles at me, and I remember her words from the car. I only have to tell them as much as I want to.

"Well, I was training as an MMA fighter—"

"Whoa, like an actual fighter? Like a UFC fighter?" Tlali asks, now back in the living room with us.

"Yeah. Well, I wasn't in the UFC yet," I say.

"You will be one day," Mandy reassures me.

I smile at her. I don't know if it's the wine that has relaxed me or how welcome Izel and Tlali have made me feel, but I find myself confiding in them openly. "I'm here for treatment. I met Mandy at the hospital."

Tlali and Izel eye each other in a gesture I am starting to understand is some sort of telepathy or *brujeria* between them.

"I have cervical cancer, and I'm on Dr. Ramirez's clinical trial. I'll be in K.C. until treatment is over."

Izel changes seats so she can be next to me on the sofa. She wraps her arm around my shoulder into a half hug. "Dr. Ramirez is amazing," she says. "You'll be fine."

"And we got you. Whatever you need," Tlali adds with a smile of her own.

My eyes sting with tears; I am so moved by this small tribe of women who don't know me from Eve but offer a safety net for when I fall. If this is what having girlfriends is like, I never want to go back. "Can we talk about something else? Treatment starts tomorrow, and today I just want to feel normal," I say as I wipe my eyes.

I don't share all my fears with them. The prospect of going under the knife for the first surgical procedure of my life is terrifying, and I'll have to follow that up with radiation. I need my mind off it all and am so thankful these girls are here to help with that.

"Of course, *amiga*," Tlali says. "What you wanna talk about?"

"Um, what do you guys do at the hospital?"

"We all have double lives," Izel says with a grin.

"What?" I ask, confused.

Izel points her chin toward Mandy. "You know how she's a research assistant-slash front desk clerk at the hospital by day and a painter by night?"

"Yeah . . ."

"Well, I'm a surgical technologist by day, and I write by night," Izel says.

"And I'm a medical interpreter by day, and I translate novels by night," Tlali says.

Mandy jumps in. "We have a master plan that we will all one day make a living from our arts and leave our day jobs. We cheer each other on to stay motivated."

"That's amazing," I say. "What kind of books do you write and translate?"

"I write horror," says Izel. "Pretty gruesome stuff," she says with a delighted grin on her face.

Tlali rolls her eyes. "And I translate proper literature. Or want to, anyway."

"So you do speak Spanish? Or are you translating another language?"

"Yeah, Spanish."

"Your double lives—it's like Superman and Clark Kent—"

"Exactly," Mandy says. "Did you know Superman is from Kansas?"

I shake my head. "No, I didn't."

We laugh and get to know each other better the rest of the night. The cousins don't ask me more about myself unless I offer tidbits, and I realize they are trying to respect my privacy.

If I make it out of this, I hope we can all stay friends. I surprise myself because, more and more, my plans post-treatment seem to shift to Kansas City and away from home.

CHAPTER 7

"**I** have to ask you one last time, Valentina. Are you sure? We can still stop." Dr. Ramirez looks at me with creased brows. I understand she's just doing her due diligence, asking about fertility again. We have the same conversation we did on our first appointment, and I don't budge.

"There are more ways than one to become a mom," I say to settle the matter once and for all. "I'm not saying I won't ever change my mind about being a mom, but if I do, I'm pretty damn sure I don't want to cook my own, if you know what I mean."

The corner of her mouth slants into a weak smile, and she sighs. "You've thought this out."

"I have. I'm young, I know that, but I also have always known what I want."

"Okay. You've convinced me." Dr. Ramirez presses the nurse call button next to my bed.

A short, slim blonde walks in. She smiles broadly and moves with jerky movements like she's had too much caffeine. "Hi, Miss Almonte. I'm Sara," she says and gives me her hand to shake.

"Just Valentina, please, or Vale if you'd like."

She smiles at me and goes over to a laptop resting on a cart in the corner of my room. "I see we have surgery and radiation scheduled today."

"First round of treatment," Dr. Ramirez says. "I have to go to my next patient. Can you take care of transport, Sara?"

"Sure," the nurse says.

"For future procedures, we'll have an orderly transport you, but for this first one, I'd like to go with you. Dr. Ramirez briefed me about you, and I'd like you to have a friendly face around."

"Thank you," I say. She brings a wheelchair into the room, I sit, and she wheels me out of the room.

"So, I hear you are a fighter?"

"Yeah. I was." I say it in the past tense for the first time.

"You box or something?"

"Mixed martial arts, but yeah, boxing is one of my strengths."

"Wow. Must be amazing to be a professional athlete."

I smile, remembering everything I left behind. She keeps talking.

"Are you nervous?"

"A little. Mostly I'm eager to put this behind me," I say. *One way or the other*, I add mentally.

"I'm not going to lie, it's going to be rough, but Dr. Ramirez and I, we got your back." She squeezes my shoulder, and the solitude I carry starts to chip away at the edges.

We get out of the elevator, and she tells me we are almost there. "When you're going under anesthesia, in that freaky alien setting, and they are asking you to count down from ten, it helps to think of your happy place or a person who means a lot to you. Think about that to help with the nerves."

"Okay. Thanks for the tip."

Nurse Sara hands me over to a technician, and I'm transferred to a bed and then wheeled into the operating room. She was right; this place is freaky and alien. I smile, thinking how this is such a perfect workplace for Izel, the horror writer. She must get excellent creative fodder from everything she sees here.

When I begin the countdown, nurse Sara's words run through my head, and I think of my happy place. I'm in the locker room, getting ready for a fight. My hair is pinned back in braids. I encase my hands with the knuckle wraps and position my mouthguard between my teeth. I stretch my neck from side to side and bounce in place like I'm jumping rope.

I'm walking out of the locker room through a sea of people calling my name—only one is distinguishable, with those unruly red waves bright in the audience. The cage calls to me like a siren's song; my opponent is waiting for me. I step into the cage, and my world goes black.

The next thing I know, I'm striking the current flyweight titleholder. She stumbles back, recovers, and kicks me in the jaw with a force that sends me flying and landing on my ass. She wastes no time in clamoring over to me, and her fists rain down on my face. I go into a defense position, with my fists covering my face for only a second. I bring my legs around her torso and my arms around her neck, placing her in a triangle choke. My grip is so tight around her, her punches weaken.

When her exhaustion weakens her struggle, I swing my body with full momentum, rolling us both over. I land on top, taking the dominant position. The crowd cheers, but somehow, one voice calling to me rises above the deafening cheers.

"Valentina? Valentina? Honey, wake up," says the voice.

I open my eyes, and my brain is in a haze. It takes me a while to remember where I am and why. My face is wet and cold, and I bring up a hand to wipe it dry. I was crying.

"Sorry," Sara says. "I normally wouldn't try to wake you, but I think you were having a nightmare."

"No," I say. "It was a good dream." My voice is husky, and my throat hurts as I say this.

"Oh. I'm sorry, then. Is your mouth dry?"

Rolling my tongue across the roof of my mouth, it gets stuck with the dryness. I clasp my throat and nod. She places a cup full of ice chips on a tray over my bed, and I suck on those.

Sara looks at the monitors I'm hooked up to and makes some notes on my chart on the laptop. "Dinner should be here in about an hour." She points to a bin sitting next to me on the bed. "In case you need it. Nausea hits at different times for different people, but be prepared for it tonight to be on the safe side."

"Thanks," I say.

When I'm alone, I pull the blankets to one side and lift my hospital gown. I can't see the incisions because they are covered in bandages. I flex my abdomen gently, testing for pain, but whatever they gave me is strong enough it never comes.

It's a strange thing, going from the perfect body to one that is cut up and radiated. I don't feel any different, and I start to hope I can get back to the cage when this is all said and done.

When dinner comes, I lift the lid to find the most disgusting-looking bowl of soup. The stereotype of hospital food being gross is no joke. Despite not enjoying the dinner one bit, nausea from radiation doesn't kick in tonight. I sleep through the night, and I wonder if I could be so lucky as to avoid the horrors of side effects.

I am so wrong.

In the morning, I devour pancakes that aren't quite as bad as the chicken noodle soup, but they almost instantly come back up.

The rest of the day is a constant race between Sara and the other nurses to rush fresh basins for my vomit. If that weren't bad enough, by the evening, I'm spewing out the other end too. How the hell can you get diarrhea when you are vomiting everything you eat?

By morning, my body feels like it's been through five fights in a row, with no breaks, and lost all of them. I finally am able to keep down some mashed potatoes. It is a triumph because it means I don't have to live in the hospital until chemo starts the following week.

"I hear you finally ate and kept it down?" Dr. Ramirez walks in, pumps hand sanitizer on her hands, and sits next to me.

"Yeah. It was pretty gnarly there for a second."

"Valentina, this is only going to get much worse before it gets better."

"I know. I'm in this. I swear."

"The standard of care is also a great option. We can go for less aggressive treatment over a longer period of time. You don't have to be in this trial if it's too much."

"It's been one day, doc. You giving up on me already?"

She laughs. "No. Of course not. It's protocol that the patient understands we can stop at any time."

"I'm not stopping. Your chances are my best chances. Do your worst. I can take it."

"Okay, then. Since you can keep your food down, you can go home this afternoon. On Monday, you have your first chemo-radiation combo. Be here at eleven."

"I know. I know," I say. "We go like that for five weeks."

"With weekends off," she adds.

"I never thanked you for breakfast the other day."

Dr. Ramirez smiles. "My pleasure. Amanda is a wonderful human. I was hoping you two would become friendly."

"We did. She's great and a total riot."

Dr. Ramirez laughs at my assessment. "That's one word to describe her. I personally use 'firecracker.'"

My phone buzzes on the table, and I grab it. It's an unknown number.

"Go ahead and take it. We are done here. I'll have discharge papers here in a bit."

"Thanks, doctor. Really."

Turning my attention back to the phone, I answer. "Hello?"

"Valentina, I'm so glad you picked up." Rory's voice sends my blood pressure through the roof. Crap. Why did I pick up? I should have known it was him.

"Um, hey." I press my hand to the phone, hoping the line doesn't pick up any of the hospital sounds.

"I'm calling about that date," he says.

"I'm not sure I'm free."

"I'll check in with you Saturday morning. We can play it by ear. If you're free, you're free. If not, we can hang out another time."

"Uh, okay," I say reluctantly. The thing is, his voice is the most comforting thing in this hospital room.

"Valentina, can I say something without you freaking out?"

"I suspect you will no matter what I say."

Rory laughs. "True." Then his voice turns serious. "I can't stop thinking about you."

Why does he have to go and say all the wonderful things? He was a play-thing, a boy-toy. I was meant to never see him again.

Tell yourself what you want, Valentina. You gave him your number for a reason.

I can't stop thinking about him either. Memories of our day together have kept me sane the last twenty-four hours. But I can't tell him that.

"You are freaking out, aren't you?" he asks.

"No. I'm not freaking out." I pout as though he can see me, and he laughs again.

"Well, I need to get back to work. I just wanted to say, have a good day, and I'll be thinking about you."

"Thank you, Rory. You have a good day too."

"And?"

"And what?"

"And, you will be thinking about me too."

"Fine. I'll be thinking about you too."

I'm a bit panicked he might walk by my door, so I press the call button, and Sara's head pops in. I ask her to close my door for privacy, and she tells me she'll be right back with discharge paperwork.

The strangest feeling comes over me as I wait. I started out this journey homesick for the gym, for Chema, and for Pili. But now, my homesickness is more about time with Rory, and Mandy, and even the cousins Izel and Tlali. It feels strangely like Kansas City is home, not Mexico. I won't deny I miss Chema and my sister, but they don't beat in the same spot in my heart that home beats anymore.

Sara comes back to change the dressing over the two small laparoscopic incisions on my lower abdomen. I sign a stack of paperwork, get a prescription for pain medication I won't fill, and take a ridiculous cab ride the two blocks to my apartment.

I'm lying down and icing my belly when I get a text from Chema. My heart sinks. He knows nothing yet. The longer I've kept him at arms-length, the harder it has been for me to give him the excuse I had planned for him. I read all his texts in Spanish.

Chema: *Where are you?*

Me: *I'm sorry. I've been meaning to call you. I'm out of town.*

Chema: *Out of town?*

Me: *Yeah. I'm in the U.S.*

Chema: *What? You never cleared it with me. You haven't trained in a week!*

I don't answer him again because I'm a chicken shit, but minutes later, the phone rings, and it's him, and he's furious.

"What's going on?" he clips as soon as I answer the call.

"Hi, Chema. Miss you too."

"Don't be cute."

"I'm sorry. You don't deserve me disappearing on you."

"What? You're disappearing?"

"I wanted to tell you in person. I thought I'd get a break soon so I could say this face-to-face, but that didn't work out," I lie. My chest constricts at the betrayal I'm about to lay on him. "I got an agent."

"That's great, Tini! Why didn't you tell me? I knew you were starting to get attention. We even had a reporter here yesterday looking for you."

"You did?"

"Yeah," Chema says, all the anger gone from his voice. I imagine his hulkish frame that never quite seems to fit his warm smile.

"That's a first," I say, surprised.

"I know. I'll email you the details so you can tell your agent. If they want to do a feature at the gym while we train, that would be great for the gym too, Tini."

"Chema," I say and feel the tears in my throat. "There's more."

"What's wrong?" His voice is all concern now.

"My agent agency. They want me to train with someone else."

"You're dropping me?"

I take a deep breath. "I have no choice. It's the only way the agent would sign me. I had to agree to the new coach and new training plan."

Chema laughs bitterly on the other end, and the sound knocks the wind out of me. "After everything we've been through? After getting you this far? This is how you repay me?"

"I'm sorry, Chema. Please believe me, I never meant to hurt you. It just worked out this way."

"You know what the worst part is?"

All of it, I think, but keep silent.

"The worst part is I remember that gangly little kid with not a muscle on her body begging me and pestering me to train her."

"I remember," I smile when I think of our start. "It took me four months to persuade you."

"You never persuaded me, Tini. You're a force of nature. There isn't a goal you set you don't accomplish. You wanted me as your coach, and you showed up at my gym daily until you willed me into being your coach."

"I'm grateful for everything—"

"Which is why I don't buy this 'it just worked out this way' bullshit of yours. If you decided to drop me, that's fine, but I deserve the respect of being your mentor—of being your friend. Hell, Tini, you're my little sister. You owed it to me to tell me to my face. I'm your fucking family."

"Chema—" I croak out, but he is no longer on the phone with me.

I roll to my side and curl my knees to my chest. A shiver runs through me, and the fetal position provides warmth. I cradle the phone in my hand, hoping he'll call back. Hoping he'll let me apologize. Hoping he'll forgive me.

But there is no call, and I fall asleep like that.

CHAPTER 8

$\mathcal{B}$eing sick sucks. The only good thing about it, and I really do mean the only good thing, is that I get to watch all the television I never got to when I was in training.

I'm halfway through the live-action version of *Beauty and the Beast* when my doorbell rings.

"Who is it?"

"It's me, girl." Mandy's loud voice fills my living room from the intercom, and I wince at the sound.

I buzz her in and unlock my door. I'm back on the couch when she enters my apartment.

"How's it going?" she asks.

"I've been better."

"I'm sure. Sorry I didn't visit while you were in the hospital—"

"It's okay, Mandy. I know you work there. I don't expect you to want to spend your time off there too."

"Wish that were it. I'm actually working overtime to get the pieces ready for the art show."

"That's right. How's that going?" I ask, and my face

scrunches up with a short-lasting jolt of pain at the incision sites.

"Where are your pain meds?" Mandy asks.

"It's nothing," I say.

"Don't give me that. Where are they?" Mandy walks over to my kitchen and starts rummaging through my cabinets.

"I didn't fill the prescriptions," I admit.

"Valentina! Seriously? You're going to need them soon."

"I'll go to the hospital pharmacy at my next appointment. Happy?"

"Barely," she says and plops on the cushion next to me. "What are we watching?"

"*Beauty and the Beast.*"

"Oh, is this the one with Emma Watson as Belle? I love this version."

"Would you like me to start it over, Mandy?"

She grins. "Thanks for taking the hint."

We both relax, and I forget all about the pain as we watch the movie. Her presence lifts me somehow and props me up. I only hope I can be the same for her if she ever needs this kind of support.

My sister would be here now if I had told her and she was able to get away from her obligations. Who am I kidding? She could only be here if her husband were to give her permission, which is a big 'if.' I didn't want to put her in that difficult position. Having Mandy in that sisterly role almost made up for Pilar's absence. Almost.

The movie is nearly over when my phone dings on the seat next to me. I smile at the nickname I saved Rory under until I realize Mandy's gaze also followed the chime, probably thinking it was her own phone. Panic overtakes my smile.

"*Big Dick?*" her eyebrow raises suggestively. "Who's *Big Dick?*"

"Oh my god. Shut up," I say and grab the phone so she can't read his full text.

Mandy pauses the movie and turns to face me instead. "Come on, give up the goods."

"Fine. Just that one night stand I already told you about."

Mandy raises an eyebrow. "You exchanged phone numbers with a one night stand?"

"It was a mistake, okay? Chemo brain."

"Oh no, you don't. You gave him your number before you started treatment. Besides, it's too soon for chemo brain. Oh," she says, and her mouth forms into a smile.

"What?"

"You *like* him."

I avert my gaze.

She relents, finally, and starts playing the movie again. I read the text that came through.

Rory: *You end up being free?*

I sigh. It's Saturday, and he is claiming his date. If only I could go with him. It's not like I don't want to go, but I have no energy. I make up an excuse. I base it on truth, so it'll be harder to slip in my story. I was having enough of a hard time casting the web of lies with Chema and Pili as it was.

Me: *Yes. But I can't. I'm not feeling well.*

Rory: *What's wrong?*

Me: *Just a stomach bug. Raincheck? I wouldn't want to get you sick.*

I'm not sure how long I'll be able to spin that lie and keep Rory at bay, but I'm not ready to say goodbye to him yet.

"*Chica*, you should see the smile on your face," says Mandy.

I roll my eyes and grab a cushion, hugging it to my body. The credits roll, and Mandy and I both sigh after the Beast.

"You know," she says over the credits' music. "There's a massive plot hole in Beauty and the Beast."

"Oh yeah? What's that?"

"Belle should have totally tapped Gaston's fine ass."

"No, she shouldn't have!" I say, appalled at the travesty she just suggested.

"Oh, come on, tell me, if you had been in a little town like that with few options, you wouldn't have had a little fun with him?"

"He is really hot, isn't he?" I ask sheepishly.

Mandy nods. "And athletic, which I'm sure is your type." Mandy stands and stretches her arms over her head. "Between your text from Big Dick and watching Gaston grunt in that fight scene, I seriously want some. I'm going to go see what Chris is up to."

"Okay. Thanks for stopping by."

"Sure thing. Oh, tomorrow night, if you're feeling up to it—and only if you are feeling up to it—I'll pick you up for dinner. We have Sunday family dinners, and you can meet my parents."

"I'll let you know if it's a good day."

Mandy leaves, and I scroll through movie options to pick my next movie when a knock at the door distracts me. It's strange because I didn't buzz anyone up. I wonder if Mandy is back for some reason.

"Did you forget something—" I start to ask, opening the door, but freeze when I see him. For a long moment, I don't know what to do. My jaw drops.

Rory stands in front of me, handsome as I remembered him, with a grocery sack in each hand. "Can I come in?" he asks.

"Um, sure. Sorry." I move aside, and he steps through, making his way to the kitchen.

"No offense, but you look like crap," he says.

"You should have just said *offense*."

He chuckles, but the concern continues to crease his brows. "You lose a fight or something?"

I laugh. "Yeah. Something like that."

"Am I ever going to get to watch you fight?" he asks.

The question saddens me more than I would have thought. The truth is, I have no idea if I'll ever get back to the cage. "What's that?" I ask as I try to peer into the grocery bags he has placed on my counter. Changing the subject is safer. I avoid sitting at the barstool because barstools and Rory in the same room are a dangerous proposition, and I'm still weak from my first round of treatment.

"Well," he says. "You said you were sick, so I brought supplies. You know I'm a doctor, right?"

"Yeah, you mentioned."

He starts pulling out items and turns them on the counter so they face me. First in the lineup is a tall white container. "Chicken noodle soup," he says. I hope it's better than what they serve at the hospital, but I stay quiet. "Crackers." He pulls out a six-pack of ginger ale and puts that in the fridge.

"You really didn't have to do all this, Rory."

"I know." He shrugs. "I wanted to. And that's not all." He keeps pulling items from the bags, and I can't help but laugh when I see the rest of his purchases. There's a familiar blue container of Vick's Vapor Rub—or *vaporú* as we call it in Mexico—and a tall candle with the *Virgen de la Guadalupe* on it.

"You're unreal," I say through a laugh that sends a small shock of pain through my incisions. I play it off and keep talking. "How did you know?"

"You okay?" He asks with concern.

I scramble through my brain for a lie. "Yeah. Just a bit of a stomachache."

He nods. "I searched online for Mexican home remedies, and these two items came up a lot. Sprite and lemon did too, but I thought it might be a bit much."

"Oh, *that* would be a bit much? How'd you think to do this?"

"Every culture has its own home remedies. It's kind of interesting to a doctor. Would you like some soup?"

I shake my head. "Not really hungry yet. Later?"

"Sure. You staying hydrated?"

"Okay, you know you're not actually my doctor, right?"

Rory's hands shoot up in surrender and then he places the soup container in the fridge too.

"Well, thanks for stopping by, and you know, checking in."

"You kicking me out?"

"No, I just—" I bite my lip and look away from him. "I can't imagine you'd want to hang out with me while I'm sick. And besides, it's kind of gross. I'm not ready for you to hear those sounds."

"If I may, I would like to counter those points," he says seriously as he counts fingers. "One, I'm a doctor. No sound to escape you should embarrass you. Two, yes, hanging out with you is exactly what I want. Three, if you are worried about getting me sick, don't. Work a year at a hospital, and you will have the immune system of a god. And four, I would cheer you up."

"Fine," I say, happier than I would have liked. "But no funny business. I'm just being lazy on the couch and watching TV."

"That's exactly what I would have prescribed," he says and kicks off his shoes before taking his spot on the couch. "Seriously, though. I'm sorry you aren't feeling well."

I sit next to him, and it must be too far for his liking because he wraps his arms around me and scoots me to his side so I can cuddle next to him. I bask in the warmth of his body, and he keeps one arm around me as we scroll through our options.

He makes me watch a sci-fi show about androids who raise children on another planet, and it isn't half bad. I make him watch the most recent female flyweight MMA championship. He's like a little kid, staring amazed at the screen. It's almost as if he can't believe women are so tough.

"I take it you don't like to watch sports?"

He shakes his head. "Normally no. I prefer to be active rather than sit and watch others be active, but that fight was pretty epic."

He picks another movie after that, but I fall asleep on him. When I wake up, I'm lying down on the sofa with my duvet over me, and Rory is in the kitchen heating up some of the soup. He brings it to the coffee table along with a small plate of crackers and a tall glass of water.

"I'd feel better if you ate something." He smiles at me, and it's all the encouragement I need.

"All right," I say. "I'll try."

The soup is eons better than the soup at the hospital, and I ask Rory where he got it so I can get some more.

"Oh no. I'm not giving you my secrets. You want this soup, you'll have to go through me."

I laugh and take another spoonful. I had been afraid to eat after my night at the hospital, but now that I was eating, my hunger opened up with a vengeance. Setting the spoon on the coffee table, I start drinking straight from the bowl like a savage.

Rory laughs next to me.

"Thank you," I say. "That was good."

He smiles. "You betcha."

After insisting with a look of warning that I am quite capable of cleaning up, I take the dishes to the sink, and soap suds drip from my hands when something in my stomach churns. I run to the toilet and barely make it in time.

The soup comes out nearly in the same state it went in, and it is revolting. I feel a hand on my back, and I push him away. "No," I manage to say. "I don't want you seeing me like this." I wave him away with my head hovering over the toilet bowl.

"Valentina, this doesn't bother me. Please, let me be here." He pulls my hair back so it's not dangling into the toilet bowl just in time for round two of the soup rejection.

I close the lid to the bowl and sit back as I wipe my mouth.

"Real sexy, aren't I?" I say, attempting a joke, but Rory's face is all concern. "I really wish you hadn't seen that."

"Like I said, it doesn't bother me. Normally I would respect your wishes, but I know you don't have any family here."

"Can I have a moment to clean up a bit?"

Rory scratches his jaw through his beard, then nods. "Yeah, I'm just out here if you need anything, okay?"

"Thanks, doc."

After brushing my teeth and taking a shower, I find Rory scrolling through his phone. He looks up at me with a face-splitting smile that melts me.

"Better?"

"Yeah."

"What else do you want to watch?"

"I'm actually kind of sick of the TV for today."

"Okay. We can just chat."

"Sure . . ." I say reluctantly. "What about?"

"Anything. Let's see. Oh, I know. What's your favorite band?"

I smile, glad for the change in subject. "Easy. *Industrial November*. I always thought my walkout song would be either *Metal Red Day* or *Welded Dragons*."

"Those would be good fighting songs. I'm surprised, though. You listen to them in Mexico?"

"They're much bigger in Mexico City than they are here, I'll tell you that much."

"Well, yeah. Maybe not so much in the Midwest, but they have fans in the U.S. too."

"What about your favorite band?" I ask, content with the easy conversation topic that is also somehow really revealing.

"I have a lot. Let's see, well, lately I've been listening to a lot of *Kidneythieves*."

My eyes widen. "What?"

"You never heard of them?"

"That can't be a real band name," I say, horrified.

"Yep. That's their name—pretty good band too."

"I don't care how good they are; that's a horrible band name."

"It's not like we play it in the dialysis clinic," Rory deadpans, and we both roar with laughter.

"You laugh at really inappropriate things."

He shrugs. "Yeah. I have a pretty dark sense of humor sometimes. I guess I understand life is grim enough without us trying to make it dimmer. You know?"

"Would you laugh at anything?"

"Probably."

"What about death?"

"Yeah. I see myself laughing at death in the right circumstances."

"What about when I die?" I ask, not giving away I'm serious. "Will you laugh then?"

He looks at me, and a smile plays at the corners of his mouth. He does that a lot, giving away he is about to tell a joke like he needs to smile before sharing it. "That depends on how you die," he says, and we both laugh again.

I yawn, and Rory carries me to bed. He returns my duvet to the bed and tucks me in before placing a glass of water on my nightstand. "I'm still worried you'll get dehydrated. Please try to keep down some water, okay?" He kisses my forehead in the sweetest gesture any man has ever displayed for me, and I nod.

I drift off to sleep with a smile on my face.

CHAPTER 9

Mandy's house is loud—so loud. Just like her. We sit at the table with her parents, Mr. and Mrs. Gomez, though they insisted I call them Enrique and Ana as soon as Mandy introduced us.

Mrs. Gomez—Ana—runs from the kitchen to the table as she piles *tortillas* onto the *tortilla* warmer in the center of the table.

"Mateo!" Ana screams at the top of her lungs, and a young man's voice bellows from down the hall in response.

"One second!"

"Sorry, Valentina," Ana says. "This kid drives me crazy sometimes." She offers me a sheepish smile, and I ask her to please not worry on my account.

"I'm so hungry I could eat a cow," says Enrique.

"Mom makes the best *albondiga* soup," Mandy says. "I thought a light broth might be good for you." She squeezes my forearm, and my heart swells that the menu was catered to me.

"Thank you," I say. "I haven't had any food that tastes like home in a while."

"Especially not at the hospital," Mandy adds.

I shiver at the memory.

"Mateo!" Ana yells again, her frustration growing on her face each time she has to yell her son's name. She tosses another pile of *tortillas* onto the heap and plops in her chair, a bit out of breath.

Ana is beautiful, and Mandy looks a lot like her. They have the same small frame with a lean muscular build, though Mandy's tanned skin is a shade darker, more like her dad's.

"Ama!" Mateo yells as he walks toward the dinner table. "I had to save my game."

"We have guests," Ana hisses.

Mateo and Ana continue to argue, and Enrique starts asking Amanda about work, ignoring the argument ensuing on the other side of the table. Each set of conversations has to raise an octave when the other conversation takes over the dining room's sound until they are all but screaming. I resist the urge to wince because it is also a little bit funny. I see now why Mandy is so loud.

The smack over his head silences Mateo once and for all, and he scowls.

"Hi, Mateo. I'm Valentina," I say to insert myself in the conversation.

"Hi," he says, looking down at his dinner.

"How old are you?"

"Thirteen," he seethes.

Mandy shakes her head at her little brother. "I'm going to have Valentina kick your ass," she says and smiles.

Mateo laughs. "She's a girl!" He snaps as if that disqualifies me from the job, and I press my lips together.

"She's an MMA fighter," Mandy says, crossing her arms.

Mateo's head snaps up with wide eyes like he can't believe what his sister just said. His gaze scans my arms, sizing me up, no doubt. "No way," he says, shaking his head. "You're too small."

"Yes, way," I say. "But I won't kick your ass. I promise."

He smiles at me, and for the rest of the dinner, he can hardly look in my direction.

"So," Ana says, "Mandy tells me you are getting treatment at Heartland Metro,"

"That's right—"

"Mami! I told you she doesn't want to talk about that," Mandy says.

"It's okay," I smile reassuringly at Ana. "I don't mind. Thank you for having me over for dinner. It's nice to eat with someone."

"All your family's in Mexico?"

I nod.

Ana's face twists like she is angry I'm alone.

"It's okay," I say. "They don't know about my treatment, or they would be here."

"I'm sure they would like to know—" Enrique says.

"Papi!" Mandy huffs, and I have to laugh. "Sorry," she says with an apologetic look of embarrassment.

"It's okay, Mandy. Your parents can ask me questions." I smile at them both. "Ana, the soup is delicious, by the way."

Ana smiles at me and digs into her own bowl.

Thankfully, Mandy manages to steer the conversation away from me. She hogs the attention, bringing everyone up to speed on her art show.

I listen halfheartedly as I watch this family that is so close my heart constricts. Why can't my family be like this? I would gladly give up the wealth of my upbringing if it meant we could have healthy relationships—if it meant we could be close.

So many 'if's' that would mean they would be here right now because I would have told them about my illness.

But I look at Enrique as he listens to his daughter talk about her art, and I know my father could never be like that. Enrique clearly has no idea what half the things she says mean, but he listens intently and offers encouraging words. Her mother, too, throws in a comment or two of support and several of pride. They don't understand Mandy's ambitions, but they support her anyway. Families can actually be like this? A longing for something I will never have creeps up and lodges in my throat.

Halfway through dinner, Mandy yells at her brother once again. "Give it back—or else!" she threatens.

"No," he sticks his tongue out at her. "You know the rules."

I blink as I stare at the fighting siblings. Enrique bites his lip as he tries to suppress his laughter, making his black mustache wiggle.

"House rules," he explains at seeing my confusion plain on my face. "Hold on to your *tortilla*, especially when the stack is getting low," he points with his gaze at the *tortilla* warmer. I lift the lid to peek inside, and sure enough, there are none left.

Ana holds on to her spoon with one hand and clutches her own *tortilla* in the other. She takes a sip of water, but to do this, she lets go of the spoon, not the *tortilla*. She raises her glass toward me, showing that she is the victor of the game. I laugh.

Mandy must have kicked Mateo under the table because he drops both spoon and what's left of the *tortilla* on the table as he chokes on his last slurp of the broth. Enrique doesn't even skip a beat. He lunges forward and reaches for the *tortilla* that Mateo dropped on the table, snagging it just before Mandy's hand could get to it.

"Dad! That was mine!" Mandy is frustrated now, and Enrique gives me a little salute with the piece of *tortilla* left, and I lose it.

I laugh so hard and so long, they all stare at me. "I'm happy to get up and heat up more," I say through the laughter.

"That's not the point," Enrique explains. "By the time whoever heats up more, they will trickle back to the table rather slowly. There are only so many *tortillas* you can fit on the stovetop at a time. You wait long enough, your food gets cold."

I nod at the simple explanation, and I can't suppress the laughter again, but they join me this time.

"So finders keepers is the rule?"

Enrique nods.

The turn of keys at the front door turns all our attention, and we watch as Izel marches in. She drops her purse on the couch and rushes to the table.

She sits next to me and gives me a kiss on the cheek like we are old friends. "Hi, Vale," she says, and I smile at the nickname —a sure sign she considers me her friend.

I can't tell if the happiness of this moment has my mind in shambles, but a swell of emotion overtakes me. It is so natural to be inserted into Mandy's life. Izel looks at me like I'm not at all out of place in this family tableau, and I almost want to cry.

I want to cry because Mom and Dad will never be like this. Because we will never be at a family dinner unless it's an event Dad would force us to go to for publicity.

If anything, this night only cements what I already knew: I did the right thing by not telling them anything.

CHAPTER 10

The treatments are going as well as can be expected, and I am faithful to the new regimen. My routine is solid. Every weekday, I go into the hospital for chemotherapy, and three times a week, I go in for radiation in addition to the chemo. So far, I've seen no signs of Rory, and no one has commented on my disguise of sunglasses and a hat as I walk through the lobby.

My body is taking a hell of a beating, but Dr. Ramirez looks at me—and at my chart—with hope, so I push through the pain.

I lost five pounds in the first week, and some days are better than others with nausea. Days when the chemo is combined with the radiation are the worst, especially the next day. Mandy was right about absolutely everything. I'm hungry and can hardly keep anything down half the time. Drinking calories has been somewhat helpful, but the pounds are still shedding off my body.

I had radiation yesterday, and I haven't been able to keep anything down today. I'm due at the hospital in an hour, and I have a raging headache.

Rummaging through the cabinet, I grab for pain meds and

stare at the vitamin bottle. Did I take my vitamins this morning like I was supposed to? I can't remember, and I panic.

Skipping vitamins one day isn't the end of the world, but so far, I've treated treatment with the same discipline I used to treat training. Missing supplements is not an option for me or for my routine.

The bottle rests next to the pain meds, and I grab them both. I stare between them, unsure why I grabbed them. My head pounds, and I remember the headache. I take two pain pills from the bottle and stare at the vitamin bottle again. What the hell is happening? My brain is misfiring, and I have no idea why. I shake my head, trying to clear it, and the movement makes the room spin.

The floor moves from under my feet, and I'm about to topple over, so I grab the edge of the counter. I try to lick my cracked lips, but my tongue is dry. Fuck. I'm dehydrated.

Holding on to the counter, I go to the sink and fill a glass. I try to chug it, but it only comes back up.

I pull my phone out to call a car. Looks like I'm heading to the hospital early today.

Nurse Sara replaces the IV fluids for the second time, and I look at her, a bit embarrassed.

"It's very common to get dehydrated when you can't keep anything down," she says soothingly.

"Yeah. I know. I'm glad I noticed before I passed out."

"You did good. You need anything else for now?"

"No. Thank you, Sara."

She walks out of my room, leaving me with my thoughts—another hospitalization. I get to stay overnight until I can keep down two full meals in a row. I'll need to make another large deposit to the hospital. Hospital stays in the U.S. are much more expensive than I thought they would be. I'm so glad I asked Pilar for more money than I thought I'd need to be on the safe side, though I have no idea how the hell I'm going to pay her back.

A new doctor I don't know walks into my room, followed closely by Dr. Ramirez.

"Valentina, how are you?" Dr. Ramirez asks.

"I've been better," I say dryly.

She nods. "This is Dr. Medina. He will be the new attending on your case."

Dr. Medina is tall and handsome, and I don't for one minute miss the twinkle in Dr. Ramirez's eye when she looks at him. I press my lips together because she can't hide her feelings at all, and it's adorable. Dr. Ramirez briefs Dr. Medina on my case like the residents do at morning rounds.

"Nice to meet you, Miss Almonte," Dr. Medina says. "I'm new to the clinical trial team, but we will see a lot of each other now that I am here."

Dr. Ramirez mentioned him earlier, when she was about to meet him. At the time, she thought he would be unattractive, but Dr. Medina is super hot for an older guy, and yet, I could see them together despite their age difference.

When he sits to read my chart and turns away, I mouth to Dr. Ramirez that he is hot, and I bang the air to get a reaction out of her. Her eyes widen with horror, and she pins me with a look begging me to stop. I press my lips together to seal the laugh inside of me.

"Thank you, doctor," I say to Dr. Medina as they excuse themselves. I can't wait to see how their relationship unfolds.

I'm bored out of my mind the rest of the day and drift off to sleep by eight p.m. The next thing I know, I'm awakened for rounds at 6 a.m. I hate hospital stays. It's been nice sleeping in for the first time in my adult life, but it never happens when I'm admitted overnight. It's as if they like to start rounds with me, so I'm the earliest every day.

The lights go on in my room, and the trail of footfalls follows. It's usually one attending and seven to ten residents and interns. I groan and pull my pillow over my face with annoyance.

Someone clears their throat, and I wave them to go on. A resident whose voice I don't recognize starts presenting my case. I hate hearing it. Every time they mention the details of my case, I feel like the stupidest woman on earth. Who skips their pap tests? Who ignores symptoms?

Me. I do all of those things, and my penance is my life. I only half-listen to the residents discussing my case. My philosophy on my involvement in my own treatment is likely as asinine as my prevention plan. I do what they say. All I ask is that they be aggressive with treatment and tell me where to be and what time.

"Miss Almonte, please," I recognize Dr. Medina's voice now as he tries to get my attention.

"What time is it?" I whine.

"Six in the morning."

I huff and take the pillow off my face placing it behind me. I stare among the residents, only half of whom I recognize.

"I hear you got a little dehydrated?" Dr. Medina asks as he glances through my medical chart.

"Yeah. I noticed it quickly, though, and came to the hospital right away," I say.

Dr. Medina faces the students, asking for their proposed plans for keeping food and water in my stomach. They have barely begun pitching treatment plans when the squeak of sneakers rushing into the room draws the attention of the small army of doctors. Someone is late.

And that someone is Rory.

He is staring down at his tablet and looking disheveled. His red hair is a mess, like he just woke up, and his white coat is nowhere near as crisp as the other doctors.

"Glad you could join us, Dr. Dennis," Dr. Medina says.

"Sorry, doctor. Won't happen again," Rory says as he squints at the room. He pats his pockets until he produces his glasses and brings them to his face.

Everything happens around me, but not to me. I'm looking into the hospital room scene from a faraway window like an out of body experience. My stomach burns, and I would grab for the bedpan if I didn't know there is absolutely nothing in my stomach that can come up right now.

Rory freezes when his eyes land on me. His hands clench around the tablet in his hands, and he looks down, undoubtedly looking at my chart, confirming the name that belongs to the patient. He looks up at my face, back at the tablet, and back to my face, freezing his hold on my eyes on the last glance. I swallow hard, wincing at the painful dryness in my throat. His hands fall to his sides in resignation. I'm not sure if it's the state of his crumpled doctor's coat, his slouched posture, or the weakness of his arms dangling at his sides, but Rory gives the impression of a crumpled napkin, discarded on a dirty old street.

The residents are mostly done with rounds by the time Rory arrives. I nod and say, "Sure, sure," not knowing at all what they have said. They trickle out of the room until only Rory remains.

His mouth parts like he is about to say something, then he shuts it again as he takes a step away from me. My eyes sting as I watch him withdraw. And it is so stupid because we barely know each other. It shouldn't matter. I don't care about him. He doesn't care about me. Not really. So why the hell has this heavy ball of lead settled low in my stomach?

"Rory, I—"

"I have to catch up to the group," he points with his thumb toward the door and leaves me alone.

THE LONG DAY DRAGS AFTER THAT. PILAR CALLS ME AROUND lunchtime.

"When can I come to see you?" she asks.

I know Felipe won't let her, so I bluff. "Whenever you want."

"I'm going to try to manage it. I think next month, I can get away for a week or so. I want to see your new place, the gym, everything."

"All right," I say, sure this will never happen.

"How are you liking it there?"

"It's great. I've made a few friends." Sticking with the positives will keep her at bay for a while.

"That's great, Tini! Tell me about them."

"Let's see, there's this girl, Mandy. She's an artist. And her two cousins, Izel and Tlali. Izel writes horror, and Tlali translates novels." I stick to describing them by their true trades instead of their day jobs. I'm afraid to even mention anything hospital-related to my sister.

"How Bohemian." Pilar sounds overjoyed. "And strange."

"Why strange?" I ask.

"All your friends here are gym rats. This is different."

"New leaf and all that," I say. "Trying new things. How about you, Pili? How are you doing? Really?"

"You know me. I'm always fine."

"Pilar, come on. I want to know the truth."

"I just miss you, is all."

"I miss you too. You should really think about making some new friends too."

She laughs, but it's bitter. "Do you think I could find some friends under the couch or in the kitchen?"

I wince. She is basically a prisoner in her fancy tower. "I'm sorry," I say. "That was insensitive."

"Don't worry about me. My problems aren't really problems."

"Just because you are wealthy and don't lack any physical comforts doesn't mean you can't have problems, Pilar."

She sighs into the phone. "I called to check on you, not to get the Spanish Inquisition."

I laugh. "Yeah. You're only okay with giving me the third degree."

"Speaking of which, did you speak to Chema?"

It's my turn to sigh. "Yeah."

"And?"

"He's pretty pissed at me."

"Were you expecting anything less?"

"No. I guess not. Do me a favor? Check on him if you can?"

"I'll try, but you know Felipe—"

"Yeah. I'm sorry. Forget I asked. I'll try to keep tabs on him with my gym rats, as you have so lovingly put it."

"I miss you," she says.

"Miss you too."

She promises she'll do her best to visit in a few weeks, but we both know better. Despite the lie, I'm glad for the call and the distraction from the boredom that is the dreaded hospital stay.

I'M NOT SURPRISED WHEN RORY COMES BACK. HIS WHITE COAT IS gone, and I'm guessing he is off work late in the evening. The door to my room is open when he shows up, and he doesn't ask to come in. He sits on a chair opposite me and leans back, his legs apart, while he bounces one foot on the floor, making his leg shake.

The armrest props his elbow up as he grips a pen. He clicks the pen once, then twice, but doesn't say anything.

Being in the hospital gown without the armor of makeup or

my knuckle-wraps, I shift in the bed uncomfortably. *Say some-thing,* I think. *Anything. What are you thinking, Rory?*

The pen clicks again as his dark green eyes pierce through me. I open my mouth to break the hollow silence, but nothing comes out. I'm not sure how to explain this, or that I even want to. Rory swallows, and his Adam's apple bobs up and down. His eyes narrow as he waits patiently.

Another click of the pen.

The sound of it is so annoying, I want nothing more than to march up to him, snatch the pen, and throw it to the ground.

Click.

Mercifully, he finally speaks. "You didn't have a stomach bug," he says, and it's most definitely not a question. I shake my head. "What is it?" he asks.

"I'm sure you read my chart already."

"No," he snaps. "I wouldn't invade your privacy like that."

"But, I thought . . . earlier, you looked at my chart."

"I did. I looked to make sure it was you. I confirmed your name, then I stopped reading."

"Oh," is all I manage.

Rory stops tapping his foot on the floor, and the sound ceases. He also sets the pen on the hospital tray between us. "So? Are you going to tell me what it is? I mean, you're on the oncology floor, so I know it's cancer." His face betrays no emotion. I need to know if he's angry or if maybe he even feels cat-fished, for all I know.

"Does it matter?" I ask.

Rory scoffs. "Yes, it fucking matters," he sneers, finally betraying his stoic composure from earlier.

"There's a reason you were meant to be for only one night, Rory. This wasn't supposed to get complicated."

"We're a little past that, don't you think?"

"It's not too late. Feelings aren't involved yet. You can go on as you were before we met, and I'll go on with my treatment.

No hard feelings," I offer, and do my best to smile in a way that might soothe him. Yet, the thought of him not being around aches in my chest.

"Is that right?" he asks, but it's clearly rhetorical. "You've decided, then? You have no feelings for me, and there's no possible way I have feelings for you?" His muscles are all tight knots, and I wince a bit because he is so wound up, I can almost anticipate him throwing something. But kind and gentle Rory wouldn't do something like that—I know that much.

"Rory, we hardly know each other. I won't begrudge you walking away if that's what you are worried about. I never wanted you to find out at all."

"That's what you think I'm worried about? That I would feel guilty about walking away now?"

"Well, yeah. Wouldn't you?"

His eyes soften, and he scratches his jaw, letting out a long breath. "Valentina, I care about you. You're right, we barely know each other, and it is too soon to talk about feelings. If circumstances were different, I would wait until we'd had more time together, but I meant what I said before. I want to get to know you and finding out you're sick doesn't change that."

"It does for me," I say, and now it's me who's angry.

"What does that mean?"

"You were never supposed to know. You were a fantasy— what I would have wanted if I wasn't sick—and I got to live it for one day. I was happy with that, but you had to keep pushing, didn't you?"

"Yeah, I did! Because I like you," he hisses. I blink because it's almost comical how he says the sweetest words with the roughest voice and so much anger. I want to laugh at how such a deep voice comes from the body of a man who has no business with that baritone.

"Rory," I plead. "Do you think I want you around for this? Especially when you know what I am without this illness?"

"Do you think you are any less remarkable because you're sick? Valentina, it only makes you that much fiercer. Don't you see? It's the fighter in you that I'm drawn to."

My vision blurs at the welling of my eyes. He says the most perfect thing he could possibly say to me, and I press my hand to my chest to soothe my aching heart.

Rory stands from his seat and lies down next to me on the hospital bed so he can embrace me. I curl up into his side like I did that night on the Kansas City grass and breathe him in. This time, it's the hospital's antiseptic scent instead of the earthy smells of the park that mingle with the smell of Rory, and it is no less remarkable because it is him. His embrace soothes like nothing in this world, and I fall apart in his arms. I break down for all the words I haven't said and all the people who don't know I'm sick. I sob into his t-shirt, and he lets me. He hugs me tight, encouraging me to let it all out.

The circles he rubs on my back bring me down from my cry, and I compose myself.

"Now, can you tell me what it is?"

"Cervical cancer," I say weakly.

Rory's chin rests on top of my head, and I'm so glad he can't see my face right now.

"Stage?"

I try to resist giving him any details, but in the end, I give in. I tell him every detail about my cancer and am relieved I don't have to explain what any of the terms mean because he already knows. His arms tighten around me like the words physically attack him.

After a long moment, I feel him shake around me. I look up, and he is holding back laughter. I wipe my eyes. "What?" I ask. "Are you laughing?"

"Nothing," he says, but this time he lets a little laugh escape.

"That's not nothing. Tell me!"

"I was just thinking . . ."

"Yeah?"

"It's a good thing you're dating an oncologist." Then he lets the roar of laughter out. I love that he can't help but laugh at his own jokes before he shares them out loud.

I smack his abs playfully. "That's not funny, Rory," I say, but I'm also laughing.

"Yeah, it is," he says and plants a sweet little kiss on my forehead.

"You really do laugh at anything," I say with a roll of my eyes.

"What else is there?"

CHAPTER 11

Four weeks of treatment down and only one to go, at least in this first round. Hopefully, it is also the only round if I achieve remission.

"I want to admit you," says Dr. Ramirez.

"No, I'm fine," I say. "I don't need any extra help."

"It's not about help. I don't like the amount of weight you've lost. It's getting harder and harder for you to keep anything down."

"How long will this hospital stay be?"

"That depends. I want to run some tests."

I wince at the prospect of a long exploratory admission. Between the apartment, treatment, and the dehydration admission, I'm getting dangerously close to needing to ask Pilar for more money. She'd give it right away, but it would make her suspicious. Her life is hard enough in her marriage; I can't add to her troubles.

AFTER EXTENSIVE TESTING, DR. RAMIREZ WALKS INTO MY ROOM with Dr. Medina, both their faces grim.

I sit up and look between them expectantly. Dr. Ramirez stands a few feet behind Dr. Medina, and it is he who speaks first.

"Hello, Miss Almonte," Dr. Medina says.

"Valentina, or Vale, please," I say with a half-hearted smile as I wait for the bad news.

"That's right. I'm sorry. Valentina, I'm afraid the tests we ran today confirmed what Dr. Ramirez feared. The radiation is damaging your small intestine. That's what's been exacerbating your GI issues more than normal."

I suck in a breath and shut my eyes. No. This can't be happening. My body is shutting down, and I've lost all control of it. The blow is devastating. I have always controlled my body one hundred percent. But this? There is nothing I can do to make this better. I don't know how I manage to not cry—maybe because anger is vying for first place in my mind, but I keep it together in front of my two favorite doctors.

"Okay," I say as it sinks in. "So what do we do now?"

Dr. Ramirez sits in front of me and squeezes my forearm. "We have to do surgery to repair your intestine," she says.

I exhale. "So there is something we can do about it, then?" Can I dare hope I will get through this? Hope is dangerous, but I want it so bad. "Is this common?" I ask.

"It can be, for cervical cancer patients who receive extended radiation," Dr. Medina says.

"And the surgery?"

"I have scheduled it for tomorrow," Dr. Ramirez says.

What follows is Dr. Ramirez explaining the surgical procedure briefly and answering some of my questions. However, both she and Dr. Medina reassure me the surgeon will stop by before the procedure to answer anything more specific. Both my doctors are confident this is the only path forward, and I have to get over the fear of major surgery because I have no other choice.

"Can I go home today?" I ask.

"I'd rather you stay," she says.

"But do I have to?"

"I really think it's best," Dr. Medina interjects before Dr. Ramirez can respond.

I'M BORED OUT OF MY MIND AND WONDER IF I PACKED A BOOK OR at least a magazine. I stand to grab my duffle bag and plop it onto my mattress so I can rummage through it. *Please tell me I at least packed my tablet*, I'm thinking, but I must have said it out loud because someone clears their throat inside my room. I spin around and smile when I see that Dr. Ramirez is back. "Dr. Ramirez!" My excitement dwindles when my eyes land on Rory standing behind her.

"Hello, Miss Almonte," says Rory. I cock my head to study him. He's never before called me that in our few interactions together at the hospital.

We never discussed it, but now I'm wondering if I could get him into trouble at work. Surely there are rules against dating patients. But we met before either of us knew . . . I doubt his superiors would see it that way. I decide to play along for now, and I'll be sure to ask him about it later.

"Valentina. Please," I correct and do my best to reassure him with my eyes that I won't give him away.

Most of what Dr. Ramirez says doesn't register. Something about consent forms that I've heard a million times, but I'm so nervous about giving him away, I'm afraid to speak.

"Well, missy, if you are that bored of my rambling, maybe I'll have the capable Dr. Dennis go over the paperwork with you. Do you mind, Dr. Dennis? I was paged."

"Sure," he says and takes the consent form from Dr. Ramirez.

The minute she leaves, I interrogate Rory. "Am I going to get you in trouble, Rory? Or fired?"

He shrugs. "Don't know. Don't care."

"Rory, please. I need to know."

"It's frowned upon. Let's put it that way. But I've never actually delivered any sort of care, nor have I broken any privacy laws trying to find out what's going on with you—not that I haven't been tempted. They will be able to tell I've never accessed your electronic record except for that first time before I knew it was you."

"What about the consent forms? Isn't you going over them with me part of care?"

"Yeah, I'll page another resident in a bit so they can go over them with you. Better safe than sorry."

"All right. And Rory? Thanks for not reading my medical chart. I appreciate you respecting my privacy."

He takes a seat and scratches his jaw—a move I've come to recognize as a sign of either concern or deep thought. "So," he starts. "You gonna tell me the truth this time, or will I have to pry it out of you again?"

"You have the consent forms, so you know it's surgery."

"No. I didn't read them."

I can't help but tell him everything Dr. Ramirez and Dr. Medina said to me about the procedure. Rory listens intently with a stoicism that I haven't seen in him yet. It's an entirely different side of him. I get the sense I'm looking at Dr. Dennis now, and not my Rory. There is no playfulness. His jaw ticks, almost as if he's angry.

After a long stretch of silence, I have to know what he is thinking. "What's wrong?" I ask.

"You."

"I'm wrong?"

"Yes. It isn't supposed to be this way. You're so young. So healthy. So . . . good. You aren't supposed to get cancer. Everything is all wrong."

"Rory—" I try to interject, but he won't let me.

"I wasn't supposed to find someone I—" His voice cracks, and he has to swallow several times before he can speak again. "Only for her to have to go through this—"

I close my eyes because I don't want to see Rory cry, and he seems to be on the brink. This is why I haven't told anyone about the cancer. I don't want this pity. I don't want it from him either.

"I'm sorry," he says, and his voice is firmer now. I dare to peek at him again, and all signs of incoming waterworks are gone. I relax and lean into my pillows. "It's just, I've seen this disease so much. I know what you're going through, more than probably even you do. I've never experienced cancer myself, but being on the other side of it, in this seat, I feel so fucking helpless, Valentina."

I let his words sink in and try to piece together what he is saying. I can't square this side of his personality with the man who, not too long ago, on hearing my diagnosis, laughed with me at his jokes about being an oncologist dating a cancer patient. His seriousness reaches a degree that leaves me uncomfortable.

I'm already in a somber mood after losing a big patch of hair this morning. Add to that happy-go-lucky Rory suddenly grim and I grow worried, really worried, that I am going to die from this. This is just too many bad omens for one day, not that I've ever believed in omens before.

"Look," I say. "Um. I've had a bad day. I appreciate you stopping by, saying hi, but I really want to be alone now."

"Yeah, um. I'll stop by after your surgery, okay?"

I nod, and he leans over me to place a short, sweet kiss on my lips.

"Bye, Rory."

~

I'm in the worst mood when Sara walks into my room, pushing a cart. I can't stand her bubbly personality today. But she's been amazing to me, and I don't dare be rude to her. Dr. Ramirez walks in shortly after. As much as I love her, I'm starting to hate seeing her. She only ever comes to me with horrible news.

"Good morning," I say, but Dr. Ramirez only smiles. "What?" I ask, confused at why these women are in my room so chipper.

Dr. Ramirez places some items on the counter in front of my bed. A few seconds later, *Girls Like You* by Maroon 5 and Cardi B fills my room from what I can now see is a speaker on the counter. I sit up on my bed, confused at what's happening, and then prim and proper Dr. Carolina Ramirez starts dancing. *Dancing.* Dr. Ramirez—dancing. Her moves are a bit spazzy, but I can tell she is having fun.

When I turn to find Sara in my room to ask her what the hell Dr. R took, I realize Sara is also dancing. Several other nurses who have worked with me poke their heads in for just a moment to sing one line of the song's chorus. I throw my head back in laughter.

They are trying to cheer me up. They don't care if they look like fools doing it. Then Rory sticks his head in and sings the chorus directly at me. My face hurts from all the smiling, then I panic. Dr. Ramirez is looking at me with an eyebrow slightly raised.

The song ends and rolls straight into the next one as Sara uncovers her cart's contents: hair clippers. I nod at her with understanding and permission. She wraps me in a cape with raised edges to catch my hair, and Dr. Ramirez takes me by surprise and starts painting my toenails.

I appreciate what they are trying to do. They're treating me like any other girlfriend on any other day—not the sick person I am. There is no pity in their eyes as Sara leaves me bald. They keep singing until they run out of energy and turn their attention to boys.

If I could have had the guarantee my family would act like this around me, like I was still me, I would have told them.

I worry a bit as they keep talking about the men in their lives. First, because Dr. Ramirez implies that Sara's boyfriend isn't a good guy. Then I worry they are going to ask me about any romantic partners. I'm not sure I could lie to them after what they are doing for me.

Dr. Ramirez is so focused on painting my nails, she never notices Dr. Medina standing at the counter by the nurses' station, watching as she and Sara tried to cheer me up. I have a clear view of him through my open door. He smiles at me and brings a finger to his lips, asking for my silence. I gave a quick, discreet nod, and he stays there, his eyes glued to Dr. Ramirez as she works to cheer me up. It seems I'm not the only one with a secret doctor crush at this hospital. I smile at Dr. Ramirez. Not until they are nearly done and putting away all the supplies does Dr. Medina sneak away unnoticed.

Sara and Dr. Ramirez leave, and though my spirits are a bit lighter than they had been before they came, I'm left exhausted. Even talking as much as we did today took it out of me.

I rummage through my purse to pull out my pocket mirror. I'm not a vain person, and I have never paid any particular attention to my hair, but it was beautiful. I say 'was' because Sara just walked away with all of it in a trash bag.

I take a deep breath and remove the blue silk scarf Dr. Ramirez tied around my head. I steel my spine as I unfold the mirror in my hand and take a peek at my new reality.

To be honest, it's not bad. I mourn the loss of such beautiful, lush, thick hair, but the baldness gives me a certain edge. I almost look dangerous. Thinking of the future, I realize it might be a good look for the cage if I ever get back to it. The way a fighter looks can certainly affect an opponent's perception and potentially throw them off their game.

Yes. Bald is the best fighting look.

CHAPTER 12

"**You** ready?" Rory asks.

"For what?"

"We're going home today." He smiles warmly.

"We?"

"Yeah, well, I'm taking you home."

"I don't need any help, Rory." I sound about as annoyed as I feel.

The scarf Dr. Ramirez and Sara brought over to cover my head helps a bit, but I'm not ready for him to see me bald.

"No, you don't *need* help, but I would like to see you home. Make sure you're good."

"Rory," I let out a long breath.

"Please, Valentina. I worry about you being alone, and I'll feel better seeing you settled."

His brows are knitted together, and his longish hair is mussed. His boyish demeanor is long gone, replaced with sunken eyes like he hasn't slept in a while. He's been worried about me. Suddenly, my annoyance feels out of place. "Okay," I relent. "You can drive me home, get me settled. But that's it." This surgery was more invasive, and I'll have a larger scar than my other laparoscopic ones from before. I can anticipate more pain than before as well.

His smile is crooked, and barely a trace of his typically wide grin, but it's something. "Thank you," he says.

When we get to my apartment, Rory makes my bed and inspects my fridge. I know he is trying to determine if he needs to shop for me, and I hate that all I can be is angry.

We went from hot lovers to something else, though what that something is has not been defined yet. Is he my doctor and I his patient? Is he acting like a parent? Or worse still—am I his *charity case?* Long gone is the sexiness of our first day together. I almost wish I had stuck to my original idea and not given him my number to begin with.

I don't say any of this to Rory because ultimately, I understand he means well. He is caring and thoughtful and wants to take care of me. Now I'm mad at myself for being angry, and it's giving me a headache.

The medication bottle rests on the counter, and I grab for it.

Rory doesn't miss it. "Is the incision site hurting?" he asks.

"No. Just a bit of a headache," I say. After taking two pills, I go to my room, and Rory follows. He kicks off his shoes and lies next to me.

If he's going to insist on bugging me, then it is high time for him to give up some information himself. This couldn't continue to be as one-sided as it has been so far.

"It's time," I say.

"Time for what?"

"I was hoping you'd tell me on your own, but you haven't, so I'm forced to ask."

"Ah," he says. "You want to know about my scar?"

I nod. "You know more about me than I ever wanted you to know."

"That wasn't by design," he says.

"I know, but if you'd like to tell me, I really want to know why your chest was cracked open."

He turns on his side to look at me before he speaks. "I was born with a heart defect," he says. "I have what's called a pericardial patch on my heart."

"That's a pretty big scar if you got it when you were a baby," I say as I trace my finger over his chest where I picture the scar under his shirt.

"Good eye. When I turned eighteen, it had to be revised. I was growing, and so was my heart."

"You outgrew the patch?"

"Exactly."

"Open-heart surgery both times?" I ask.

Rory nods.

"Will it have to be revised again?"

"More than likely. Eventually, it will wear out."

My own heart skips a beat, and my mouth goes dry and not because of dehydration. Rory must see the worry plain on my face because he reaches to smooth out the crinkle between my eyebrows with his thumb.

"My cardiologist keeps a good eye on it. You don't have to worry," he says.

I purse my lips, and I can't tear my gaze from his chest.

"Is that why you became a doctor?" I ask.

"Mostly," he says.

"And?"

"And what?"

"You said mostly, so there's another reason."

He sighs.

"You're intimately acquainted with my medical chart, and with noises you shouldn't be familiar with this soon in the relationship. I think I deserve to know why you became a doctor," I say.

Rory grins, pleased with himself. I have no doubt it was me

referring to us as being in a relationship that has him smiling. "Oh, grow up," I say, rolling my eyes.

His smile is gone when he speaks again. "I promise you'll know that part of me. Probably sooner than later, but do you think you can be a little bit patient?"

"It's not really my strong suit," I say dryly.

Rory scoffs. "Yeah. I've noticed."

"What's that supposed to mean?"

"You're a little bullheaded," he says.

"Occupational hazard."

Looking at Rory in my bed under the current circumstances makes my blood boil. The anger is quickly followed by guilt about being angry when nothing is his fault. Nothing is my fault. Nothing is our fault.

None of that is true. It's all my fault. If had only . . . so many things. If I had gotten my pap test when I was supposed to, or if I had gone to the doctor when the back pain started.

But I was built and trained to push through pain. It was nothing, I convinced myself, until it was too hard to ignore.

It's also my parent's fault because there is a vaccine for this cancer. If only they had agreed to get me the vaccine. Why won't parents give their children a cancer vaccine if it's available? My parents had only daughters. They should have known better. And even if they'd had only boys, they should have gotten the vaccine for them to protect their future girlfriends and wives. But who am I kidding? If we had been boys, we probably would have gotten the vaccine.

My family is estranged to begin with, but my resentment played a massive part in not telling my family what is happening to me.

Now, I'm lying in a bed with a wonderful man I wish I could keep, knowing I can't—a lover who gave me a taste of the life that still awaits. A lover I can't make love to.

"Hey," he whispers. "Where's that head at?" He smooths his fingers over my forehead again, and I blink my tears away.

"I'm sorry," I say.

"What do you have to be sorry for?"

"You're in my bed . . . and—I want to want you, but . . ."

"But you don't," he says.

I shake my head. "No. Sorry."

"Oh, Valentina. I know how this goes. Your sex drive will come back eventually. You have to be patient."

"Even if I had my sex drive," I explain, "I wouldn't want to. Not while I look like this." I avert his gaze, and Rory reaches to scoot me to him. His arm wraps around my waist, and he kisses my forehead.

"You silly woman. You're so beautiful, dontcha know. If you ask me, losing your hair and getting a little pale is only fair to other women." He chuckles. "They have a slightly more level playing field, but even then, you shine over all of them."

"You're just saying that."

Rory shakes his head. "Not even a little."

"It's hard for me to tell when you are joking, being sarcastic, or being serious."

"Always assume I'm serious and I'm joking. It's that pesky sarcasm you gotta look out for."

"Well, that narrows it down," I scoff.

"Can I ask you a favor?" Rory asks.

"Sure," I say.

"Mind if I take your apartment key and make a copy? I'd feel better that if you were to need anything, I could come in."

"That's sweet, but Rory, I'm feeling really weird about you taking care of me so much. We hardly know each other."

"I disagree. We know each other intimately."

I narrow my eyes, but he continues.

"I know, for example, that you prefer when I bestow attention on your left breast over your right. When I tease your left nipple, your back arches, and your toes curl. Nothing happens with the other one—"

"Oh, my, god, Rory!" I laugh—this man.

"I know you're embarrassed by your morning breath—don't think I didn't notice you sneaking to brush your teeth. I know you drink your coffee black but prefer it sweet. You've added increasing amounts of sugar each time we've had coffee together," he explains. "I know you have a lot of anger, and that's partly why you don't want your family to know you are here—"

"I—"

"I know that you're too stubborn and bullheaded to ask for help," his eyebrow arches high above the rim of his glasses when he says this. "And I know you don't feel beautiful bald, but I need you to know that you're more beautiful than ever—especially to me."

A sensation I can't identify lodges in my throat, and I have no words. What do you say to a beautiful man who says the most beautiful and comforting words? Nothing, that's what. You just hold on tight to that man.

RORY'S COMFORTING ARMS ENVELOP ME AS I FALL ASLEEP, DRAWN in by the warmth radiating from his body. I don't know how long I've slept when movement in my living room wakes me.

The footfalls of more than one person alert me, and I hear voices. What the hell? Rory is not next to me anymore, so at least one of the voices has to be him.

I sit up and wince at the pain at the surgical incision. Looking at my phone, I realize I missed taking the last dose of my pain medication.

I readjust my headscarf that fell off while I slept. "Rory?" I say as I walk to my living room.

The apartment door is ajar, and Rory talks to another man

who is bringing in a duffle bag. They both turn to face me as I walk over to them.

"Valentina, I'm sorry. Did we wake you?"

"It's okay. I had to take my meds anyway. What's going on?"

"Uh," Rory cups the back of his neck like he does anytime he is nervous. "This is my roommate, Neil. Neil, this is Valentina."

The tall, dark, and handsome man, who reminds me of Mandy's Chris, sets the duffel on the floor and extends his hand. His black eyes shine as he looks between Rory and me, and his grin spreads wide on his face. "Nice to meet you," he says, "Neil Campbell."

I wince at the movement as I shake his hand. "You too," I manage to say.

Neil's face turns to concern. "Are you in pain?" he asks.

I scoff. "Great. Let me guess. Another doctor?"

Neil chuckles and nods. "Yeah, but I'm in the surgery department."

Rory wastes no time in getting to my side. "Are you in pain?"

I nod. "I didn't wake up in time for pain meds."

Rory rushes to the cabinet, searching for them while Neil grabs my hand and leads me to the couch. "This all right?" he asks as he props a cushion behind my back.

"Yes. Thank you."

Rory offers a glass of water and two pills. I smile and take them. "Rory?"

"Yeah?"

"Why are there bags in my living room?"

"Okay, please don't get mad."

"Somehow, that statement alone makes me mad—"

"Well, that's everything from the car," Neil says. "I'm going to get going, man." He claps his hand on Rory's back and shakes his head as I watch him leave the apartment.

"Spit it out, Dennis," I say with little patience.

"You need help."

"I can hire a nurse."

"I can help while you get the nurse hired, and even then, the nurse won't be here twenty-four hours a day. You had major surgery. You shouldn't be alone, at least the first few days."

Looking between the bags and Rory, realization of what he has done sets in. My eyes widen with horror. No. He can't. I won't let him.

"So you moved in with me?"

"Well, um—" He at least has the grace to avert his eyes. "Just temporarily," he says.

"You didn't think you'd have to run that by me?"

"You have the extra room—"

It's barely a whisper as I manage to tame my anger. "Get out."

"Val—"

"Out, Rory! I don't want you here for this."

"Valentina, no."

He tries to stand his ground, but I know he sees the depth of my anger in my eyes. I stand and take a step toward him. He rears back only one step as he shakes his head.

"Out," I hiss and point to my door.

He doesn't budge, and I open the door. When he doesn't step out, I press my hands to his chest and shove him out. I am weak, but he follows the direction of my push voluntarily until I slam the door on his face.

Even that small amount of activity has me nearly panting, and I've never felt so weak. I rest my back on the wall next to the door, and the coolness of it is inviting.

A sob I didn't realize was building escapes me, and I can't stop it. My legs are noodles, and I slowly slide down toward the floor, my back gliding down the wall.

I'm a crumpled mess on the carpet of my rental apartment. My entire family and support system is a country away, and I've kicked out the only human I care for who knows about my cancer.

I never looked into hiring a nurse because I thought I could do without one for a while. I hadn't known then that I'd be having major surgery on top of everything else. Now was the time, though. I couldn't keep feeling sorry for myself.

This is that moment in the fight when every fighter is so tired and beaten up, you consider giving up. But then you remember that the other guy is feeling the same and considering giving up too, so you push just a little more until you rise.

I set my jaw and tighten my fists. Cancer is the other guy here, and I have to rise because soon, the other guy will be giving up. I move to place my legs under me so I can stand up, but the movement shifts my abdominal muscles, and a searing pain radiates from the incision site, forcing my legs to stretch out again. All the air leaves my lungs, and I pant until the pain ceases. I guess the medication hasn't kicked in.

The frustration deepens, and I fling my head to the wall. In my mind, I do this with force, but the effort is weak, so my head only gently taps at the wall.

Luckily, my phone is still in my pocket, saving me a trip crawling to it. I grab it, searching my contacts through my vision blurred by tears, and I call. It only rings once.

"I'm sorry," I say. "I can't do this alone. I need you. I need . . ." Saying the actual word is more challenging than I would have imagined. "I need help," I say, ignoring the pride that wouldn't let me say it until now. The weird thing is, saying the word out loud . . . is liberating.

The doorknob turns, and Rory is once again in my apartment. I smile weakly because I know he never left the other side of the door.

He crouches in front of me, and plants a kiss on my forehead. "Thank you," he says.

"For what?"

"Letting me help. I know that was hard."

"You do?"

"We're so much alike, you don't even know. I have a hard time asking for help too."

Rory places his hands under my armpits and lifts me like a doll. I wince at the sudden movement, and when we are both on our feet, he bends to place one arm under my knees, lifting me off the ground. I cradle my face in his neck and let him carry me back to bed.

"You've lost too much weight," he comments.

"*Et tu, Brutus?*"

Rory chuckles. "I'm guessing Dr. Ramirez already laid it on thick?"

I nod. "There wasn't much to begin with. You have to remember, my body was a fat-burning machine."

"In the morning, that's the first thing we will work on."

Once I'm settled, he inspects the room to make sure I have everything I need.

"Thank you, Rory. I'll hire a nurse tomorrow."

"You betcha, and no rush, really," he says with a wide smile.

"I don't want to keep taking your time like this."

"Valentina, you can have all my time, any way you want it."

I laugh. "Even in my sickbed?"

"*Especially* in your sickbed."

My heart sinks a little when I hear him settling in and taking all his things to my guest room instead of mine. It's for the best, though. I'm not sure what crazy thing my body will do next, and I probably don't want him right next to me all the time. He is respecting my privacy and trying to preserve what little dignity I have left.

CHAPTER 13

I hardly remember the next two days after Rory quasi-moves in with me. The pain from surgery has only gotten progressively worse, and I can do nothing but lay in bed.

Sleeping lets me forget about the pain, so I spend most of my time doing just that. I have a fleeting memory of Rory trying to wake me up. He had small, cool cubes of watermelon in his hands as he tried to feed me. The coolness of one pressed against my lips nearly tempted me, but ultimately, I pushed it away in favor of sleep.

The next vague memory is a blurry collage of the hospital lobby, Rory carrying me in, and a flurry of hospital images and sensations; the pinch of the needle going in, tubes of blood drawn, and the IV line set up.

When I wake, I'm not surprised to be at the hospital, knowing I would only be lucky if it had all been a dream, and luck is not on my side these days. It's morning, and my room is empty. How long have I been out? Is he back at work? I thought he took vacation time for a while to stay with me.

I lick my dry lips with a dry tongue and wince a little at the stiff skin peeling off my lower lip. They are so cracked it almost hurts. My throat is shut tight, and I'm thirstier than I ever have been. How long was I out?

The hospital remote rests conveniently by my side. I pick it up and press the call-nurse-button.

"Valentina, you're awake! That's great." A sunny Sara walks into my room and reads from some of the monitors next to me. "Welcome back," she says.

"How long have I been out?" I rasp.

"Oh, you must be thirsty. One sec." She comes back with a cup filled with water and adds a straw before handing it to me.

"Dr. Dennis brought you in last night. You don't remember anything? You were somewhat conscious when he checked you in."

I shake my head, trying to bring back memories, but nothing swims back. "What happened?" I ask.

"You spiked a fever. They think an infection from your incision. The docs put you on antibiotics, and you should be good as new soon. I'll have Dr. Ramirez come in and explain in more depth later today."

"Thanks."

"It was lucky Dr. Dennis was there." Sara places her hands on her hips and looks at me suggestively. "So you and Dr. Dennis . . .?"

I glance away from her, then return my eyes to meet hers. "I don't want to get him in trouble," I say.

Sara smiles. "He's not your doctor, and he can't be involved in your treatment moving forward. It's not exactly against the rules, but—"

"But what?" I ask with wide eyes.

"It's frowned upon," she says.

I nod, understanding. "If it helps, I didn't know Rory was a doctor here when I first met him—"

"Listen, you owe me no explanations. I won't judge you," she pauses then adds, "for anything."

Sara says the word 'anything' pointedly like she has caught me with the hands in the dough, as Mom would say.

"Thanks . . ." I'm not sure I should ask her what she meant by that comment, so I trail off, hoping the silence will force her to fill the void.

"It's none of my business," she says finally, "but Rory left."

"Oh," I say.

"He was here all night."

"He stayed overnight?" I ask, and my heart swells.

"He did, until . . ." Sara trails off, and it's her who can't meet my eyes now.

"Until what, Sara? What aren't you telling me?"

"Until your husband showed up."

"Until my what?" I nearly yell. I shake my head. What the hell?

"Like I said, it's none of my business, but I do have to ask, Valentina, do you feel safe at home? Is that why you moved away from your family? Is your husband abusive?" Sara places a hand on my forearm and smiles warmly, inviting me to confess. Is this woman insane?

"There's a mistake, Sara, I don't have a hus—" I don't finish my sentence because a massive figure blocks the entire doorway to my room. I swallow hard.

Shit.

Chema stands with his arms crossed over his chest, looking at me with a face full of tension only reserved for when he is upset with me for slacking off during training.

Sara must confuse my look of panic with confirmation of her fears because she assumes a defensive stance between my bed and Chema. I twist in the bed so I can reach for her and gently pat her arm.

"No, it's okay," I say. "But he's not my husband."

Sara keeps pinning him down with a glare, and I'm in awe that Chema actually flinches. I've never seen him do that before.

"Did you lie to hospital staff to get patient information?" she asks defiantly.

"She *is* family," he says with an accent even thicker than mine.

Sara throws her hands in the air and finally turns to face me again. "Do I need to call security? Do you want him out of here?"

I shake my head but have a hard time finding my voice. "He's, um, he—is right. He's family. He can be here."

Sara's brows knit together, but she lets it go when I smile at her. "I'll leave you to it, then. Call if you need anything," she says before leaving my room and sending one last nasty glare Chema's way.

Chema walks forward, his nostrils flaring, and I can't help but recoil as I wrap my middle with the blankets. I wouldn't want to be his opponent in a fight.

I close my eyes for a second, then take a deep breath. He is going to yell. He looks so mad, so betrayed. I roll every lie I ever told him on a loop in my brain and know he has every right to be angry with me.

I've betrayed him.

But he doesn't yell.

Instead, he drags a chair to the spot next to my bed, and it's only when he sits that his shoulders collapse, and he buries his head in his hands. His shoulders start shaking, and I would think it's laughter, but the sob that escapes from deep in his chest leaves no room for interpretation.

"Hey, Chema, love, no," I say, switching to Spanish for him and place a hand on his shoulder. "I'm here. I'm okay."

His head snaps up, and his jaw sets with a fury I know all too well. "You are not okay," he hisses.

The tears streaming down his face deflate me. "You're right. But I'm working on it, okay? I am still here."

"What if you died and nobody knew, Valentina? What the fuck were you thinking?"

"I didn't, Chema, I'm right here," I say a bit louder, hoping the words get through to him.

He sits back, and it is only then, with his hands folded over his lap and the light flooding through the window illuminating his face, that I see his puffy, bloodshot eyes and red nose, like he has been crying for hours.

Or days.

"Chema, I'm sorry. I didn't want you to worry; that's why I didn't say anything."

"Worry? Valentina, you are going to send me to an early grave. I almost had a heart attack when I saw you."

"Lucky you were in a hospital, then," I say and grin. Chema glares at me with icy eyes, and I realize Rory's dark humor is starting to rub off on me, and it is not for everyone. Rory. Where is Rory?

"Chema?"

"Yeah?"

"Where's Rory?"

"You mean the *flacucho* who was here before I arrived?"

I nod.

"He left."

My eyes widen with horror. No. "Please don't tell me he thinks you really are my husband?"

Chema studies me until the smallest corner of his mouth extends into a hint of a smile. "Seriously, Valentina? A gringo? And a lanky one at that? I have more muscles in one *nalga* than he has in his entire body.

"Not true," I say. "He is deceivingly fit," I proclaim, and just like that, I'm in Chema's mind-game.

He grins. "You've seen these muscles?" he asks and raises an eyebrow.

I huff. "No. He's a runner. That's why I say that."

When my first text goes unanswered, and he sends me to voice mail on the first ring, I decide I have to go find Rory. I start shuffling blankets off me and trying to get to my feet when Chema pushes me back into bed with one finger to my shoulder.

"What do you think you're doing?" he asks.

"I have to find him, Chema. He thinks I'm married. I have to explain."

"Don't worry. He'll be back."

"How are you so sure?"

"He told me."

"*What?*"

"Yeah, he said he was getting a few things from your apartment, and he'd be back to drop off the key."

I sink back into the bed as my heart plummets low in my chest. "You shouldn't have told him—"

"Let's not start begrudging who should have told who what," Chema hisses.

Great, the two most important men in my life are mad at me at the same time. That thought jars me. When did I start thinking of Rory as equally as important to me as Chema? Chema, who is family at this point.

Rory is coming back, so I try to calm down in the meantime and shift the conversation away from him.

"How did you find out?" I ask, finally.

"Pilar called me."

"Pilar? How does *she* know?" A fresh wave of panic hits me. Do my parents know too?

"What did you think was going to happen, Valentina? Huh? You leave your family and your dreams for a half-baked plan to train away from home. Of course, she was going to get suspicious. If you signed on with an agent, why would you need the kind of money she gave you?"

The extensive web of lies I cast is starting to ensnare me. "Chema," I croak, unable to voice the question I am dreading. "Do my parents know?"

He nods. "They are on a flight as we speak."

I shut my eyes. No. The last people on earth I want to be seeing right now are my parents. "You had to tell them?"

"They had to know. But it wasn't up to me. Pilar made that call."

"Is she coming too?"

"No. Felipe, he . . ."

"Yeah, I know. Don't worry." The day she leaves that slime ball will be the happiest day of my life.

"I can't believe she told Mom and Dad," I say.

"Really? That's what you're worried about? God, Valentina, you can be so selfish sometimes." Chema shakes his head and stands to pace the small space in front of my bed. "We thought you were dying. Which, I guess you kind of are . . ." He trails off, and his bottom lip quivers.

"Chema, I didn't mean to . . ."

"I know." He sniffs. "You've always been too proud to ask for help, but I never thought you would take it to these extremes—"

"It's not about pride," I say in a small voice.

"Then what?"

"So many things. It's hard to explain."

"Try."

I want to tell him the truth. I never wanted this disease to define me. I didn't want to walk into a room and be the cancer girl. The sick girl. The dying girl. I've always been the strong one. The fighting one. The athlete. This is not who I am. I don't want to tell Chema I was afraid he would stop coaching me after—if there will even be an after. Or that I feared potential sponsors losing interest in my career. I didn't want them to see the failure of my body, because I wasn't a failure. But most of all, I want to tell him how angry I am. I don't say any of it. "I didn't want my parents to know. That's all." I say.

"Why not?" Chema wants answers, and he will not relent until I give them to him.

"Because I'm so angry at them, okay? I can't stand to look at them." That's not a lie, and I'm hoping a partial truth will appease him.

His eyes soften, and he retakes his seat next to me, cupping my hand not trapped by the IV line in his. "Did something happen before you were diagnosed?"

"You know it's always been strained between us. Dad had a lot of resentments toward me even before this happened. And I won't lie. I have a lot of resentment for him too. But Chema, that's not even it. There's a vaccine for this type of cancer. They refused it because they said it was for *sucias* only."

"And if you'd had it, you wouldn't have gotten cancer?"

"No. I wouldn't have."

"Then you have every right to be angry at them. Hell, I'm angry, but tell them that, Valentina. Don't shut the rest of your family out because you're mad at your parents."

Chema is right, of course. I'm bottling up so much anger for my parents, anger I've accumulated for so many years, anger that stretches far beyond their inability to give me a simple vaccine.

At first, the anger started when I was old enough to understand Dad's general disinterest in his own family. His business took up most of his time. His lovers took the rest, leaving nothing left for his wife and daughters.

For her part, Mom retreated into herself with the help of various little pills that a new doctor friend of hers prescribed. She slept or was awake but high—those were her two operational modes growing up. She became a hollowed-out, inactive participant in her own life, and I couldn't stand to watch her weakness. I was only fourteen when the dynamics of my family finally fit together in the jigsaw puzzle.

I swore I'd never be that weak and decided instead to be strong. I chose mixed martial arts in my quest to find my own strength, and I thought I had found it until my body told me otherwise.

"Chema, I know what happens next with my parents."

"What's that?"

"I will be an inconvenience for my father who has to be away from his *commitments*, and my mother will play the part of the perfect martyr whose daughter is sick. It's nauseating."

"Why don't you give them the benefit of the doubt?" He asks.

"Because I know better."

SLOWLY BUT SURELY, I GET THE FULL STORY OUT OF CHEMA. PILAR became increasingly suspicious and decided to engage the services of a private investigation company. They found me out, easily tracked my mobile device, and took pictures.

Pilar hadn't thought to let me know, she simply wanted to know I was safe, but she knew I was sick when she saw the photos. I make Chema show me the images they've seen. He has them saved to his phone. The PI took pictures as I left the hospital. This was before I lost my hair. The image of the girl in the photo is unrecognizable even to me. She is me, but with no indication of muscles ever having existed, sunken eyes, and a greyish pallor.

The truth is, if at this moment Chema showed me a picture of Pilar looking like that, I would move heaven and earth to find her and make sure she was okay. I can't begrudge them for caring. Even if it means my parents were on their way.

How could I ever confront them? Neither of them will care about my anger and instead only be angry at me for hiding this.

Not once, in my brief adult life, have I let them dictate what my life would look like—an ever-irritating sore on Dad's side, and this will only give them more ammunition to try to convince me they know what is best for me.

I take a deep breath. *Don't worry about them until you have to.* Instead, I focus my attention on my sister. I owe her an explanation. "Chema? Could you give me some privacy? I need to call Pilar." He nods and is about to go on a quest for decent coffee when Mandy rushes into my room in a whirl.

"Is it true?" she asks hurriedly. She brushes the hair off her face and eyes Chema up and down with a glint in her eye. "You're married? Way to keep a secret, woman," she scorns.

"He's not my husband," I say and glare at Chema. "He's my coach and more like family."

"Then why does the entire oncology floor think you're married?"

"I lied to be able to see her," he admits and hangs his head.

"Is that right," Amanda says, grinning at him and tossing her hair over one shoulder.

"Mandy! Stop it. You're with Chris." I can't believe this woman. She flirts with anything that moves.

"It's not serious, and we have never said we are exclusive," she says to me but looks at Chema the entire time. I roll my eyes.

"Well, I'm in a serious relationship. Afraid I'm—"

"Taken," I cut Chema off.

His eyebrows shoot up when he looks at me, but he extends a hand to shake Mandy's, and her face falls with disappointment for a beat before she takes it. "Chema. Nice to meet you."

"Yeah, you too," she says.

"Mandy, I need to call my sister. Chema was on his way to search for coffee. Give him the lay of the land?"

"Sure," she says and smiles encouragingly at me. I know she is happy I'm finally letting my family know.

THE VIDEO CALL RINGS ONLY ONCE, AND PILAR GLARES AT ME through puffy, red eyes that match Chema's. She opens her mouth to speak, but I beat her to it.

"I'm sorry," I say.

"We've been so worried, Tini. You have no idea."

"I'm so sorry," I plead.

"I knew whatever you needed the money for was important, so I gave it to you even knowing you were lying out of your ass. But I never imagined it was life or death or I would have—"

"Would have what, Pilar? Come to see me? To help?"

She crosses her arms and looks away from the camera. We both know that's not an option, if her controlling husband has anything to say about it.

"I don't know," she says finally. "But I would have done something. You're my baby sister. You are a big part of the tiny light that exists in my life. I can't make it without you, Tini. Please don't ever pull shit like this again. You hear me?"

"I hear you. I promise I won't." And for the first time, I mean it. The heartbreak evident in my sister's eyes hurts more than any chemo and radiation side effects. She has been hurt enough in her life, and I can't be yet another person to let her down.

"I'm sorry. Mom and Dad are on their way," she says.

"I know you shield me from them as much as you can."

"You've noticed that?"

I nod. "Pilar, if I've learned anything from all this, it's that life is short. I hope I don't die from this, but even if I do, as brief as my life has been so far, I got to do what I loved. If you were in my shoes and you were facing death, could you say the same?"

"So that's what you're going to do. You're going to play the cancer card and hold it over everyone around you?"

"Only the ones I love," I say and smile.

Pilar doesn't engage the topic I tried to broach. Instead, I bring her up to speed on my treatment and we say our goodbyes and end the call, both of us sad but also a bit hopeful.

There's nothing left to do with the rest of my day but lay on my hospital bed and rehearse what I want to say to my parents. They need to know that while I share a big part of the blame for pushing off my regular checkups, they could have prevented it all. They need to know what a mistake they have made. And maybe, if I'm brave enough, I'll tell Dad precisely what I think of him. I was always too intimidated by him to do that. My young age and dependability prevented me from confronting him with his failures as a father, but now I am old enough to know better. My spine has strengthened, and this experience with cancer has matured me more than just physically. It would be now, or it would never be.

I'm saved from having the dread of time suffocating me by Rory finally showing up.

"Hey," he says but can't look at me.

"Rory!" I smile at him.

"Just came to drop off your key. I got all my stuff out of your apartment, and you don't have to see me ever again—"

"Rory, you don't have to—"

His voice deepens. "Yes, I do. I have to."

"Chema is my coach. Not my husband."

His head snaps up, and his eyes narrow, searching for the truth.

"He only said that so he could get my medical information."

"He can be arrested for that," Rory says.

"No. He won't. I'm okay with it. Frankly, I've put him through hell."

"So you two, you were—"

"No," I shake my head. "He is my coach and a good friend —that's it."

Rory doesn't seem fully appeased, but he takes a step forward, giving me hope.

Chema walks in then, clutching a mammoth cup of coffee that still looks puny in his hand and a bag with something that smells wonderful. "Brought you some breakfast," he says cheerily. "Hello." He smiles at Rory as he hands me the paper sack.

"Hello," Rory says but blinks as he tries to make sense of the situation.

I open the bag to find what I can only assume are burritos.

"Can you believe they put eggs in burritos?" Chema asks.

I shake my head and chuckle. My dear friend is about to have the same rude awakening with food I had when I first arrived. The truth is, I haven't eaten a burrito but a few times in my life. The last I remember was when my father had a trip to Chihuahua in Northern Mexico, where the burrito is king. It was one of those rare occasions when he brought his cumbersome family along. But those burritos had delicious grilled meat and beans with fresh avocado slices. Not eggs and cheese so greasy it leaks out of the flour tortilla rendering it soggy.

Still, I'm famished and take a healthy bite, which I have to admit, is not half bad. "I guess you two met while I was out of it?" I ask through the chewing.

Both men nod.

"I explained to Rory you're my coach," I say to Chema, "and not my husband."

Chema looks at Rory a bit sheepishly but still sizing him up with his glare. I'm proud when Rory stands tall, not at all intimidated by the meathead in the room.

"I'm sorry about that, buddy," says Chema. "I'm her coach. Actually, I'm—"

"Also a good friend," I say. Chema side-glances me.

"Oh." Rory cups the back of his neck.

"Sorry for the misunderstanding. As you can imagine, Valentina here had me and her family worried. I had to take drastic measures."

"Right, um, well, anyway, I assume you are staying with Valentina for a bit?" Rory asks.

Chema nods.

"Good. I'll be less worried," says Rory.

The proposed plan is appealing. The man I have the hots for doesn't have to see my physical decline, and one of my best friends can help me if I need it. I'm not sure when I became okay with the idea of help, but I did. It might have to do with the fact that not letting the people in my life who love me help me was in fact hurting them. I was hurting them, and I don't want to keep on hurting them.

"Chema? Are you staying for a while?"

"Until you're out of the woods," he says.

"And the gym?"

"It's taken care of. Don't worry."

"Well, um. I gave Valentina her spare key back. You can take that. I can show you to her apartment if you'd like," says Rory to Chema.

"Why don't we wait for me to be discharged, and we can go together?" I ask, suddenly nervous about leaving them together alone.

"They're keeping you overnight for observation, making sure you're responding well to the antibiotics, but you look much better, so I'm sure they'll discharge you in the morning," says Rory, who I know had to ask Sara for that information.

It's not ideal, but I have no further objections. At least not persuasive ones. I reassure Chema I'll be fine while he goes to freshen up and catch a nap before coming back.

"Rory?"

"Yeah?"

"I'll see you soon?" I ask because it is a question.

Rory's mouth upturns into a crooked smile, almost as if he were upset by the new arrangement. "Yeah, soon," he says.

Rory walks out of the room first, and Chema lingers for a bit.

"You aren't going to tell him I'm—"

"Don't you dare tell him," I warn my gentle giant, and he smiles knowingly at me. "Chema, thanks for coming. I'm glad you're here. Really."

"I'm always here for you, Tini," he says and walks out of my room after Rory. I can only imagine what they will talk about.

CHAPTER 14

"Oh my god," Mandy squeals. "You guys need to see him. He is so hot," she informs Tlali and Izel who are both huddled around my bed.

As soon as evening visiting hours started and everyone got off work, my room filled up. Chema is still at my apartment, but my new girlfriends keep me company. Sara even lingers after she checks on me to catch some of the girl-talk. When I first came to Kansas City, I never imagined I'd end up with a hospital room full of friends. I was prepared for lonesome and restless long stints in the hospital, but that has been the furthest from the truth.

"Is he coming back?" Izel asks and grabs a potato chip from a bag inside her purse.

"God, I hope so," Mandy says dreamily.

"Stop it," I warn. "You are taken. He's taken."

"You sound a little possessive there," she says and isn't even a little discreet when she glances at Rory, who is sitting in the corner of the room.

Rory's jaw ticks, and he stands up, probably not wishing to continue to let Mandy target him with her directness. "I'll leave you ladies to it, then. Valentina, I'll swing by tomorrow. I'm guessing you'll have your plate full tonight."

He tries to jab at the girls, who all giggle, but I already told him my parents would be showing up soon. "Yeah. See you later."

He steps past Mandy, and lands a peck on my cheek, then smiles at me. As he walks away, I don't miss Tlali looking between us as she presses her hand to her heart.

"He is so sweet," says Tlali.

"I couldn't believe Mandy when she told me you were dating a doctor here," says Izel.

"In my defense, I didn't know he was a doctor here when I met him at the bar."

"He looked a bit jealous," Mandy says with a mocking smile.

I smile back.

"I knew it. You are trying to make him jealous," Mandy accuses.

"No. I'm not *trying* to make him jealous," I say. "But I'll admit I'm not mad about it. He's kind of cute when he's angry, isn't he?"

"Guys, you're all missing the bigger picture here. Not that Dr. Dennis isn't super cute and everything, but Chema! We need to get back to Chema. Is his relationship serious?" Mandy asks. "Because I'd love to move to Mexico."

I roll my eyes.

"What does he look like?" Izel asks. "Like, compare him to a celebrity so we can have an idea."

Mandy's index finger taps her chin, and she chews the inside of her lip for a second. "I got it," she says. "He is ripped. And I mean *Ripped*. Think of the body of a young Arnold Schwarzenegger. His face, it's a cross between the manly features of Antonio Banderas, and the sculpted jaw of Henry Cavill." Mandy nods, pleased with herself.

I think about that description and picture, Chema. She kind of nailed it.

Sara laughs. "That's pretty accurate," she says, then excuses herself to check on other patients.

"Okay, *that* I have to see," Tlali says.

Mandy proceeds to fill us in with updates about Chris and her upcoming art show. I'm hoping I get to go. Izel and Tlali don't have much to report, though they continue to motivate each other with their artistic projects even after their long shifts at work. I'm glad they squeeze time to come chat with me here in there, as busy as they all are.

The conversation is upbeat, and I'm so grateful that my body's ailments are forgotten, if even for a moment. I don't see the sick Valentina reflected in these women's eyes. The hospital walls melt away from my periphery, and I can almost see myself having this conversation at a bar over dirty martinis. In my mind's eye, I'm healthy, pink at the cheeks, and my hair is still long. The distraction of this conversation is so welcome, I'm even glad Chema hasn't returned.

The happy mood doesn't last because late that afternoon before Chema has a chance to come back and be my reinforcement, I have two new visitors show up.

The last two people I wanted to see me sick.

My parents.

We are laughing and in the heat of our conversation when a booming voice fills the room, silencing us all.

"Valentina?" His voice is deep and cool, making my stomach drop.

We all turn to the door, and I freeze. My father walks in behind my mother.

"Hi," I say. All the levity that had been in the room evaporates, and Mandy, Tlali, and Izel all suddenly look at their purses, the floor, or their shoes. Anywhere except at my parents or me.

"Um, we'll get going," Izel says. "Come on, guys." She gestures for Tlali and Mandy to follow her. They both act like mutes, which is the first time Mandy has been at a loss for words. "Mr. and Mrs. Almonte, it's really nice to meet you." Izel is the only one with a functioning brain now, apparently. They all trickle out of the room, herded out by Izel, who closes the door.

I face my parents and attempt a smile, but I know it's awkward. My mom brings her hand to her mouth to hide her gasp. Her hair is mussed, something I've never seen before, and her designer outfit is rumpled. They came straight from the airport, then. Her eyes are swollen and red-rimmed. She grasps my Dad's arm for support like she can't stay upright if she lets go.

On the other hand, Dad breaks away from her hold and steps forward toward the side of my bed. His gaze sweeps my body from feet to face, and he falls to his knees.

"Dad?" I'm momentarily concerned he has fallen, but he takes my hand in his.

"Honey. We were so worried."

I don't remember the last hug from my Dad, or the last gesture of kindness between us, so my hand in his is awkward—at least for me. For him, it looks like it's the most natural thing in the world.

His harsh, black eyebrows are drawn in with concern, and I notice the stubble starting to shade the lower part of his face for the first time. He never goes unshaven. Or out of his suit and tie, for that matter. He wears a polo shirt and jeans that don't look out of place here but would have him stick out like a sore thumb any other day back home.

He lets out a sob, and I don't know what to do. I look at mom for help, but as usual, she is useless. She takes a seat and clutches her chest like she can't breathe, as if she were the sick one and not me. I knew this would happen.

"Dad, it'll be okay."

He wipes a tear from the corner of his eye and kisses the top of my hand. I blink at him, unsure what to say. He stands then and grabs a chair to sit next to me.

"Valentina Almonte, how dare you keep this from your mother and me?" I can tell he is aiming for scorning, but his voice cracks, giving him away.

"I'm sorry. I would have told you if the treatment failed. I swear."

"And you would have robbed us of time together," he says.

"*Virgensita*," Mom says and looks to the ceiling. She makes a cross over her chest and starts muttering prayers toward the sky.

This is it. The dreaded moment. The moment of truth. I am sick, but I am still me, and my illness hasn't erased all the harm done to our relationship before now.

"You've never cared about time together before now, Dad." I don't mean to sound as harsh as I do, but I know that's how it's received because Dad winces. He knows it's the truth.

"I'm sorry, *Mija*. I've let work consume me, and I've overlooked so much. I'll make it up to you. I swear. Tell me what I can do to make it up."

"Why don't you start by taking Mom to your hotel so she can freshen up and let her have her feelings there. We can talk tomorrow when you're both rested and more calm."

We both look at Mom, who is rocking back and forth in her chair with a rosary dangling from her clasped hands, tears dripping from her chin.

Dad shakes his head. "No. We want to see your doctor. I want to know everything. All Pilar said is that you have c-c-cancer. That you've had it for God knows how long, and she didn't know how bad it was."

"Look, I'm getting treated now. I got myself in a very aggressive clinical trial. You can relax and know I'm being taken care of. As for the doctor, you'll want to talk to Dr. Ramirez or Dr. Medina. They're the team leading the trial and most familiar with my case, but Dad, it's late. They've gone home, and they'll be here in the morning."

Mom finally comes and crouches over me, placing a hand on each of my cheeks. I'm smothered, but I don't protest. "*Mijita*, when you get through this, I'm going to give you the spanking of a lifetime," she says. Her tears are dripping onto my face, but I don't wince. Now, in a span of twenty-four hours, Pilar, Chema, Dad, and now Mom all shed tears for me.

I wonder what it's like for them. Do they feel defeated, like this cancer will consume me? I'm still in fight mode, and I refuse to switch to flight until I know there is nothing else I can do. I'm not dead yet.

"Mom, stop. Please. I'm alive. Save your tears."

"Until you're dead? Is that what you're trying to say?"

She always exaggerates. "Yeah, Mom. But it won't be today or anytime soon."

She smiles weakly and dries up her tears. I know she's trying to keep them in, but she fails miserably.

"Okay," says Dad. "I'll take her to the hotel. We just had to see you. Make sure you're okay. You understand?"

"I do. And for what it's worth, I am sorry about how you found out. I wanted to tell you myself, if it came to it."

"You've always been so strong, Valentina. I never realized you would use that strength to pull something like this. But we'll talk more tomorrow. Okay?"

They both kiss me and walk away, though they glance back as they walk out the door. I take a deep breath. Okay. We can do this in small bites. We've ripped off the Band-Aid, and tomorrow we can do the rest.

～

RORY GETS TO MY ROOM BEFORE MY PARENTS. HE WEARS HIS scrubs and doctor's coat. Being hospital staff provides him the liberty to avoid visiting hours.

"How are you?" I ask and smile at him.

His face brightens when he sees my smile. "Good. How about you?"

"Feeling a bit stronger. But it won't last. I get chemo tomorrow, and that usually knocks me out for a few days."

"Think of it this way," he says. "You're almost halfway there."

He is right. I know this. The trial is a five-week treatment plan, and I'm entering week three. I hadn't let myself search for the light at the end of the tunnel, but there it is, reflected in Rory's bright green eyes.

Rory places a vase of yellow and pink tulips on the counter by the window.

"I love tulips," I say. "Thank you."

"Do you? Or are you just saying that?"

"Would I lie to you?"

"You *have* lied to me. And you seem to lie to a lot of people."

A kick to the jaw would have been less painful.

"I'm sorry," he says. "I'm new to being on the other side of this. Usually, I'm the doctor. Navigating everything else . . . that's harder," he says.

"I understand."

Rory takes a seat next to my bed and takes my hand, rubbing the top of it with his thumb in circles.

"I hate that you see me like this," I admit.

"Like what?"

"Sick. I look awful."

"Valentina, you have no idea how beautiful you are. I don't think you'll believe me, but I have to say it anyway. When I look at you, I don't see a sick person. I see *you*. And you are strong, and yes, beautiful. I don't care if you think I'm superficial."

My eyes mist over for the first time because Rory Dennis

says the only words I want to hear. He hasn't let this disease alter his perception of me.

"Hey, don't cry," he coos.

"I'm not crying. You're crying." I shake my head to center myself and smile at him again.

I squeeze his hand, and he leans forward to land the sweetest and softest peck on my lips. It's not a passionate kiss like what we shared before, but the tenderness and rawness of it plunges us into a different level of intimacy. I place my hand on his cheek as our lips pull away, and he presses his forehead to mine. We're sharing this tender moment when a booming voice has us jumping and pulling away from each other.

"What is this?"

As he turns to face the door, Rory keeps my hand tight in his.

My father glares at him, his nostrils flaring, and his hands at his sides bunch into fists. His body shakes with fury, and my heart races.

"Dad, hi. Good morning."

He says nothing and takes a step toward us.

Rory lets go of my hand to stand and adjust his posture as he faces my father. "Mr. Almonte, it is a pleasure to meet you. Rory Dennis." He stretches out his hand, but my father doesn't take it, never breaking his glare from Rory's face.

"What is the meaning of this?" Dad asks.

"Dad, Rory is special to me. He helped take care of me when I was alone and has done nothing but help me and be kind to me."

Rory's rejected hand goes into his coat pocket, but he doesn't let my Dad intimidate him. "Valentina is very special to me too, sir."

Dad's mouth opens to speak, but he is interrupted when Dr. Ramirez walks into the room.

"Valentina, good morning," she says brightly. "Oh, hello. I'm

Dr. Ramirez," she shakes my Dad's hand, but his glare stays frozen on Rory. "Dr. Dennis, good morning," she says, smiling despite the questioning look on her face.

"Dr. Dennis?" Dad roars, and his chest rises faster with each breath.

"Yes, sir. I'm a physician here."

Dad turns to Dr. Ramirez, an accusation in his eyes. "Is it common for doctors here to kiss their patients?"

Dr. Ramirez's gaze scans the room from Dad's face, to Rory's, to mine, finally understanding what's going on. "Dr. Dennis isn't one of Valentina's doctors, Mr. Almonte. I can assure you, no lines have been crossed."

"Excuse me?" Dad huffs. "No lines have been crossed? My daughter is sick. He's clearly taking advantage—"

"Dad, no one's taking advantage. Please sit down so we can talk."

Dad shakes his head. "What kind of a sick bastard preys on cancer patients?"

"Dad! He didn't prey on me. He didn't even know I was sick when we met."

I can tell Dad's resolve wavers a bit, but he's also the person I inherited my stubbornness from, so I know he won't relent so easily. "I will sue," he hisses. "No one takes advantage of my daughter."

"No one took advantage of anyone, Dad. And you are not suing. If anything, you owe a wealth of gratitude to everyone in this hospital, including Rory. They have all made me very welcome knowing I was here alone."

"Mr. Almonte, I'm sure you have questions. I'll be back in an hour when everyone is calmer." Dr. Ramirez doesn't let Dad answer her before she is out of the room. I don't blame her for her quick departure, because the showdown taking place in my room is awkward as fuck. I don't even want to be in the room myself.

Dad takes a deep breath. "I need you to leave," he tells Rory.

"He's not leaving," I say and grab Rory's hand to make myself perfectly clear.

Rory never breaks eye-contact with Dad, and Dad's glare moves from him to me and back to him again.

"*Please*," Dad says. "I have to speak with my daughter and her doctors." His voice is more placating now, and I'm more receptive to it. Rory looks at me, checking with me it's okay if he leaves. I nod.

My eyes widen with horror when Rory bends to kiss my lips one last time before heading out. When he stands, I look at Dad, who is fuming. Rory Dennis is a brave man to have made that move.

"Mr. Almonte, I'll be back later. I'm sure you'll want to chat with me too."

Dad looks stunned and frozen in place as Rory leaves the room. He starts pacing, pausing to glare at me every few steps, just as Chema had done. He seems a little better than he did last night when he first arrived. He has shaved, and his clothes are crisp once again, though more casual than what I'm used to seeing him wear. My mother is nowhere to be seen, and I'm not surprised. She's never handled family situations well. Avoidance being her modus operandi, I know she has knocked herself out cold with pills back at their hotel room. I don't have to ask Dad for confirmation.

We switch to Spanish for the rest of our conversation. "Dad, can you sit down? You're making me dizzy."

He stills and at last sits, taking the chair Rory vacated only moments ago.

"What on earth were you thinking?" he asks. "Were you even thinking? Men like that prey on weak—"

"Dad! Stop. You don't know him. He didn't prey on me."

"You're sick. Any man trying to, to . . ." He trails off, not able to finish his thought.

"Any man trying to be with a sick woman is trying to take advantage? I don't deserve to be loved if I'm sick?"

"That's not what I'm saying," he says and runs his hands through his hair, pulling on it with frustration.

"Then what, Dad? Please. Explain."

His head hangs for a moment before he looks back up at me. "I don't know, *Mija*. This is all too much of a shock. Seeing you yesterday like this, and then seeing that—" he points to the door in reference to the man who just left. "Love, huh?"

My eyes widen. "What?"

"You said he loves you."

Did I? "Um, well, I don't know if he does, I was just—"

"Do you love him?"

That takes me aback. I had used the word *love*, though I'm not sure why. "I don't know, Dad. I've only known him a few weeks. I don't think we can say we're in love yet, but he's special. And I owe him a lot."

"What do you mean?"

"He took care of me after surgery."

Dad shuts his eyes, his brows knitted together in pain. "You had surgery?" he asks as his gaze fixes on me once again.

I nod. "I'll let Dr. Ramirez fill you in on anything medical going on, but Rory, he took care of me and brought me to the hospital. If he hadn't been there—"

"Don't finish that sentence. I don't even want to know what could have happened."

I smile. "See? It's good he's been around."

Dad's shoulders finally droop with resignation. "I'll apologize to him later, though I don't like this. Not one little bit."

"Thanks, Dad."

When Dr. Ramirez comes back, I sign paperwork granting her permission to disclose my medical record to Dad. I ask them to leave the room so I can nap because I'm too tired to go through my entire medical history. Besides, I'd rather Dad ask

Dr. Ramirez a million questions instead of me, and I'm glad she's more than willing to take one for the team.

When I'm awake again, he is in my room, smiling at me, but I can tell he's been crying from his puffed-up, red eyes, and I don't know how to feel about it.

He acts like the strain between us was all in my head, but I know it wasn't. Dad has never looked at me like this before, at least not in my adult life. It was always disdain and disappointment because I refused to marry the men he lined up for me.

He told me once that no man would want to marry a professional fighter—a woman who had more muscles than him. I told him that's exactly the kind of guy I would never end up with. When Pilar married, he finally stopped pushing me toward the destiny he'd drawn out for me since my birth. Since then, we've hardly spoken, and if we have, it has been mainly to argue.

Now, he is here pretending like that history never existed. Like I imagined it all. He is doting and loving like he had been once long ago when I was just a little girl. I bite my lip hard to hold back my emotions. I hate that it's taken me getting sick for him to care again. Why couldn't he show me his love before now, when it might very well be too late?

CHAPTER 15

The next day, Mom comes to visit with Dad. I'm feeling a bit stronger and glad they are here together because I have quite a lot to say.

But first, I let Mom nag and nag about keeping the secret from her.

"Are you done?" I ask after her tirade.

"I'm not even close to done, *señorita*—"

"Cecilia!" Dad snaps. "That's enough. This is hardly the time."

Mom's lips disappear into a thin line. Just once, I'd love to see her talk back to Dad. Today would not be that day.

"I'm angry too, you know," I say finally.

Mom glares at me. "*You're* angry? After you pulled this?"

"Mom, calm down. I'm trying to have a conversation with you. I'm angry about a lot, and for once, I wish you would just listen to me before you check out."

She looks away from me and shakes her head like I'm talking nonsense.

"Hear her out, Cecilia," Dad says, and I'm surprised he's on my side. Unfortunately for him, I'm angry at him too.

Mom takes a seat and crosses her arms. She taps her foot as she waits for me to speak.

I take a deep breath and decide to start with the easier one. "I'm upset you're never there for Pilar or me. You're like a ghost, Mom. We've never had your support, so I don't understand how you'd expect me to go to you for something like this when you always avoid hard situations."

"That is not an excuse—"

"Mom, Mom. Please. Just let me finish."

Mom glares at me but keeps her mouth shut. "Thank you," I say. "Neither of you has ever come to see me fight—"

"We didn't want to encourage—" Dad starts to say, but I cut him off.

"Dad, I know it's hard, but let's pretend for a moment this is the worst-case scenario, and I don't make it. Aren't you glad, as short as my life has been, that I got to do the one thing I loved most in the world?"

The silence hovers over all three of us like a dark cloud. Dad's eyes turn glassy, and he swallows hard.

"Wouldn't you wish, then, that you'd gotten to see my greatness? I know you don't think it was much compared to your business or Pilar's marriage, but Dad, I was good. So good. They don't call mixed martial arts 'arts' for no reason. I was an artist with my body. It's fighting, yes, but it's also a dance, and it's so beautiful. I was beautiful. And you never got to see it."

"You're not going to die, Valentina," he declares like he can somehow control it.

That's not what I wanted them to get from what I said, but I'm not surprised. They will never support my dreams unless they are dreams I share with them. I know now that if—when— I beat this thing, they will not change. It's time for me to move on from the hope that we will ever be close.

"I'm sorry you're angry," Mom says. "But I've done the best that I could."

"I know, Mom," I give her a sad smile because I believe her, and knowing that was her best is a bit disheartening.

Now for the harder one. The one they won't want to so much as hear me out on.

"That's not the only reason I'm angry."

Both my parents look at me intently, waiting for me to go on.

"This cancer is your fault—"

"Great. You're going to blame us for this—" Mom says, exasperated.

"Mom! Please, listen." I wait a moment, and when she doesn't speak again, I continue. "You could have prevented this if you had given me the HPV vaccine. I wouldn't be here right now if you had done that one little thing."

"I don't know about that sort of thing," Mom says dismissively.

"My doctor told you about it. I was there. You turned it down. Tell me I'm wrong."

"You have to understand. That vaccine is for young girls who are lost causes."

I shake my head, and I'm furious. "No, Mom. It's for everyone. Men and women. Everyone needs to get it when they're young—*everyone.*"

"Everyone who does . . . *things,*" she argues, not willing to put it into words.

"Say it, mom. Say what you mean."

She just shakes her head, and Dad's face is buried in his hands.

"You want to say it's only for whores," I snap.

"Watch your language, *niña.* These are not things we talk about." Mom stands and takes the small medallion on her gold necklace between her fingers so she can play with it as she paces.

"Mom, most women get HPV in their lives. It can take years

to turn to cancer. Pilar could get this cancer too."

"No," Mom says. "Really, Valentina, I can't believe you would talk about this and with your father present. You have no shame. Besides, Pilar is married."

"Good. I'm glad Dad's here. He needs to hear this too. Pilar can get this cancer even if she's married, Mom. She could have gotten it before—"

"No!" Mom shakes her head. "She didn't get it before."

"She could get it from her husband, Mom! You could get it!"

Mom stops and blinks at me. She shakes her head. "I can't believe we are talking about this—especially in front of your father. Valentina Almonte, you were raised better than to talk about this."

I'll never get through to her, but at least Dad displays some form of shame. He hangs his head and pulls on his hair as he listens to me. At least I know he feels somewhat guilty.

"Mom, I haven't been a virgin for a long time. Why is that so hard to talk about?"

Mom turns to Dad, swinging her purse over her shoulder. "Benjamin, please take me to the hotel. This conversation is over." Then she turns to me. "If you want me to come back, missy, none of that talk. *No seas cochina.*"

At that moment, and with those words, I give up on my mother. "No, Mom. I don't want you to come back."

"Valentina!"

"I mean it. Dad, you are welcome back if you'd like, but don't bring her with you. Not unless she regrets not getting us that vaccine before it was too late." He nods, and I add, "I know you feel bad about this, Dad."

He clears his throat. "Um, I'll see you tomorrow, then." He kisses my forehead for the first time in I don't know how many years and looks back at me as he leaves the room.

～

THE NEXT MORNING, I'M HAPPY TO FIND DAD HAS RESPECTED MY wishes and left Mom at the hotel, though I'm sure she didn't protest. After speaking with Dr. Ramirez yesterday, he looks less forlorn, though he admits he carries guilt for not being more involved in our health and leaving it up to Mom, who, let's face it, didn't do a good job. I tell him I forgive him because I really do.

"Why can't you forgive your mother too?" he asks.

"Because she doesn't believe she did anything wrong."

I'm relieved when Dad lets it go. I change the subject and tell him about all the people I have met besides Rory. He smiles when I describe how Mandy, Tlali, and Izel welcomed me and have kept my spirits up.

"This place suits you," Dad says.

I smile. "It does. Doesn't it?"

I tell him about Rory, though I only give him the PG version, and he laughs when I describe the confrontation between him and Chema.

"And he didn't flinch?" he asks about Rory.

"Not even a little."

Almost as if we had summoned him, Chema walks into my room. He hadn't come back after I texted him that my parents were here. For obvious reasons, Mom and Dad loathe Chema.

Which is why it takes me by complete surprise when Dad stands and hugs Chema. Towering over Dad, Chema looks over his head at me. His eyebrows float up in question, and I can only shrug. I mouth, *I have no idea.*

The men part, and I take the somewhat happy opportunity to give Dad my one request.

"Dad, Chema has agreed to stay and help me out while I finish the last few weeks of treatment."

"I don't know how I'll ever repay you," Dad says.

"I love Valentina like family," Chema reassures him. "I wouldn't take any type of payment."

"I'd like for you and Mom to go home—" I start to say.

"Out of the question." Dad shakes his head like he can't believe what I just asked him.

"Dad, please. Chema promises he'll call if things go south. But if not, and everything goes like I'm hoping it will, then what's the point of you and Mom being here, living in a hotel?" He's unsure, so I drive it home. "You know if she comes back, we'll just fight—and that's the last thing I need right now."

"*Mija*, I want to be with you."

"I know, but I promise I'll video call often, so it'll be just like you are here."

He reluctantly agrees after I swear I'll keep him in the loop, but I see his relief to be able to get Mom away from me—like this is the one thing he can do for me, so he will do it.

Dad hasn't done much for me in my life, but this small gesture means the world to me.

The olive branch extends from my hands, and he takes it in the first fatherly act of my adult life.

CHAPTER 16

After my parents' departure, I stay in the hospital for two days during my next infusion. I spend the two days in bed without any energy. Luckily, it is Chema who sees me like this, and he keeps Rory at bay as much as possible, though the weasel sneaks in here and there.

On the third day, I have a burst of energy that Dr. Ramirez takes as an excuse to finally discharge me.

When we get to my apartment, I see Chema has made himself at home. He upgraded a bit of the decor so everything isn't so cream and beige. There are burnt orange cushions on the sectional sofa and several clear food organizers on the kitchen counter displaying oats, nuts, and shredded coconut. A few abandoned takeout containers sit on the coffee table, and Chema's many pairs of tennis shoes litter the carpeted floor. It's a mess, and it feels more like home than it ever has.

We settle on the couch, and I grab the remote.

"Wanna watch a movie?" I ask.

"No. Actually, my telenovela is on now. Mind if we watch it?"

Telenovelas don't appeal to me quite as much as they do to

Chema, but I owe him too much to say no. "Sure. Which one is it?"

Chema takes the remote and fills me in excitedly. "It's called *Curvas Peligrosas*. With Erica Moran. She's that new actress who's really popular right now."

"The curvy one who looks like she just stepped out of a fifties movie?'

"That one! It's so good."

We are watching the show, and I soon realize she is an anti-hero. She uses men as boy-toys, and they call her the man-eater because no man can tame her heart. I can see why Chema loves the show so much. It breaks away from every telenovela trope I've ever encountered. The actress is stunning, and she is also plus-sized. Not that there aren't gorgeous plus-sized actresses, but they usually play the best friend, not the main character.

I'm going over this character analysis in my head when I get a text from Rory.

RORY: *PLEASE DON'T KILL ME.*
  Me: *What? Why?*
  Rory: *I swear it's not payback for making me meet your parents.*
  Me: *What did you do?*
  Rory: *My parents want to meet you.*
  Me: *Um, okay.*

I don't say I think it's too soon to meet the parents or that him meeting mine was a fluke thanks to my sister, but fair is fair, after all. I take a deep breath.

  Me: *Okay. Set it up.*
  Rory: *Already done. Open up.*
  Me: *What?!*
  Rory: *We're downstairs. I'm so sorry. They insisted.*

MY HEART RACES. "I'M GOING TO KILL HIM."

Chema's eyes don't tear away from the screen as he asks, "Who?"

I snatch the remote and shut off the television.

"Hey, what gives?" Chema's annoyed glare pins me.

"Pay attention. Rory's downstairs."

"So?"

"With his parents."

"Okay . . ."

"Chema!" I whine. "This place is a mess!"

"Oh." Realization lands on his face. "Oh. Shit. Sorry." He kicks it into gear and picks up shoes from the floor and trash from the coffee table as quickly as he can. Everything gets tossed in his room. I'm not able to help with much, but I go over to the intercom to buzz them up.

"I'm going to take a nap," Chema, the coward, tells me and shuts his bedroom door.

When I open the door, Rory stands in front of a couple a bit shorter than him, neither of whom is a redhead.

"Valentina, hi."

"Come in, please." I adjust my headscarf and straighten my sweatshirt.

"This is my Mom and Dad. This is Valentina," says Rory as we stand awkwardly by the door.

"Oh, she is darling, Rory. You didn't do her justice." Rory's mom takes me in for a hug that is so tight I have to suck in air. "Oh, I'm sorry, dear. Didn't mean to crush you."

"Hello, Mrs. Dennis. It's very nice to meet you."

"None of that nonsense. Call me Lisa. And this here is Tom."

"Lisa. Tom," I say and smile at them. "Please take a seat, make yourselves at home."

Lisa Dennis has dark brown hair and a light-olive skin tone.

Her eyes are brown, and she is short and stocky. Nothing about her looks like Rory. Tom Dennis is only a few inches taller than his wife, and both his hair and eyes are a dark brown that is almost black. Neither of them has Rory's signature freckles.

"Your mom is right, son," says Tom. "She's a lot prettier than you said."

"Dad! I'm sorry, Valentina. Don't believe anything they say. They are both liars."

I laugh. I'm glad I'm up for company today.

"I'm sorry to spring up on you like this," says Lisa. "We wanted to surprise Rory with a visit, and he confessed he met someone special. He didn't want us to meet, but then the weasel told us you are sick and alone and, well, we had to come check on you. He's a sneaky one, dontchaknow." Lisa shoots daggers at Rory with her eyes, and I almost feel bad for him. Almost.

It's so strange to have his parents here and to have them so concerned about me—a complete stranger to them. I search Rory's eyes for a possible explanation. Rory just shrugs, not understanding the question I failed to ask telepathically. He must have said something to them that made me seem impor-tant enough for them to want to check in on me. But wasn't this move exactly like something Rory would do? He always shows up if he thinks I might need any help, whether he's been invited or not. Now his parents are doing the same. He gets it from them, and I'm starting to understand that this is simply how his family operates. It's intrusive . . . and loving.

Then I turn my focus to what his mom is saying. I remember Rory using that phrase before. Dontchaknow. The syllables running into each other like they are all one word. When he used the phrase, he had been talking about home. Now I know where he gets it.

I study Lisa with curiosity. I don't understand what made them visit with such urgency once they found out I was sick.

They don't know me enough to care. *What did you say to them, Rory?*

"Oh dear," says Lisa. "We've really put our foot in it, haven't we? I only mean Rory's been through enough in his life. If someone he cares about is ill, we want to be here for Rory."

"And for you," Tom says, looking at me.

"I, um—I don't know what to say," I admit. I look between the three of them, trying to find some sort of resemblance between Rory and his parents, but there is none.

There is no similar curve to his nose like Tom's, and his wavy red hair couldn't be further from his mom's brown curls. I look like my mom—a lot, and still, I have a bit of Dad around the eyes.

"You haven't told her," Lisa says to Rory but keeps her gaze on me.

Rory shakes his head.

"Tell me what?"

"Well, we can get going if you two want to have a chat," Tom starts to say, but Rory cuts him off.

"No. It's fine. You can be here when I tell her."

"Tell me what?"

"I'm adopted," Rory says. "It's the rest of the scar story I promised I'd tell you one day."

"Oh," I say. "Wow. I mean, um. I don't know what to say."

"No need to say anything, dear," Lisa says. "We know he is our son, and so does he. There's no difference if I carried him or if I didn't. Rory Dennis is mine and Tom's."

Rory takes his mom's hand in his, making me smile.

"I'm confused," I say. "What does that have to do with the scar?"

"When my biological mother learned I had a heart defect and would need open-heart surgery as soon as I was born, she gave up her rights to me."

"The poor thing was very young, and a sick baby was more

than she could handle." It's nice to see Lisa doesn't seem to carry any resentment toward Rory's biological mother.

"At the time, we had been praying for a miracle," Lisa continues. "When we got the news about him and that he had a heart condition, well that hurt as if he were ours. Because he was ours."

Tom listens to his wife tell the story with a small smile, letting her do all the talking.

"Is that why you wanted to be a doctor, because of your heart?" I ask Rory.

He nods, and I imagine a teenage Rory, feeling rejected by his biological mother and wanting to be a doctor so no other child would have to go through the same thing.

"Why oncology, then?"

"The plan was pediatric cardiology, but then I came to Heartland Metro and met Dr. Ramirez."

"Ah," I say, understanding. "She inspired you."

"Yeah. You could say that. I've had many passionate teachers before, but to her, fighting cancer is like a personal battle. She recruits physicians into oncology like she is drafting for war. She's a force to be reckoned with."

"No need to explain further," I say. "You never stood a chance."

Lisa and Tom both laugh like they already know everything Rory is saying and all about Dr. Ramirez. Does he talk to them about everything? I wonder what that's like. To have parents you can speak with and who listen—parents who support your dreams, even when they change. Rory may be adopted, but his parents are closer to him than my biological ones ever will be to me.

Lisa stands, inviting herself to my kitchen. She opens the fridge door, and meeting with scarce options, declares it won't do. In a blur, and before I can stop her, she goes into my room and comes out with a dirty clothes bin. "I'll take care of these for you, dear," she says.

I'm about to protest, but she glares at me with a look I don't dare confront.

"It's best if you just let it happen," Tom says and winks at me.

"Tom, would you drive me to the grocery store? I want to fill the fridge and—" Lisa starts to say.

"It's really not necessary. My friend Chema is staying with me. He's helping."

When I mention Chema, the corner of Rory's eyes tighten a bit.

"I don't see him anywhere," says Lisa.

"He's napping," I say.

"Good. While he naps, I'll get the laundry going and go get some things so I can make some soup."

"Mom's chicken noodle soup is magic," Rory says.

"Uh . . . Thanks. For everything," I say.

"You betcha, dear," says Lisa with a smile.

Lisa and Tom say a quick goodbye and leave my apartment, though Rory lingers for a little while.

"I'm sorry about all that," he says. "They mean well."

"Don't be. They are fantastic, Rory," I say.

Rory smiles and plants the customary peck on my lips before leaving. It feels familiar already, like we've known each other for years, and this is how we part ways.

I don't like it. Not one bit.

Rory was meant to be temporary. A tiny blip in my life, when everything was said and done. But somehow, he has already cared for me in my sickbed, met my parents, introduced me to his, and told me about his biological mother and his heart defect, which couldn't have been easy for him.

He thinks this thing between us is serious.

It can't be. Not unless I know I'm in the clear. If death weren't staring down at me, I know I'd let this happen, but everything is so much more complicated because of my stupid, stupid cancer.

Rory beamed when he introduced his parents to me. He was so proud for us to meet. He was not scared like I was when I was forced to introduce him to mine. My life is much too complicated to let this happen. His feelings for me are growing, and I can't break his heart.

I need to nip this in the bud.

CHAPTER 17

$\mathcal{R}$ory pulls the wheelchair from the trunk and places it outside my door.

"Have I told you how beautiful you look tonight?" Rory asks.

I chuckle. "Yes. When you picked me up, remember?"

"Yeah. Right."

He is lying through his teeth, but I know he's just trying to make me feel good.

I dodged him after his parents went back to Minnesota, but we both committed to going on a date to Mandy's art show. I figure I can break it off with him after one last date.

If I'm honest, I want to see him one last time. One last time when we are both happy.

I feel okay today and insisted I wouldn't need the wheelchair, but Rory didn't want to push my luck with my energy levels. At the tail end of treatment, I only have one week to go, and then all that's left is to wait and see if it comes back. Finally leaving chemo and radiation behind me will be one of the best days of my life. I just hope I'm putting treatment behind me for the last time. I'm not sure I can put myself through this again.

I'm swimming in my wrap dress. I tied it as tightly as I could to make it seem more my size, though it's not fooling anyone. Rory looks dashing in dark slacks and a maroon button-up shirt that makes his beautiful green eyes pop. I'm going to miss him, but I try to focus on one last night together, enjoying his company for now.

Rory pushes my wheelchair into the nearly-empty gallery. The space has a modern vibe, and every wall is filled with colorful oversized landscapes and much smaller portraits.

Tlali and Izel huddle around Mandy, talking to a tall woman whom she introduces as the gallery manager and her art dealer, Debra.

"It's nice to meet you," I say.

"You too, enjoy the show. I have to check on a few things," Debra says and gets to work.

I turn to look at Mandy. "Are you nervous?" I ask.

Mandy nods. "A little. I've been working on this for so long. It's always a little nerve-racking putting work out there, hoping no one will trash something you've poured your heart into."

"It'll be great; you'll see." Tlali half-hugs Mandy and rubs her shoulder. "The paintings are great. You'll get rave reviews. I just know it."

"Thanks. I hope you're right," Mandy says, and nervous isn't a look that suits her.

Izel walks over to the hors d'oeuvre table and plops a tiny tart in her mouth, then grabs a glass of white wine. "You look good, Valentina," she says. "I'm glad you felt up to it."

"Me too. Thanks."

A few more people trickle in, and Mandy leaves us so she can greet them. Izel and Tlali both make their way to various paintings to admire, and I ask Rory to push me around so I can see them all.

One half of the room is hung only with portraits. I recognize depictions of Tlali, Izel, and Mandy's mom. The rest of the portraits are all women, though I don't recognize any more of them. Mandy's style is a bit abstract up close, but the further you step back, it's almost photorealistic. I'm no art expert, but despite my untrained eye, I can tell these are good.

I've seen modern art before. I don't understand most of it. A lot of it seems like things children would do, but somehow, Mandy has managed to merge classical-style painting with a modern twist. It's unlike anything I've seen before.

"She's really talented, isn't she?" I say to Rory.

"She sure is," he agrees. "One day, when I'm making a good salary, I'll commission a portrait of you from her."

Who knew that little package of loud would be this good an artist? I've always pictured artists as tortured souls suffering for their art. In my head, it was the Hollywood depiction of alcoholics and drug addicts starving for their art, only gaining recognition long after their death.

Mandy couldn't be further from what I envisioned an artist to be. Her life is chaotic, but she is fulfilled. She holds a regular job to support herself and has friends who support her.

"Take me over to the landscapes?"

Rory obliges, and we get in line behind a few people to start the procession in front of the significantly larger landscape paintings. The gallery is nearly full now, and I'm relieved for Mandy.

Her landscapes are crafted in a similar style to the portraits but on a grander scale. I can tell this is the playground where she experiments with light. The landscapes exude a feeling the portraits lack, and I know, just know, this is where her true talent lies.

We reach the end of the room to find a single painting larger than all the other landscapes. It's technically a landscape because I see land below, but clouds engulf the vast majority of the canvas, more like a skyscape.

I squeeze Rory's wrist, asking him to let me admire it a little bit longer. I haven't seen much art in my life, but I understand now why people seek it, travel for it, suffer for it. It moves something inside you. It makes you feel alive. It gives you a reason to live.

My eyes sting with tears as I take in the painting. I haven't seen enough. I haven't seen enough art. I've never seen clouds like these, sunrises like these—places like this. I've spent all my life in a big city surrounded by high-rises—a concrete jungle encasing me. While I love my city, there is so much more I haven't seen; not enough natural wonders, foreign countries, or art. I've never seen so much as a waterfall in real life.

I take a deep breath and swallow back my tears before they spill. Craning my neck to read the small card next to the canvas, I read: "Untitled, Not for Sale."

"That one is my favorite," Mandy says as she reaches Rory and me.

"Mine too," I agree, eyes still glued to the painting. I'm relieved the conversation distracts me from my fatalistic thoughts. "I was thinking about buying it, but it's the only one not for sale. Why?" I ask her.

We walk back to the food table as we keep chatting.

"I don't know," Mandy shrugs. "There are some paintings that you're just full of some sort of emotion while you work. You know? And then when you're done, it's like you can't believe you made that—that you have something like that inside you."

"No," I shake my head. "I have no idea what you are talking about, but I'll take your word for it."

"It would just be too hard to part with it, that's all. Though, I do think eventually I'll end up selling it."

Debra walks over to our spot and clutches Mandy's forearm. She speaks in small conspiratorial whispers, but Rory and I are close enough to hear too.

"You are not going to believe this, but we have someone wanting to buy the landscape that's not for sale."

"I do believe it," Mandy says. " It's my best work, but it's not for sale."

"He really wants it and is ready to prove it. He said to name your price."

"Who is it?" Mandy asks, scanning the gallery past Debra.

Debra points to a giant man almost as tall as Chema, though not quite as beefy. He is stunning, but in more of an Enrique Iglesias kind of way. My jaw drops, and I look over at Mandy, but her face is all scrunched up. "What's wrong?" I ask her.

Her jaw twitches, and I can tell she's grinding her teeth. "That's Dr. Bel."

"Wait, you know him?" Rory asks.

"Yeah. He's a surgeon at Heartland Metro."

"Why do you look like you are about to kick him in the shin?" Rory asks.

"He's a complete jerk. I've seen him every day for years, and he never remembers having seen me before if I say hello. Not that he'd say hello first. He basically fits every arrogant, god-complex, surgeon stereotype." Mandy's nostrils flare at the end of her rather picturesque description of Dr. Bel. "No way in hell I'm selling him my favorite painting."

"Hold on just one minute," Debra hisses. "Think about it. He asked for you to name your price for that landscape. You can make as much as you want here."

Mandy's resolve wavers, but in the end, she shakes her head. "No. I'd burn the painting before *he* could have it—"

"Mandy, hold on." I try to reason with her. "Why don't you set a ridiculous price no one in their right mind would agree to? That way, he'll probably say no and no harm done. And if he agrees, then you can make a small fortune at his expense."

"But he'll have the painting," Mandy says.

"But you'll have his money at a premium," I smile wickedly at her.

Most of the landscapes are priced at around fifteen-hundred

dollars, depending on their size. I'm sure the gallery takes half of the sales price. She has the opportunity to make a killing on one painting alone.

Mandy bites her cheek as she thinks, then looks at Debra. "Fine. Valentina makes a great point. Tell him twenty thousand dollars—firm. I'm not going to haggle with him, Deb. I meant it."

"Are you kidding?" Deb hisses but plasters on a fake smile. "That's ridiculous. He'll never agree to that. You're not that established yet. One day maybe, but not—"

"I'm not trying to sell the painting, Deb. You agreed to this. We only included it because it's part of the narrative we were going for."

"Okay. Okay, but you're killing me here."

"Unless he agrees," Mandy smiles. "In which case, I just made you a shit ton of money."

Debra glares at Mandy, and I know she doesn't think Dr. Bel will buy it.

Rory, Mandy, and I all stare at Debra walking toward Dr. Bel. We can't hear anything they are saying from the other side of the room, but we see Dr. Bel nod. His head snaps up to look in our direction, and the three of us break our formation to pretend we were talking the entire time.

Debra walk-runs to us in the most comical way, a huge smile spread on her face. "He said yes!" she squeals.

Mandy's jaw drops. "What?"

"He said yes! He's buying it."

"We didn't set the price high enough?" Mandy asks, her brows creased.

"I honestly think he would have bought it no matter the price. He really wants it."

"See, that just makes me angrier. I just validated that he can get anything he wants," Mandy hisses. "And he gets to keep the one painting I didn't want to part with. It feels a lot like losing."

I nudge Mandy's arm. "Hey, you just made a shit ton of money. You can certainly be happy about that. And he paid a ridiculous amount for it. You have the upper hand here. Twenty thousand dollars, Mandy."

She smiles. "You're right. I can do a lot with that money."

Witnessing my friend's success shifts the mood of the evening, and I feel lighter now. I'm dreading the end of the night when Rory takes me home, but the rest of the time in the gallery is lighthearted. The gallery announces the sale of the untitled landscape and toasts Mandy with champagne. Within the hour of the announcement, the landscapes sell out, as well as a good portion of the portraits. Mandy's face must be in so much pain from all the grinning as she walks from patron to patron, explaining her artistic choices and thanking them for their support. I couldn't be prouder of her.

"Are you getting tired?" Rory asks, and I'm not too fond of the concern on his face.

"A little. Do you mind if we go home?"

"Don't ask me stupid questions, Valentina."

"I'm sorry. Yes. Please, take me home."

"Would you like to say goodbye to your friends?"

I shake my head. "Mandy's busy, and I don't want to distract from her happiness. Let's just go."

The drive to my apartment is short, and we don't say much. This is the moment of truth. I have to tell him. I sneak a text to Chema so he'll help me up to my apartment when we arrive. I don't want Rory to go into my building once I leave this car. I can't see him anymore. My pride can't take it, for one, and I can't part this world knowing I've broken his heart. I've let this go on far too long. I never considered myself a selfish person, but what I'm doing here with Rory—it takes the cake for selfishness.

CHAPTER 18

"We need to talk," I say as Rory parks. I glance over at my building, where Chema is sitting on the stoop. I signal for him to wait.

Rory takes off his seatbelt and faces me. The city's night lights render him more handsome than ever, and I know this will be harder than I thought. "Okay," he says with a wide smile.

"I want to thank you for being there for me and forcing me to accept help when I really needed it."

"Okay." Rory runs a hand through his hair, mussing it up in the sexiest bedhead way. "You've already thanked me for that. Valentina, I was happy to do it."

"You're amazing, and I really did need . . . someone, even if I wouldn't admit it."

"I know. What's really going on?" he asks.

I suck in a deep breath to strengthen my spine. "Now that Chema's here, and treatment's almost over, at least for a while, I'm set. You don't need to check in on me anymore."

"That's not what I'm doing here. I'm not checking up on you. I want to spend time with you—"

"Rory—"

"Don't you like spending time with me?"

"That isn't the point."

"That's exactly the point because that's all I'm doing."

His piercing gaze lingers on me, but I don't cower under those angry eyes. He knows what's coming. He has to.

"Rory, I don't want to keep spending time with you."

"Bullshit. You do, and I know you do."

I shake my head, though I know I'm trying to persuade myself as much as him. "I don't. Chema has agreed to stay through the end of my treatment. I'll also have Mandy and the girls around, so I won't be alone."

"You being alone is not what I'm worried about."

"You don't have to worry about anything. That's just it. I'm taken care of."

"Dammit, Valentina. I'm not trying to take care of you. I'm not your fucking nurse, and I'm not your fucking doctor. I'm just a man who has feelings for you, I—" he runs his hand through his hair more angrily now, then his eyes narrow. "Valentina, I'm in—"

"No. Don't say it. I can't handle it if you say it."

Rory's eyes remain narrow slits, but he stays quiet. I knew it almost the minute he started looking at me differently. It was a shift in his eyes when he would drift off, and I knew he was making plans for us—for our future together. He's taken steps, meeting my parents, bringing his parents to meet me—all of it to show me how deeply he cares about me. I should have stopped it sooner, but I couldn't.

I love him.

I love the man who didn't bat an eye to stay in bed with me and just sleep because I was too tired. The man who fed me watermelon cubes when I was nearly delirious with fever and hadn't eaten in days. The man who stood proud as he pushed me around in my wheelchair, never once giving off any indication that he was embarrassed by the sick woman with him during our date tonight.

But I can't tell him. He can't know I'm in love with him because I won't saddle him with a dying woman. My eyes prickle with tears, and for once, I don't draw them back in. I'm giving up perhaps the most perfect man in the world.

That small excursion to the art gallery, as brief as it was, took all the energy I had for the day. I'm a prisoner in my own body—the very body I once commanded with pride—and there isn't so much as the briefest hope of escape from this prison. I mourn for the loss of my health, the loss of what my body once was—what Rory got to enjoy so briefly so many weeks ago and that I will never be able to gift him again.

"Hey, hey, what's this?" Rory coos, all the hardness in his face gone. He adjusts in his seat to be as close to me as he can and wipes away the tear rolling down my cheek.

"I don't want to keep spending time with you. Before, you were just a meaningless one-night stand."

Rory shakes his head. "That's not true."

"And then I let you hang out because I didn't know anyone here, and I was bored. You were a distraction, Rory."

"You're lying."

"No. I am grateful, *I am*, to you for helping me when you did. I know that if you hadn't been there when the infection set in, I'd probably be dead. I'll always be grateful for that. But Chema's here now. I won't be alone, so you don't have to worry."

Rory's jaw sets, and he drops his hand from my face. He glances out the window past me and his nostrils flare. I know he sees Chema behind me. Then he focuses his gaze back on me.

"I know you don't want to hear it, but you have to. Valentina Almonte, I am so fucking in love with you."

My mouth dries up. I knew he wanted to start a serious relationship with me, and I know I love him, but I never imagined this outcome—that he already loved me back.

"Do you think maybe, your compassionate and caretaking nature as a doctor is bleeding over and clouding your feelings?"

"No. I love you, Valentina. Not sick Valentina. Not the athlete Valentina. None of that fucking matters. I love *you*. The person inside."

"Um, I'm sorry, I don't . . ."

"You don't what?"

"I don't know what to say."

"Just the truth. Do you have feelings for me? I know the answer, but you'll need to convince me otherwise if you're really breaking this between us off."

I clear my throat and sit up as straight as I can manage in the car. "I don't have feelings for you." I look him dead in the eye when I say it.

Rory chuckles, but it's bitter. "That's such bullshit."

"I'm sorry I let you think there was more here, but there isn't."

"Just stop, Valentina. We both know you are lying. Now I just want to know why? Is it because you feel bad for me, being with someone as sick as you, or is there another reason?" When he is done speaking, Rory glances past me again at Chema.

"What?"

"Do you have feelings for more than one person?"

I blink, trying to make sense of his words. "What are you talking about?"

"The way I see it, either you think you are self-sacrificing on my behalf and saving me for some reason, or you have feelings for someone else also. I say 'also' because I very damn well know you have feelings for me too."

"Stop telling me what I feel. I don't have feelings for you,

Rory. Not like that. I'm grateful like I said, and I'll happily consider you a good friend and a good memory from my time in KC, but stop putting words in my mouth."

"Then answer the question. Is there someone else you care about?"

I turn and look at Chema, who stands and puts his hands in his pockets. His eyebrows are drawn together with concern and a questioning look in his eyes. I signal at him again to wait. I see now what Rory sees. He thinks I'm in love with Chema. This is my out. I swallow hard. I know if I take this step, if I dare utter this awful lie, I'll be putting the nail on the coffin of Rory's brief chapter in my life.

But for Rory, I do it. Because I love him, I can't tell him the truth. "You're right," I say finally. "I have feelings for someone else."

"Chema . . ." He says with a voice that cracks.

I turn to Rory again, and his eyes are glassy. I find no anger in his features, only hurt. I did that. I hurt him. But this hurt is less than the pain I would have caused by my death or by saddling him to a sick woman who would do nothing but take and take.

"Yes," I lie. "Chema. He will take good care of me, so you don't have to worry."

Rory takes in a deep breath and lets it out slowly. "Well, that changes things."

"I know. I'm sorry. I should have said sooner."

"No, it's fine. I'm glad we had the time we did," he says. "Does he love you?"

I don't lie because Chema does love me, even if I know it's not the same type of love Rory is asking about. "Yes. He loves me. And I love him."

Rory's eyes draw shut, and he drifts his head to the headrest. When his eyes open again, he smiles weakly.

"Does he love you more than I do?"

"That would be impossible to know, wouldn't it?"

"No, it wouldn't—" Rory takes me by surprise, holding my head in place so he can kiss me. His lips are tender at first, pressed against mine gently, until his tongue coaxes my lips open. He conquers my mouth hungrily for a few seconds, and I push him away, even though it's the last thing I want to do.

"I'm sorry," says Rory. "I believe that you love him. But I don't believe you don't have feelings for me too. If you weren't sick, and it wouldn't put you through hell, I'd fight for you. I'd do everything to make you see that my love is greater. But I don't want to put you through yet another emotional wringer."

"Thank you for respecting my wishes."

"I will. For now. But Valentina, once you beat this thing, all bets are off."

My eyes widen with panic. "What?"

"Go ahead and be with him now. Let him be your emotional support and caretaker until you get better—because you will get better, whether you believe it or not—and when it's all said and done, I'll be here. I'll be loving you. No amount of time will change that."

I turn from him, not able to look him in the eye after all those lies. I open the car door and call Chema over. Chema is at my side in an instant, and he ducks to get me out of the car. I'm only on my feet for a moment before he takes me in his arms like a child. I rest my head on his chest, as tired as I've ever felt.

"You okay?" Chema asks.

I nod. "I will be."

Another car door opens and shuts. "Chema!" Rory calls when we are almost at the door. Chema turns, so we both face Rory.

"Take care of her for me, okay?"

Chema nods and squeezes me a bit in his arms. "Always have. Always will."

Rory nods and gets back in his car.

CHEMA SETS ME DOWN ON THE BED, AND I CURL AROUND MY pillow, letting the sob out. "What happened?" Chema asks.

"We broke it off," I admit, the words like hot daggers searing my throat.

"Why? It looked like things were going so well." The bed shifts as Chema sits next to me. I stay facing away from him because I don't want him to see me cry.

"He said he loves me."

"And that's why you broke it off?"

"No, I, I—"

"Do you love him?"

I nod and keep sobbing into my pillow. Even the energy required for a good cry exhausts me. Chema's beefy hand wraps around my shoulder, and I put my hand over his.

"Then tell him that."

"No," I cry. "He can't know I love him."

"Why?"

"Look at me, Chema."

"I'm looking."

"How could you possibly think a man like that could be with someone like this?" I hiss out the question.

Chema shifts me on the bed so I'll face him and knows I can't fight it off. "Someone like what, Valentina? Someone strong and brave, smart and loving? Why wouldn't anyone deserve someone like that?"

I snort. "I'm not any of those things. I'm shriveling up and dying. Don't you all get that?"

"You are not dying."

I smile. "I used to say that when I first started treatment. I was so hopeful and thought I would live, and I'd say 'I'm not dead yet' a lot. I haven't thought it in weeks now—"

"Valentina, treatment is almost over. Just one week to go. Of course it was going to take its toll on you, but hear me when I say, 'you are not dying,' and I'm not going to sit here and listen to you tell me how you are going to die. I won't do it—"

I raise my chin so I can stare at my friend in awe. His voice crackles, but his face is furious. Fuck. I'm hurting him too. There is not a single loved one I've managed to spare from the circus that is cancer.

It takes all the strength I can muster, but I bring my hand to his cheek. "I'm sorry," I say.

"Don't do it again," he orders.

"Are you coaching me through the final week of treatment? Is that what this is?"

Chema wipes the tears pooling in the corners of his eyes and smiles. "Yeah. Guess I am. Now, rest."

He shuts the lights off before leaving my room. I hug my pillow once again. I want his optimism, an optimism I shared when I first started, but my body is so far gone, I can't imagine ever being what I once was. I was so naive to think I could hide this from everyone, that I could go back to fighting like nothing had ever happened. What a child.

My body will be altered for life, internally and externally. I will bear the scars as proof of this battle whether I die in weeks, months, years, or decades—I'll always carry the reminders.

I lie in bed and have a breakdown unlike any I've experienced so far. I'm surprised at how far I've made it, from what Mandy had told me. I let the tears flow as I mourn for the life I'll never get back even if I do live. I mourn the loss of the body I was once so damn proud of. I grieve for the loss of my physical strength.

The crying leads me into the early hours of the morning, and

I can't stop the breakdown because I also mourn for the only person I could ever imagine being the love of my life.

My heart is bruised.

Contusions in every ventricle sending waves of pain with each heartbeat because Rory's gone. And no amount of ice baths, salves, or massages will ease the hurt.

I mourn for the loss of my love with Rory Dennis.

SIX MONTHS LATER

CHAPTER 19

WINTER

"I have an opening at three tomorrow. Does that work?" The hospital scheduler asks.

"Yeah, I'll be there."

I hang up the call, and my blood runs cold. Is it back?

It couldn't be, though, could it? I feel great. My energy is back, food tastes good again, and I've even put on some weight. My hair is growing in, including my eyebrows, and I thought, really thought, this was behind me.

Then I got the call to go back in for results from the tests I took last week. This is the news I've been waiting for so I can finally go home. Instead, I know they'll be telling me the cancer is back. Then they'll be suggesting another round of treatment —but I can't. I won't do it again. I would rather die than go through that again.

They asked me to come in. I know what that means. Bad news. If it was good news, Dr. Ramirez would have told me over the phone. But they asked me in instead, so it's bad news.

I squeeze the armrest on the sofa to ground myself to the time and place. My apartment looks much the same and also different. It's much neater now that Chema's gone. He left after three months of concluding treatment. He refused to leave until I proved I could go up the flight of stairs in my apartment without getting winded. When I finally managed it, he fought me on it, but I didn't want to keep disrupting his life, not when I was finally starting to feel fine.

He made me swear I'd call him to come back if there were any setbacks. Should I call him now? No. First, I need to hear it. I won't believe it until Dr. Ramirez says the words out loud.

I WAIT IN EXAM ROOM FIVE, AND THE MINUTES FEEL LIKE HOURS AS I wait for Dr. Ramirez. Her face twists in concern when she sees me.

"What's wrong?" Dr. Ramirez asks. "Are you not feeling well?"

"You tell me," I say.

"Nothing's wrong, Vale, but you look like you saw a ghost."

I share my suspicions with her.

"Oh, Vale, honey—"

"It's back, isn't it?"

"No!" she nearly yells. "Valentina, I wanted to give you the good news in person. That's all. Please stop reading about treatment or procedures online. It's not the first time it's gotten you in trouble." Dr. Ramirez arches an eyebrow, almost making me cower.

"Good news?" I ask with all the hope I'll allow myself.

"Yes, Valentina. Good news." Dr. Ramirez grabs my shoulders and squeezes for a moment. A smile spreads the width of her face. "Six months remission. It's a great milestone."

"Really?" I have to confirm because it feels like a dream. I don't even know when I started crying, but I feel the tears rolling down my face.

"Really," she says. "I thought we should celebrate. I'm not

working right now. Let's go across the street to the bar. Champagne. My treat."

I'M RELIEVED TO SEE SOFIA WORKING THE BAR WHEN WE GET there. In the last six months, I have come to the bar quite a bit—at first with Chema, who started to feel cooped up all the time in the apartment. Since he left, I've spent quite a bit of time with Mandy and the girls at *La Oficina*, though I didn't quite partake in any of the drinking myself.

Over that time, I've got to know Sofia pretty well. I haven't grow quite as close to her as I have to Mandy or Izel or Tlali, but she sure is one of the friends I have been lucky enough to make during the most horrific time of my life, and I am grateful for her. I'm glad she's here to celebrate this moment.

"What we celebrating?" Sofia asks when Dr. Ramirez orders champagne. Dr. Ramirez just looks at me, and I know she is waiting for me to answer. She can't divulge my health information unless I give her the green light.

"Six months in remission," I say proudly. This is as much Dr. Ramirez's victory as mine. From what I hear, the clinical trial is promising, despite being in its early phases.

"Wow. Congrats!" Sofia says, a face-splitting grin taking over her features.

When she comes back with two flutes filled to the brim with champagne, she sets them on the table. "On the house," she says. "All cancer ass-whipping is rewarded at *La Oficina*."

Sofia leaves us to our drinking, and Dr. Ramirez and I are grinning like idiots at our table.

Then, Dr. Ramirez's gaze shifts above and behind me.

"Dr. Dennis," she greets, and I freeze at the sound of his name. Does he know it's me sitting here?

"Please, Dr. Ramirez, call me Rory outside of work."

"Okay, then please call me Carolina."

Rory shifts to stand at the side of the table so he can see both our faces, and I panic. I remember I didn't wear a scarf today and wonder if my pixie hair is pointing in all different directions. I try to tame it with my hand discreetly, but I don't know if it's helping. Why did this joint have to be all classy and not have any mirrors?

"What are we celebrating?" Rory asks.

"You want to tell him?" Dr. Ramirez asks.

I look at Rory for the first time. I haven't seen those green eyes in six months, and I don't know how I keep it together. He's as handsome as ever. I have always regretted that we didn't take any photos during our brief time together to remember him by. Though honestly, I wouldn't have wanted to be in them at the time. But it would have been nice to have recorded our time at the park for posterity.

"I, um—" I clear my throat. "Remission. Six months," I say and sink a little in my chair, though I keep my plastered smile, hoping it looks natural.

"That's great!" Rory all but shrieks.

The pang of guilt forces my eyes to the ground. I should have messaged him at some point to tell him I was better. I force myself to look him in the eye again, and his smile never dissipates.

Our eyes are locked when Dr. Ramirez interjects in the exchange. "Rory, why don't you sit with us?" she asks.

Rory looks at me, waiting for me to echo the invitation. Part of me doesn't want to open this door again, but I know it's the part that will lose because I've missed him, and I need to know how he's been all this time, so I nod.

Dr. Ramirez gets another champagne flute for Rory, and the three of us clink glasses.

"To kicking the shit out of cancer," says Dr. Ramirez.

"To kicking the shit out of cancer," Rory and I both echo.

It's hard to include Dr. Ramirez in the conversation because we both have a lot of catching up to do, but we don't want to be rude, so we steer clear of any heavy subjects for the time being.

"So, I saw your fight with the Russian—what's her name?" Rory asks.

"Galina," I say.

"Yeah, that's right. It looked like you won. I can't believe the judges gave her the fight."

I smile, remembering that fight. At the time, it had seemed like the most unfair thing I'd ever go through. I hadn't been diagnosed yet. Now, it seems so minor and unimportant. "You weren't the only one," I say.

Rory keeps babbling about the fight, and I look over at Dr. Ramirez with concern. She is looking at her phone with her face scrunched up, and those eyebrows of hers are drawn together into twin frowns.

"Is everything okay?" I ask her.

"I don't know," she says. "I, uh, have to go. Do you mind?"

"No, please. I hope everything's fine."

Dr. Ramirez kisses my cheek warmly in a gesture I know is crossing a line, but I also think she is telling me she is no longer my doctor because I no longer need her. This was always the plan—for me to return to Mexico and get follow-up care close to home. Watching her leave the bar, though, makes my chest constrict a bit. I'll miss her immensely.

"So, you look good," Rory says.

"Thanks. I'm starting to feel a little like my old self."

"That's great," he says.

"Though I finally resigned myself to the fact that I'll never be what I once was—"

"Don't say that—"

"No. No, it's not a 'pity me' thing. It's the truth. My new reality is finally sinking in. A lot of things are different."

"You're more beautiful than ever," Rory says and winks at me.

"Rory—" I take an exasperated breath.

"Sorry," he says and hangs his head, but I can tell he is smiling.

"I'm different now," I say.

"Yeah?"

"You know how it is. My body's different. There are things it can't do anymore, and don't get me started on chemo brain."

Rory's eyes soften. "Yeah. I know how it is," he admits. "But you're looking a lot better than the last time I saw you. That alone is reason to celebrate."

We clink glasses again and each take a drink.

I don't give him details, but one of the worst changes to my body is chemo brain. I forget little things, can't find the right word sometimes—only made worse by my bilingualism. I shake my head, thinking of what a snob I used to be when people would speak in Spanglish and how sometimes I'm forced to do that now when I can't find the word in one language but can in the other. My reaction time has slowed, and I'm hoping I can work on correcting that if I have a shot in hell at fighting again. Now that I know I'll live, I have to at least give it a shot. If I didn't, I wouldn't be me.

"Thank you," I say. "For everything. Really."

Instead of his regular 'you betcha' that he customarily uses instead of 'you're welcome,' he says, "Stop thanking me. It pisses me off." But he is smiling.

"This is the last time. I promise. Thank you for respecting my wishes back then. I couldn't bear to have you around while I was going through that."

"I know. It killed me to stay away. But I know." Rory's hand reaches across the table to take mine. His thumb grazes over the top of my hand, and we smile at each other. God, I've missed him.

"I missed you," he says as if he is reading my mind.

I won't tell him I missed him back. I don't want to give him hope again. There is no point. I'm leaving for Mexico in a week or two—as soon as I can arrange everything—and then Rory Dennis will be nothing but a sweet memory from my time in KC, as I always knew he would be.

"You look good too," I say.

"Valentina Almonte, are you flirting with me?"

I draw my hand away from his and shake my head. "No. I'm just glad to see you looking so well."

Rory's smile falls for only one second before he regains it. "I'm sorry. I shouldn't have said that."

"It's okay. We're allowed to be happy to see each other."

"I'm glad you're happy to see me," he says.

I stand and put on my coat. Grabbing my purse, I toss it over my shoulder. Rory stands after I do, and I surprise us both by taking him into a hug. I take in his smell one last time. He doesn't know this is goodbye for good this time. "I have to go," I say. "Chema's waiting for me," I lie.

"Right. Say hi to him for me, will you? I think I owe him big time." Rory smiles weakly at me as I turn to walk away.

I leave him at the bar, holding my heart without his knowledge.

CHAPTER 20

SPRING

The water rolls down my face as the shower fills with steam. I don't mind much that Chema never installed women's locker rooms. There are so few of us, and if the men didn't mind me here, then I had no complaints.

My parents never had to know.

I dress and try to try to rush past the front desk. My sister is expecting me for lunch, and I'm running late. I fail to sneak past Chema, though. He is at the front desk, wrapping up with a customer. He smiles as I try to dash past the desk.

"You did a great job today," he says.

Pausing to say goodbye, I face him. "Stop lying," I admonish.

"The best since you got back."

My smile is weak, and Chema picks up on my defeatist attitude.

"It's going to take a while, Valentina. We'll get you there."

"You know we won't, right? This is it. This is as good I'll ever be again."

"It's only been four months. Can you at least give it a little time before you throw in the towel?"

Nico comes up behind Chema and wraps his arms around Chema's waist. "What's this I hear about someone throwing in the towel?" He asks.

Chama pats him gently on the arms around his middle until Nico unravels his embrace and steps forward so we can both see him. He is wearing an athletic tank and shorts that complement Chema's outfit. They are so cute I feel like punching them in the face.

"Valentina's getting a little frustrated," Chema explains.

"Oh, honey," Nico says. "You don't remember when you first started, but I do. You were way worse than this."

I burst out laughing. Leave it to Nico to put things into perspective. I'll always be grateful to him. He was more than generous sharing his partner while Chema was in Kansas City taking care of me. Nico managed the gym while Chema was away. I hope I can one day have what they have—that kind of supportive partner with complete trust.

At least, I hope I'll have it again because I'm sure I got close to it once.

"Thanks, Nico," I say. "I don't know if that makes me feel worse or better."

"Any time, honey." He blows a kiss at me and kisses Chema for real before going off to teach a self-defense class.

Chema does his best to give me an empowering speech, and I try to hear it, but I think somewhere deep down, we are both aware I'm at the end of my professional fighting career. I know I'll always be in this business. Maybe I'll coach like Chema does or sponsor other fighters at some point, but *me* fighting, I know I'll have to let go of that notion real soon—if I haven't already.

"I'm going to see Pili," I say to Chema.

"Say hi for me. Tell her we miss her."

"I will. I have to swing by my place first, though, to pick up a present I ordered for her."

"A special occasion?" Chema asks.

"I don't need a special occasion to do something nice for her, especially after everything she has done—is doing—for me."

"You're late," are Pilar's first words when she opens the door. Her posture is impeccable, and her sensible, expensive outfit is well put together. Pilar is a mini version of our mother. I dealt with our Mom by avoiding her and leaving home as soon as I could, but Pilar tried, keeps trying, to earn her love by trying to mimic her. I don't think she realizes she's doing it, the mirroring effect, but it's such a big part of her personality, I doubt she'll ever be able to break it.

"I'm sorry," I say. "I was training." I follow her into the living room, where she has laid out artful canapés and an icy pitcher she pours from into our glasses.

"How's that going?"

"What?"

"Training, Valentina. Where's your head at? Seriously."

"Sorry, um—" I look around, trying to find a spot for the enormous gift I'm holding. "I brought this for you."

"What is it?"

"It's a gift, Pili."

She rolls her eyes and crosses her arms. "I know that, Tini. But what is it?"

"Well, open it and see."

Pilar can be such a smart-ass when she wants to be.

"I'll open it later. Set it down, and let's chat for a bit. Or do you have to go soon?"

The concern in her eyes melts away any of my criticisms of her. I'm the only human contact she's allowed other than her husband, parents, and many servants. "I can stay for a bit," I say and smile.

"Well, tell me about training."

I take a deep breath. "I'm improving, but it's slower than I'd hoped."

"It's only been four months. I'm sure it'll take time."

"Yeah. That's what everyone keeps telling me." I push a canapé around my plate with my fork.

"You're not hungry?"

"It's not that. I, um. I just think it might be time to give up. I'm a little disappointed I haven't accomplished much."

Pilar laughs, and I glare at her icily.

"I'm sorry," she says. "That is such bullshit."

I press my lips together, waiting for her to elaborate, though it's killing me not to pick a fight with her right now.

"Before you got sick, you won almost every fight. Your record was unreal. And we both know, if you hadn't gotten sick, the next step was the UFC. Don't kid yourself about that, Tini."

"But I did get sick."

"Yes. You did. And you beat it."

"It sounds a lot like you are saying I almost accomplished something, which isn't quite the same as accomplishing it, is it?"

Pilar raises an eyebrow in warning. "And you don't think beating the shit out of cancer constitutes accomplishing something?"

She looks a bit angry, but I can't bring myself to goad her further. I owe her too much. She was my first sponsor, when I first started fighting. She funded my training, bought my apartment, and paid a stipend so I could reach my dreams. Then I failed her when I couldn't make them happen, despite my best efforts. The cherry on the cake was asking her for a ridiculous amount of money for my treatment. Even then, she didn't bat an eye.

Didn't she care that I had nothing to show for it? I would if I were in her shoes. Wouldn't I? I had failed more than myself. I failed her and everything she has invested in me. Now I have no idea how I'm going to pay her back. I don't think I could even if I were to live several lifetimes.

"What is it?" she asks.

"What?"

"You went into your nothing box."

My 'nothing box' is what my sister calls it when I space off on her, which happens a lot since I got back.

"I'm sorry, Pilar. Your investment tanked."

"What on earth are you talking about?" Pilar asks.

"Yes, what investment?" We both turn to see Felipe now in the room.

Felipe Conde could be considered handsome by anyone who doesn't know him better. He is tall and muscular, and his face's chiseled quality wouldn't make the average woman gag—until they got to know him, that is.

My brother-in-law walks over to my sister, bends to kiss her on the cheek, and takes a seat next to her. He smiles knowingly at me, and I bite the inside of my lip so I don't sneer. Felipe crosses his legs and takes Pilar's hand in his possessively, as if it were another man and not her sister sitting in front of her. To put it plainly, Felipe Conde is a ridiculous man.

"What investment were you talking about?" he asks and looks between Pilar and me.

Pilar clears her throat nervously, and I shift in my seat. There has been exactly one thing Pilar ever allowed herself to defy her husband on. That was her sponsorship of my career. She tried to hide this simple fact from me, but Felipe hints and alludes to his dissatisfaction at her use of her own money to help me.

"Valentina is feeling guilty about me paying for her treatment. I was just about to tell her how ridiculous that is." Pilar pats Felipe's hand in a way that makes me think she is trying to placate him.

"Nonsense. You're family; of course we're happy to pay for your treatment."

He uses the word 'we' as if Pilar had used his money, or communal money, but all three of us know that money is, and always will be, Pilar's and Pilar's only. No one has ever openly admitted that simple fact, but I love that this is just one more thorn on Felipe's side. I love those thorns. Whenever I get a chance, I enjoy twisting them.

"Yes," I say. "Thank goodness Grandma Almonte had the foresight to secure Pilar's economic independence so she could do that. I'll always be grateful to her and Pilar." My words are pointed, and I try not to smile when Felipe's jaw tightens. His face twitches, barely, but I don't miss it. His presence dampening my time with my sister is almost worth it for this one moment.

"Yes, well. That's what we were talking about. Valentina thinks it's a wasted investment, and when you walked in, I was just about to tell her that her staying alive has been the best investment of my life."

My sister's sweet words change the mood in the room. I have to hand it to her. After years of marriage, she has mastered the art of diffusing tension. She talks about me beating cancer as if it was just another fight in the cage—as if it was something I accomplished, and I'd never thought about it like that before.

"I agree," Felipe says. "Best use of *our* money I can think of."

"Thank you," I say, if only to drop the standoff between us. I'll pick my battles with this idiot.

"What's that?" Felipe reaches for the present and flips it from side to side, likely looking for a card.

"A present for Pilar."

"A present?" he asks.

"Yes. You know, as a thank you for everything."

Felipe hands Pilar the gift and shifts further from her on the sofa so he can see the contents once revealed. Pilar shoots me a questioning look laced with panic, and I smile reassuringly that it's not something that could anger Felipe.

My smile is all it takes for Pilar to rip apart the wrapping paper like a savage. She has always loved presents and surprises, and this is both.

When she turns the canvas around, Pilar gasps. "Oh, Valentina. It's lovely."

"I'm glad you like it."

Pilar sets the painting down so she can stand. She comes over to my side of the room so she can sit next to me and take me into a hug. "I love it," she whispers in my ear.

"Yes, very lovely," Felipe says and stands. "Valentina, you look good. I'm glad you're feeling better. I do have to go to work, though."

"Thanks," I say.

"Working on a Saturday?" Pilar asks.

"Yes. I have a meeting," he hisses through his teeth, and my sister recoils a bit in her seat.

"Okay. Well, message me if you are coming for dinner so I can make sure it's ready for you."

Felipe delivers another kiss on Pilar's cheek, and I almost shiver.

We wait until we hear the door closing behind him before we continue our conversation. Pilar shakes her head at me but smiles.

"You could stand to be nicer to him," she says.

"He could stand to be nicer to me," I counter.

"I just wish you could get along better."

"I don't."

"Valentina!"

"I'm sorry," I say. "Let me just say this one last time. I know you don't believe it, but just because he doesn't physically abuse you doesn't mean he doesn't abuse you—"

"Not this again—"

"Please hear me out. Pilar, I love you, and if cancer has taught me anything, it's that you shouldn't waste your time on things and people you don't love."

"What makes you think I don't love him?"

"Please," I scoff. "I know you don't. He *is* abusive, Pilar. He has isolated you, made you lose all your friends, and even limits how much your own family can see you. He belittles you. It's subtle, but it's there. This is psychological warfare, and you need to start fighting back."

"Did you start watching telenovelas with Chema? Is that where this hysteria is coming from?"

Pilar knows all about Chema and Nicolas and the gym. Not because she is friends with them or interacts with them, or because she's ever come to the gym. She knows about them because her only connection to the outside world is me, and she doesn't realize she lives vicariously through me, but she does.

"Pilar—"

"I heard you. Okay? Thank you for your concern, but I'm a grown woman. I can take care of myself. Okay?"

I nod. "Okay."

This is a discussion we've had many times before. We fought the first time. Then I kept bringing it up, hoping slowly I could open her eyes. For now, I decide to change the subject.

"Where are you going to hang the painting?"

We both look around the walls of the grand room. For a cage, this mansion is rather lovely.

"I don't know," Pilar says and stands while holding the painting and admiring it. "Who did you say the artist is?"

"I didn't say. It's Mandy. You know, my friend I told you about. She helped me quite a bit when I was in Kansas City."

Pilar's gaze snaps from the painting to me. "Oh," she says thoughtfully.

"Is that a problem?" I ask.

"No. It's great. I like landscapes. You know that."

"Pilar, come on."

"What?"

"Wait, are you jealous of Mandy?"

"What? No!" Pilar scoffs and sets the painting down again. "Why would I be jealous?"

"Gee, I don't know. She was there when you couldn't be. I confided in her instead of you. She visited when I was in the hospital—"

"Okay, okay. Maybe a little. I do wish I had been there, Tini. I swear."

"Then why weren't you? Mom and Dad visited. You could have gone with them."

Pilar's face hardens.

"Oh, that's right," I say. "Felipe wouldn't let you go see your sister while she was sick. Is this the man you want to defend?"

"Valentina!"

"What if I had died?"

"You didn't."

"What if I had, though? You wouldn't have seen me for the last time. All because you're a prisoner here. When are you going to see that?"

"I'm not a prisoner."

"No?"

"No."

"Shopping with a security detail does not exactly scream freedom, but whatever. I'm tired of having this conversation. Just think about that for one second. If I had died, how would you feel toward Felipe right now? Don't tell me. Just think on it."

A long moment of silence stretches between us, and Pilar takes a few bites from the tray in the center of the room.

"How are Chema and Nicolas?" She finally asks, changing the subject.

"Good. I think Chema has finally given in and let Nico start coordinating their outfits in the morning. It's like they are blending into the same person."

"Gross," Pilar says.

I roll my eyes, but am smiling. "Tell me about it. I'm the one who has to see it."

We both laugh, and our pattern repeats itself. We have the same fight, we don't resolve anything, and instead of acknowledging that, we change the topic to something we can both laugh about. It's not healthy, but nothing in our family ever is.

"Tell them hi for me," she says.

"I will."

I stay at Pilar's for three hours, and Felipe never comes back from his 'meeting,' though I'm doubtful that's where he went.

The similarities between Felipe Conde and my father are astounding. I have no doubt that's why Dad selected him as the winner from everyone who was courting Pilar at the time. I don't use the term 'courting' lightly. It's what my parents called it.

"I have to get going," I finally tell Pilar.

She finds a spot in one of the many guest rooms for Mandy's painting. I never imagined she would take the gift as she did. At least in the guest room, she won't have to look at it every day, reminding her she was not in Kansas City with me through one of the roughest times in my life.

Pilar knows everything—I've always told her everything.

Except about Rory.

I'm not sure why. I carefully left him out of any conversations we had about my time away and about my treatment. Dr. Ramirez, Dr. Medina, Mandy, and even Tlali and Izel featured prominently in all the stories I told her when I got back, but I was always careful to leave Rory out of those conversations.

I keep him all to myself.

Most nights, I close my eyes and envision him lying on the bed next to me. He's facing the other direction as I trace patterns over the freckle constellations scattered across the creamy skin of his back. The memory of him is so fresh in my mind, I can almost feel him under my fingertips when I think of him.

I spend my days back home suppressing my thoughts about Rory, hoping I can meet someone who'll help me forget.

Un clavo saca otro clavo.

CHAPTER 21

My hair is almost at my jawline and matted to the sides of my face with sweat, distracting me. I miss being able to pull it into braids. I breathe out with each blow I deliver. Chema positions the boxing pads in a jab-cross-jab combination that I follow easily. We repeat this several times, and I know he is starting off light.

He already made me run a mile before pad training, which is significantly less than he used to. By my pre-cancer standard, it's embarrassing, but this is the most my body has accomplished since concluding treatment.

After the fifth round with the same combination, he reaches for me, and I block with my shoulder, but I'm too slow, and he ends up hitting my shoulder with the pad.

"Agh!" I growl and step away from Chema. I shake my head to clear it.

"It's okay. We just got started. Come on."

I turn back to Chema and keep aiming for the pads. I successfully block with my right shoulder on his second try. We both smile.

"Chin down," he scolds.

"Sorry."

"Come on. Keep moving."

His commands are obeyed in this gym, so I start fluttering in a circle around him as he positions the pads in the air. He switches the combination; it's still a jab-cross-jab, but this time he wants a ratio of 3-2-3, and I can't pick up on it quick enough.

The never-ending haze, like walking through the cloud of my brain where my reaction time resides, envelops me. I know the combination Chema seeks, and once I had this muscle memory, but it's all gone now. I try again, messing up after the last cross before switching back to a jab. Fuck. Fuck. Fuck.

It's so incredibly frustrating. I step back and use my teeth to rip the Velcro on my gloves to yank them off.

Chema removes the pads from his hands and drops them on the mat. "Come on. Sit with me."

We sit cross-legged, facing each other on the mat.

"I'm sorry," I say out of breath.

"What for?"

"What do you mean what for? For fucking up!"

"You're not fucking up. Stop being so frustrated. Don't you see? This is the best you've done since we started training again."

"I know, but it's not fast enough."

"Think to the first day back at the gym. Did you think you'd ever be able to run a mile again? And here you are, in your gloves after running a mile. This is huge. You need to acknowledge that."

"I do. But I also acknowledge that I can't do a simple switch of combinations. My reaction time isn't there. Chema, we might be able to improve it a bit, but I don't think it will ever come back."

"We don't know that." He shakes his head, not wanting to believe it yet.

"I think I do. The glitches in my memory are minor, but

they're there. It's like I can see the word I'm looking for, hovering just in front of me, but I can't grasp it. My synapses are short-circuiting. Eventually, my brain does what it needs to, but I can't fight like that. I can't ask my opponent, 'can you hold on just a sec, my brain is catching up?'"

"Don't give up. Not yet."

"I think it's time for my dreams to change. I can't keep mooching off Pilar forever."

"She'd be fine with that, you know?"

I smile. "Yeah. I know. I was only okay with it before because we had an end-goal in sight. I'd be sponsored soon and maybe even be able to pay her back. But I don't think that's the goal anymore, Chema. I don't think we can get me there."

"In time—"

I shake my head, and he doesn't finish his sentence. His bottom lip quivers, and I watch as his Adam's Apple bobs up and down.

"Are you sure?"

"Yeah. I'd like to keep training, I'll keep fighting, just for fun, but I'm done competing. It was beautiful while it lasted, but it's time to move on."

"What are you going to do?"

I shrug. "I don't know. Maybe I'll give you a run for your money and open up my own gym."

Chema laughs. "I'd love some competition, Tini," he says and musses my hair like I'm a child.

"Only Pilar is allowed to call me that."

"Uh-huh."

Something, or someone, catches Chema's attention from behind me, and he nods. I twist around to look where Chema's eyes are focused, and a stone so heavy drops in my stomach that I fail to stand up when I try.

Chema stands first and reaches out a hand to help me to my feet.

Too stunned to form words, I follow Chema wordlessly off the mat until we both reach the spot where Rory Dennis stands.

"Hey, buddy," Chema says and takes Rory into a hug.

I blink. 'Buddy?' What the hell is going on?

"Hi, Chema. Nice to see you."

"You too," says Chema. "Let's talk soon, but right now, I'm going to, um—I'm going somewhere else for absolutely no reason. Valentina, take my office if you want it."

I can only shake my head.

Rory's face lights up as he takes me in. "You look so good, Valentina."

"Um, thanks." I tuck my unruly hair behind my ear and start unwrapping my knuckle wraps with shaky hands. "What are you doing here, Rory?"

"Thought I'd check out the gym. Thinking about picking up boxing." He blinks at me when I stay quiet, staring at him.

Nothing's changed about him, while I look entirely different from the last time he saw me. Luckily, it's a change for the better.

"I'm joking," he says finally. "I'm here for you."

I peer around us to see if anyone is within earshot. Chema is on the other end of the gym with Nico, probably telling him everything about Rory. It's the off hours at the gym, my favorite time to train, so only a couple of other people are around.

"Here for me?" I ask.

"Yes. I can't stop thinking about you." Again I say nothing to that. "Do you think I could get a hug? I've missed you."

As if I have no control of my body, I step forward and wrap around him, resting my cheek on his chest right over where I know his scar is. Neither of us comments on my sweat dampening his shirt. His arms envelop around me and squeeze tightly while his cheek lands on top of my head. Being in his arms like this feels like finally being home. I thought I'd feel that way when I returned to my apartment, my friends, and family, but it hadn't. That feeling eluded me until right now, cocooned in Rory's arms.

"I'm so happy I don't have to be careful, worried about crushing you."

I pull away from him only long enough to look into his green eyes. "You're here."

"Yes. I'm here. I've missed you."

"I missed you too."

"Is it okay that I'm here? I know you wanted me to stay away, and I respected those wishes as long as I humanly could."

I shake my head. "No. I mean, I'm glad to see you, but I wish you hadn't come."

"That makes no sense."

"We live in different countries. I don't believe long-distance relationships can work."

"That's not what I'm proposing here."

"It's not?"

"No."

"Then what are you proposing?"

"This," he says and pulls away from my arms. He drops to one knee and looks up at me. He produces a small box from his pocket, and I take a step back, shaking my head.

"Valentina Almonte, I've had to face the possibility of losing you more times than my poor, scarred heart can take. I don't want to spend another second of my life without you. Will you marry me?"

I haven't yet processed his presence in this gym in Mexico— I certainly can't process the life-altering question he has asked me.

It suddenly dawns on me that he and Chema have been in contact with each other. How else would he know where to find me? Where I'd be and when? Chema. That's how.

"You've been talking to Chema?"

Rory's face falls, and he stands. "I'm sorry," he says, clasping the back of his neck. "I had to know you were okay. Please don't be mad at him. It was all me."

"How did you even get his number?"

"We did spend quite a bit of time together in waiting rooms."

I find Chema sitting at the front desk, grinning at me, but his grin disappears when he sees the daggers my eyes are shooting his way.

He stands and walks over to us. "Is everything okay?" Chema asks with a worried expression.

"You knew he was coming, and you didn't tell me?"

"I didn't know specifics, but I knew he would be coming to see you at some point."

"You two have been talking about me?"

The two guilty expressions look at each other, then they both hang their heads and stare at their shoes.

"I see," I say and take a step back, not sure what to make of all this.

Rory looks at Chema with a wide grin. "Full disclosure," Rory says to Chema, "I asked her to marry me."

"I saw that," says Chema with a grin of his own.

"I have to say, I thought you'd be angered by that," says Rory, looking confused.

"Why would I be angry?" Chema asks.

"I thought you—"

"Honey," Nico walks up to Chema. "I'm heading out early. I want to get groceries before heading home. I'll have a special dinner for you tonight." Nico winks at Chema and gives him a peck on the lips. "And who is this handsome fella?" he asks, reaching out to shake Rory's hand, scanning his body.

"Valentina's fiancé," Chema says.

"Valentina's what?" Nico's eyes widen with surprise.

"Well, she hasn't answered yet," Rory says, "but, um—you are . . ."

"Gay?" Chema asks. "Yeah. I'm gay."

"I thought you and Valentina—"

"Nope. Never," Chema assures Rory.

"Wait, he thought you and Valentina what?" Nico asks with a raised eyebrow.

Rory clears his throat and suddenly can't look at the two men standing next to us. "I'm sorry, I made assumptions—"

"Wait, you thought Chema and Valentina . . . No!" Nico squeals and lets out a roar of laughter. "Have you never met a gay man before?"

"Amor," Chema says, "we're ruining their engagement. Come on, let's go—"

I finally snap out of my stupor. "No," I say. "I'm glad you two have planned out my future without discussing it with me, but you have failed to recognize that I'm not property, and neither of you owns me."

The nerve.

I storm toward the locker room and don't hear the steps behind me from Rory following. I'm pulling my bag out of my locker when he finds me.

"I'm sorry. That's not how I intended things to go," he says softly.

"Really? You didn't intend to propose when I've been at the gym sweating my ass off? You didn't plan all this with Chema? Tell me, Rory, did he help you pick out a ring?"

"No, that's not what . . . um, I was going to ask you to dinner and propose then."

"Why did you do it here, then?"

"I saw you."

"So?"

"That's it. I saw you, and I couldn't stand it. I couldn't stand you being with anyone other than me for a second longer."

"Like property," I say.

"No. Not like property. I'm in love with you. That hasn't changed. And damn it, Valentina. I know you love me too. Be honest with yourself. Be honest with me. And don't get me started on how you let me think you and Chema—"

"Let's suppose for a moment you're right. It changes nothing. You live in Kansas City. I live in Mexico City."

"I'll move here, if that's what it takes."

I rear back and blink at him. "You would?"

"Yes. Nothing's more important to me than never again spending a minute apart from you."

"What about your residency?"

"I'll start over. Here."

I roll my eyes. "You don't speak Spanish."

"I'll learn."

"So let me get this straight. You're willing to drop your residency, move to a foreign country, get married, and practice medicine here? But to do all that, you'll learn Spanish first?"

Rory nods, and the corners of his mouth quirk up. He takes a step forward and cups my cheek in his hand. "I'm way ahead of the curve. I already know how to say *lagaña*."

I punch his middle playfully, and his abs are hard on impact. "I'm being serious," I say.

"I don't know, Valentina. If I can't, then I'll find something else I can do. None of that matters so long as you're healthy and by my side. We can work out everything else."

"You really mean it, don't you?"

"I do." He pulls out the box again. "Now, please. Will you *please* marry me, you stubborn woman?"

I grab the box and cradle it in my hand. It's open, and a simple round diamond glistens in the center, set in a minimalist gold band. My eyes mist over because I never imagined this outcome. I'd pictured every other outcome for my life, or my death, but not one where I lived *and* got to keep Rory.

"It was my mother's," Rory explains. "She gave it to me as soon as I told her what I was about to do."

"Oh, Rory. It's beautiful." I bring my hand to my mouth to hold my gasp.

The tears in my eyes blur my vision, so I have to bring the box closer to my face so I can keep looking at it.

"You haven't given me an answer," Rory says, his voice deepening with his frustration.

I want to scream, 'yes!' But I can't. There's too much at stake. Too much to consider. "Can I think about it?"

His face falls for a second, but he recovers quickly. "I guess I shouldn't have done this in a locker room, huh?"

"No, it's not that, it's just—we'd have to figure some things out before—"

His head snaps up as his mouth curves upward into a smile.

"I didn't say 'yes,'" I clarify. "Let's talk, and then we can decide if we are ready for this step. Okay?"

He answers by pulling me toward him and kissing me.

I missed kissing Rory. The sweetness with which he always starts and how it turns hungry so quickly without fail. Every single time.

Rory pushes me back against a locker and lifts me by my ass. I wrap both legs around his middle to stay up. I feel him hardening through his jeans, and my body awakens. It feels alive for the first time since before I started treatment. This part of me has been dormant for almost a year now, and only Rory has the key to free it.

His hand drops to the hem of my shirt, and I panic. Not only am I already self-conscious about being sweaty and smelly from my workout, but now I also have to worry about him seeing my scars. No one has seen those except my doctors.

Then there's the fact that anyone could walk in at any moment, plus the more important fact that I have no lube with me. I wince just thinking about Rory's size.

"Um—Rory. Please stop."

He listens and pants, his forehead pressed to mine. "Sorry." He says. "Got carried away."

I smile. "I know. Me too." I drop my legs to find the ground and give him one last quick kiss. "Want to see my place?"

Rory chuckles. "I'd love to see your place."

CHAPTER 22

We go to his hotel first to pick up his bags. I drive. I insist he shouldn't stay in a hotel but should stay with me instead. Rory is quick to grab his luggage from his room and check out. He is back in the car with me in no time, winded.

He smiles at me and kisses me on the lips like we have been apart for a long time instead of the fifteen minutes it took him to get back to my car. He keeps his hand on my thigh the entire time as I drive to my place.

Pilar's generosity has extended to getting me suitable living arrangements, but I've insisted on staying on the modest side, at least the 'modest side' by my family's standards.

We pull up to my apartment building, and I park in the lower-level garage.

"Well, this is it."

I help him with the smaller of his bags, and we make our way inside. I twirl the keys in my hand as we ride the elevator to the sixth floor. When we get inside my apartment, I glance around, hoping I haven't left anything terribly embarrassing lying about.

For the most part, I keep the place clear of clutter. I'm a fairly neat person, but it comes as second nature from the years of disciplined training more so than from an actual desire to keep a clean home.

"It's great," says Rory. "Mind if I look around? I want to see what kinds of things you like for when we move in together."

"*If* we move in together," I correct.

"Right. Assume I mean 'if' when I talk about plans, okay?" He asks.

"You could move in here," I say nonchalantly.

"Sure. Then you need to see my place for the kinds of things I like."

My apartment is small, with only one guest bedroom, and I follow Rory as he glances around every room. He enters my bedroom last, and I follow him there too.

Rory picks me up in his arms and carries me to the bed.

"I don't know if we'll live here or not, but just in case, I'm pretty sure I'm supposed to carry you in."

"I'm not a traditionalist, Rory."

"You sure?"

"Positive," I say and chuckle into his neck.

He sets me down gently on the bed so I can sit on the edge. He sits next to me and cradles my face in his hands. He kisses my forehead, but it's sweet, not sensual. He peppers kisses down my face until he reaches my neck. In that crevice between my jaw and my neck, the kisses turn hungry, and I feel his tongue tasting me. Rory lets out a groan from deep within his chest.

"Now, where did we leave off at the gym?" he asks. He reaches for the hem of my shirt, and I know he wants to take it off.

"Rory, wait. We have to talk."

"Uh-oh. I know the sound of that."

"No, it's just . . ." I trail off, unsure how to word this for him.

My brain flashes back to our first time together. We had

stood in my apartment, and he'd seemed so scared and afraid that I would judge his body for the scar on his chest. It had broken me a little bit at the time that he had something on his body he had no control over that he had to explain before any sexual encounter.

In a mirror-opposite situation, I now have to explain my scars.

And the scars are just the tip of the iceberg we will have to climb together if we are ever to be intimate again.

"Rory—" I say, but my voice hitches. "I want to give you an out."

"An out?" he asks.

"Yes. An out. My body has changed significantly since we were together like this the last time."

"I'm aware," Rory says matter-of-factly. "I know how your body has changed."

"It's one thing to know it, though, isn't it? And another to experience it."

"There's nothing about your body I won't love."

"Don't say that. You don't know."

Rory brushes a loose strand of hair from my face. "Tell me what you need to feel comfortable—no—tell me what you need to feel as sexy as I see you."

This man is unreal. He can't be real. I clear my throat. "We can be intimate, but only if you promise that after, if you change your mind about proposing, you'll tell me."

"That's stupid, but from the look on your face, I think I better agree to this, if only to make you feel comfortable."

I nod. "You do."

"Okay. I promise if I change my mind, I will tell you, but I can tell you now there isn't a shot in hell—"

"Rory! Stop." I chuckle.

"Do you remember what you told me last year?" he asks.

"Can I get a hint?"

"Before I took my shirt off for the first time?"

I shake my head, unable to think about anything except Rory Dennis, naked and mine.

"You told me fighters find scars sexy as fuck."

"Oh," I gasp. I hadn't been expecting that. I'd forgotten those words from what seems like a lifetime ago.

"Is that what you're worried about? Because you don't need to be. You're a fighter, and if you're sincere when you tell me you find my scarred chest sexy, then you have to believe I'm sincere when I tell you that your scars of being a survivor are also sexy as fuck to me."

I nod. How could he know what I'm feeling without me saying it? He chips away at every insecurity I have. I was afraid he'd think my apartment is shitty compared to my apartment in KC, but he loves my home. I was worried he'd find my body lacking in its new form, but he is a doctor. He knows how much my body has changed, probably more than I do.

"That's part of it," I say finally.

"Look. I know you have tiny laparoscopic scars in the lower abdomen. I also know you had additional surgery and a larger scar in your torso. The small scars will match the dimples on your lower back that drive me wild, and the larger scar, well, that one will point me home. I'll love every inch of your body, even if it is covered in a hundred scars. I promise."

Bunching his shirt in my hands, I pull him in for a kiss because that little speech of his deserves to be rewarded. "Okay," I say. "If you trusted me to see your body, I'll trust you to see mine."

I hate that the confidence I once commanded is all gone, but somehow, the fact that it's Rory who is about to see me naked soothes me. I stand in front of him while he sits on the edge of my bed. I take a deep breath and pull my top over my head. The lights are on, and every cell in my body commands me to turn them off, but I refuse. I will trust Rory Dennis with my body because he once trusted me with his. I hadn't let him down then. I'm hoping he won't let me down now.

His hand floats upward to my breast, and he caresses me over my sports bra. His fingers wander and trail down my abdomen until they land on my scars. He traces the scars as he studies them, and I turn to the ceiling, not wanting to see his reaction. A rejection would hurt too much.

The heat of his mouth covers each scar, one by one, as he dusts kisses between them. His mouth leaves my body for only a second. "My little fighter," he whispers and continues to kiss and lick my body. I look down at him, kissing my abdomen. I stare at his red hair, and I run my fingers through it, encouraging him.

"Rory?"

"Yeah?"

"Make love to me," I plead.

His body stills. "I have plans for you, Valentina. I promise. But I'm not making love to you."

I step away from him and search for my discarded shirt. "What?" I knew it was too good to be true. I knew it was too much to ask. Why did I ever think this could work? The hot woman he had sex with is long gone, and this is all that is left of her.

"No. Come here." He takes my hand and forces me to sit on his lap so he can look me dead in the eye. "I don't want to hurt you," he says.

He's worried about hurting me? I take a moment to consider that. "You won't hurt me."

He shakes his head, then smiles sexily. "I have many filthy ideas . . . Oh, Valentina, the things I will do to you . . . don't worry—"

"No, Rory. I—um—I mean, you can do those things too, but I want you to make love to me—"

"Valentina, I can't hurt you. I won't do it."

"Why do you think you'll hurt me?"

"You are all scarred inside from radiation. It's too soon."

I cock my head to the side to study him. He thinks I can't take his massive size. I grab onto his shoulders for support.

When I first concluded treatment, I told Dr. Ramirez my sexual life was a priority to me. She immediately got me started on dilator therapy to stretch me. The first and smallest dilator almost had me quit, but I pushed on. Months passed, and I kept with my therapy until I graduated to a larger dilator, then a larger one, until Dr. Ramirez suggested I graduate to a full-size vibrator.

Rory knows nothing of this. He was no longer a part of my life during that time post-treatment.

"You won't hurt me, Rory," I plead with him.

"We are not having penetrative sex, Valentina. I won't hurt you. I can't do that."

"Rory—"

"No. We can eventually get there. For now, there are plenty of things we can do to each other." He pulls me to him and whispers in my ear, "I promise I'll please you."

It's hard to pull away, but I do. "Will you just listen to me for one second."

Rory's lips disappear into a thin line, but he nods.

My face bursts into flames at having to discuss this at the worst of possible times, but it has to be done.

"I started dilator therapy as soon as treatment wrapped up."

Rory winces. "That sounds painful."

"It was at first. But that's what the therapy is for. I've kept up with it, Rory. I'm fairly certain I can take you."

He shakes his head. "I can't risk hurting you. Can you see my point of view here?"

"So long as we use plenty of lube, I'll be fine."

"No—"

"Rory, I want you. Do you want me?"

"I do, but—"

"Then can we at least try?"

He kisses me again, long and deep, leaving me breathless, and I forget what we are even arguing about for a moment.

"You're killing me, woman."

I grin at him.

"Fine," he says. "But only on one condition."

"Okay, what's the condition?"

"You promise you'll tell me if you're in pain. The minute it becomes too painful, we stop. That's the only way I'd be willing to try."

I suck in a breath. He is only trying to take care of me, even if this conversation spoils the moment's sensuality. I have to remind myself he is an expert and has seen it all. I try not to take it personally—this is not a rejection of my new body.

He loves me.

Everything he is doing—everything he is saying—is because he loves me.

The least I can do is reassure him.

"I promise I'll let you know if I'm in pain."

"Thank you," he says.

His hands snake around the back of my head until his fingers tangle in my hair. His mouth leaves mine only so he can lick and bite my neck playfully. The feel of his lips and tongue on my skin sends goosebumps of recognition down my body. His touch feels better than what I remembered.

We needed to have that conversation, but it didn't seem so bad once it was over. If anything, I think Rory and I now have a deeper understanding of the other's needs. It was embarrassing —I wanted to burrow my head into the dirt—but now there is nothing left to get in the way.

Rory's hands slide down my spine until he finds my bra strap and unclasps it. I spring free, and my muscles twitch with the reflex to cover my chest, but I don't. I have to let Rory in if I intend to say yes—because I really want to.

"Valentina," Rory whispers as he studies my body. I stand, and we keep undressing each other.

I'm shy in a way I've never been before. I know he senses my trepidation because he moves slowly, gently.

I lose my balance as he pulls me into him, and I land on his lap again, straddling him.

He runs a hand through my hair. "It's growing in great. I love it. You look beautiful."

My cheeks feel three-hundred degrees, and I bury my face in his neck.

"You mentioned lube?" He asks.

"Yeah, it's in the nightstand." I reach for the drawer and pull out the bottle and a condom, setting both items next to us.

I stand to help Rory out of his boxer-briefs, and I gulp when he springs free.

"We don't have to—" he says softly.

"No, it's fine. You promised me we could try."

He nods, but his brows are drawn inward, and his face is twisted with concern.

I take some lube in my hand and wrap it around his shaft, stroking him slowly. His face instantly relaxes, and his eyes draw shut. I can only hope I've broken through his concern.

"Valentina," he says my name in a raspy voice.

"Yes?"

"That feels so good."

"Does it?"

"Mmm-hmmm."

"Open your eyes, Rory."

He obeys and watches me take more lube. I return one hand to him, and his eyes widen when he sees me starting to pleasure myself with the other.

"Fuuck," he growls. "That is so hot, baby."

I take his mouth in mine so I can lead him to lie on his back and position my entrance over his hardness. I give it one last squeeze, and I swear it hardened even more in my grip.

"You promised," he pleads one last time.

"I promised. Let me drive; I know best how much I can handle."

Rory nods and lays perfectly still. So still, I almost laugh. This is not the time to tease him, though, so I keep it in.

He is a bit larger than my vibrator, but not by much. I would never admit I searched for a toy that resembled his anatomy, but I also couldn't deny the similar size.

I place my hands on his chest for support. Taking a deep breath, I brace myself and take the tip of him inside. I say a silent prayer this won't be painful because I want nothing more than Rory Dennis filling me to the hilt at this moment.

Dilator therapy isn't sexy. I hadn't felt sensual since the last time I was with Rory. But with just one look at him naked, my libido reared its head, and there is no way I want to tame it again.

I lower further until he is halfway in me, and so far, no pain. I take in another inch slowly, then another, and keep going until there is nothing left to take in. Rory bucks his hips upward once.

"Sorry, so sorry," he stammers. "I couldn't help it."

I shake my head. "It's okay. I'm fine."

"You are?" He looks up at me, so hopeful, I'm not sure I could tell him I was in pain even if I was. Lucky for me, there is no pain, and I don't have to lie.

I hadn't realized how tight I had clenched every muscle in my body. I relax and loosen myself. I clench experimentally around him, earning me a sexy growl from Rory.

"How does it feel?" he asks.

"Good," I say. "Really good." I circle my hips slowly, and Rory's hands drift up to grip my waist.

I grin down at him and lick my lips. I support myself with his chest as I ride him until I am spent, and our bodies are slicked with sweat. I know Rory strained himself, trying to keep still so I could have my way with him, and it took a toll on him too—his face and neck are pearled with sweat.

The room feels hotter, and my hair is nearly dripping with sweat. We are weak with exhaustion when Rory presses his thumb against my clit, and I shamelessly grind against it while he's inside me. I unravel around him as I come and collapse on his body. Rory pumps inside me twice more and steels with his own release. He rolls his head back, giving me a glorious look at his neck and the veins that bulge with his pleasure.

I pant to the rhythm of his chest rising.

"So, no pain," Rory says with a breathy voice.

I shake my head. "Only pleasure."

IN THE MORNING, I WATCH RORY AS HE SLEEPS IN. IT'S BEEN hours, and he has the sweetest little snore. I manage to get out of bed and back in again without him so much as stirring.

It's late morning when he finally wakes. "Hmmm," he moans.

"Good morning," I say.

He smiles. "Morning. How're you feeling?"

"Great."

"Great?" he asks.

"Yeah," I say.

"I need the truth, Valentina. Please."

"Very slightly sore. But no pain. I swear."

Rory smiles and draws circles on my shoulder with the pads of his fingers. "Good," he says.

He rolls up and over me so he's on top, and he kisses me. "Now," he says. "Almonte, what is it you need to think about to say yes?"

My face falls to the side, and Rory pushes it back by my chin, so I look at him. "If we get married, I'd like our marriage to be one of good communication. That starts now."

I blink. He is right. After last night, I don't think there's anything I couldn't talk to him about. I bite my lip. "Lots of things," I say.

"Okay." He kisses me gently, urging me to go on.

"I wanted to be with you last night so you could change your mind if you didn't like it."

Rory's eyebrow raises. "Did it look like I didn't like it?"

I giggle. "Right. Well, I guess that's a non-issue, then."

"Good. One down. What else?"

"I can't give you children," I admit.

That gives Rory pause, though I'm sure he had to know. He rolls off me and onto his side next to me, so we face each other. "Do you want children, Valentina?"

I shrug one shoulder. "That's not a future I ever envisioned, but when Dr. Ramirez asked about freezing eggs, I declined."

"Why?"

"It didn't seem important. There are so many children without parents—I guess I figured if I ever really wanted children, it wouldn't be important if they were biological. I'd rather give good parents to a kid with none."

Rory tucks a strand of hair behind my ear. "Valentina Almonte, you couldn't be more fucking perfect if you tried."

My eyes search his, and he smiles at me.

"Rory, don't lie to me. If children are important to you, this can't work—"

"They *are* important to me. And I intend to have them. With you. And they will be adopted, but they will be our children, same as if we made them the other way."

I laugh. "The other way?"

"You know what I mean."

He has already thought about this. Of course he has. Even if he didn't have access to my medical chart, he had to have known I'd more than likely fried my ovaries despite how hard we tried saving them. "You don't mind, then, if you can't have a child of your own blood?" I ask.

He shakes his head. "My children will be mine because they were meant to be. Just like you're meant to be their mom."

"Okay," I say.

"Okay?" Rory's eyes are wide.

"I'm not saying yes yet."

"What else do you want from me, woman?" We both laugh at his frustration.

"For one, I'd like a proper proposal. Preferably not in a locker room surrounded by the smell of feet."

"Noted. Won't happen again. Is that it, then? Are you saying yes?"

I shake my head. "I'd like to live together a little while first. Make sure we both want this and that we're committed to spending a lifetime together, because if I marry you, Rory Dennis, it'll be for life."

Rory smiles wide. "We can live together for a while first. I'm okay with a long engagement."

I turn to face away from him so he can spoon me because I don't want to see his face for what I'm about to tell him next.

"I have to confess something," I say.

"What's that?"

"While you were sleeping, I called my sister."

"Okay—"

"She wants to have you over for dinner. Meet you."

"That's not so bad. Why do you sound nervous all of a sudden?"

"She didn't say, but I'm pretty sure she intends to have my parents over."

"Oh."

CHAPTER 23

"I don't approve," says Dad. Rory is on the other side of the room, talking with Pilar. Dad's eyes are narrow as he looks at him and swirls the whiskey in his glass.

"I know," I smile and am surprised at how relaxed I am. I'm done caring. I no longer have to live my life for anyone other than myself.

"You know?" Dad asks.

"I know, Dad, but things are different now. Now it's about what I want. Not about what you or Mom want," I say matter-of-factly.

He'd never admit it, but I swear I saw the hint of a smile on the corner of Dad's mouth.

"Does he make you happy?" Dad asks

"He really does," I say.

Dad lands a peck on my cheek and walks back to his place next to Mom, but he seems happy in a way I'm not accustomed to seeing him.

Rory couldn't believe my sister's house. I hadn't seen it from an outsider's perspective in a long time. From his eyes, my world is new and filled with a wonder I have long taken for granted.

"Is she royalty or something?" Rory had asked as we'd walked up to the door.

Pilar's house is almost a palace. Her life lacks love from her partner, but in many ways, she has everything most women dream of—the perfect home and husband. My parents are happy and approve of her life, and I'm glad they have someone to approve of because I know it will never be me.

"He's great," Pilar whispers when she comes over to me. Rory is talking to Felipe about the home's architectural elements, even though I know Rory is faking it.

"I know," I say. "I'm happy."

"Are you?"

"What? Happy? Yeah, Pili. I'm happy in a way I never thought was possible. I only hope one day you can find that same level of happiness."

"What do you mean?"

"Do you really think Felipe is your happiness?"

Pilar's body stiffens, and I can decipher to the second the moment when her guard comes up. "This night is about you," she says. "Leave me out of it just this once. Please?"

I bite my lip. "I'm sorry," I say, and I am. This night is for Pilar to get to know Rory, and I have to keep reminding myself of that.

A maid announces dinner, and we all make our way to the dining room table.

Mom is a freaking painting. Beautiful, but a mere ornament on Dad's arm. Felipe and Dad monopolize the conversation, and I squeeze Rory's hand under the table. I whisper reassurances that him not feeding into their superficial bravado is perfectly fine.

"So, Rory, how much longer is your residency?" Felipe asks.

"Two more years" says Rory.

"That soon?" Felipe asks.

"Yeah. If all goes well—"

"And your plans after that?" Dad asks.

Rory clears his throat and swallows the bite of steak he is on. "Well, I'm not really sure. We have to decide where we want to live first—"

"Well," says Dad, "You'll be taking my daughter with you. I don't quite see how it would work for you to move here—"

I jump in. "Dad! Can we please not talk about this?"

Dad throws me a stern look of warning. "What? It's perfectly natural for your family to worry—"

"No, Dad. It's not. Things are different now. Everything's changed."

Dad shifts in his seat but has the decency not to comment further.

"Dad, I'm sorry," I say. "I just . . . I have to make my own choices."

"You always have," Dad says.

He looks at me but with no remorse. It's a fact. A simple fact. If he couldn't tame me before my outlook on life changed, he could never manage it now.

It's a relief when Dad changes the subject. He and Felipe turn their attention to business. Mom eats dinner, dainty and quiet for the most part.

Pilar can't stop smiling as she looks between Rory and me. We can't stop smiling ourselves.

Dad's passiveness the rest of the evening surprises everyone. Pilar and I half expected he would blow a gasket at my choice in a mate, but he doesn't. Dad had wanted me to marry an important businessman, lawyer, or politician from Mexico. Someone with influence. Someone who would add a certain type of value to the family that Dad craves. In the end, I think he sees how much I smile around Rory, how he holds me protectively by his side. There's also not a chance he has forgotten everything Rory did when I was in treatment even though he had absolutely no obligation to help.

Dad walks us to my car and takes Rory's hand to shake, but then holds it there. "I've told my daughter this, so I won't lie to you," Dad says. "I don't approve of this match. I am bitter that my daughter is leaving—"

"That hasn't been decided—" Rory tries to explain.

"As good as. And despite that, I see Valentina is in relatively good hands. I'm glad she'll have a doctor—someone who knows what to look out for . . ."

Dad trails off as he chokes on his words. I know what he is asking Rory. He wants him to watch out for recurrence of my cancer. To keep a watchful eye.

"I promise I'll take good care of her, sir."

Dad nods. "I'm sure you will," he says. "The alternative is a hell of a lot of trouble from me, son."

I bring my hand to my chest at hearing Dad call him 'son' even if it was a threat. Dad finally got the son he wanted in Felipe. He hand-picked him himself. But I know, deep down, Dad knows he doesn't make Pilar happy. And even though Rory is the furthest thing from what he wanted for me, he will be a better son-in-law than Felipe could ever hope to be.

My family, as expected, dragged out the dinner much longer than it needed to be. Pre-dinner drinks, five courses, port and cigars after dinner for the men who went off into Felipe's study, and endless, mind-numbing conversation. By the time we get home, Rory and I are exhausted. Rory barely brushed his teeth, and his head hit the pillow.

"That was better than I thought," I say.

"What dinner were *you* at?" Rory's voice is laced with sarcasm.

"I guess I should say, by my family's standard, it went better than I thought."

"They hate me."

"Not Pilar," I say with an encouraging smile.

"No, I guess not Pilar, but your Dad—I mean, I'm a doctor. He knows that, right? It's a noble profession, and no, I won't be a millionaire, but I will be financially stable. He talked to me like I was a, a, uh—"

"A what?" I ask.

"A chimney sweep," Rory says, satisfied with his analogy.

"A chimney sweep?" I laugh. "What is this? Oliver Twist?" I lay down next to Rory and take his hand in mine. "Poor little orphan boy is going to be a chimney sweep."

Rory's jaw drops, and he tries to break his hand away from mine. Then I realize what I said.

"Rory, no, I—that's not what—I just meant . . ."

"Yeah, go on, backpedal faster." Then he bursts out laughing.

"Come here, you." He grabs me and pulls me closer to him on the bed. "I'm not sensitive about being adopted. You should have seen your face, though."

I gently smack his shoulder. "That wasn't funny."

"I know. I'm sorry."

"Thank you for meeting my family."

"They're my family now, I suppose."

I haven't thought about it like this until Rory mentions it, but he is right. They are his family now too—poor thing.

"Even Felipe," I say.

"Yeah, that dude gives off a bad vibe."

"You are like a puppy," I say.

"What do you mean?"

"Dogs can sense evil without having to know a person."

"You're saying he is evil?"

"In his own way. I don't want to talk about sad things right now, though."

I catch Rory watching me sleep the next morning, as if we're taking turns with this ritual. He smiles at me, and I can't help but feel like I am exactly where I am supposed to be. His smile even feels like home.

"That's kind of creepy," I tease.

"You watch me sleep all the time."

"How do you know that?" I ask.

"I'm not always asleep."

I narrow my eyes at him, and he laughs.

"Can I ask you something?" He asks, his arm tightening around me.

"Yeah."

"Tell me about Chema and Nico."

I suck in a breath. "Are you upset I let you think we were together?"

"No. I know why you did it."

I squeeze his arm, thankful he's not mad about the second biggest lie I ever told him—the first being that I didn't love him back. But we don't dwell on those bitter moments anymore, so instead I tell him about Chema and Nico.

When I met Chema and Nico, they'd had the gym open for barely a year. Chema was coming down from the height of his fighting career after an injury, and has made his gym very successful since.

And because Rory will very soon be part of our inner circle, I need him and Chema to be friends. I need both of them in my life. So I also overshare on Chema's life; on how he and Nico were high school sweethearts in secret because their families didn't approve. They were both on their school's soccer team and were caught kissing by one of their teammates. The following day, three of their teammates cornered Nico alone and beat the shit out of him. Once he healed, Chema vowed he'd never let anyone hurt him again. They both took self-defense classes, and Chema fell in love with the sport. The fact that he could pummel anyone who dared look at Nico the wrong way was an added bonus of his profession.

When I'm done telling Rory the story of Nico and Chema, Rory's smiling at me. "Chema's really amazing isn't he?" he asks.

I nod. "Hopefully you'll learn to love him like I do."

"I already do. He took care of my precious girl when I couldn't be there."

"Precious girl?" I tease.

"Don't mock. You're precious to me, and Chema guarded you."

I smile, hopeful for the potential of our life together, and I lean in to kiss him. Shifting under the covers to get closer to him, I reach for the hem of his shirt, but he stills my hand. He shakes his head as he looks deep into my eyes.

"Why not?" I ask.

"You were sore yesterday—"

"I'm perfectly fine today."

"I'm sure you are, but can we please take it slow? I need to make sure you stay okay."

My instincts turn to anger, but I can't let it out because I know he only wants me healthy. It's coming from a good place, even as infantilizing as his desire to control my health is. We are both going to have to adjust.

"We can take it slow," I say finally. "Within reason. At some point, you have to trust me too."

"I know," Rory says. "We'll work on it. In the meantime, can loving each other be enough?"

$\mathcal{R}$ory has some sort of plan he isn't telling me about. Our flight was delayed, and everything Rory has done since we got to his apartment has been rushed. I'm tired from the long day of travel and can't imagine how he has all this energy.

"We're going out tonight, so get ready," he says.

I frown. "I'm too tired to go out."

"Please. It's important."

I cross my arms in front of me. "Rory Dennis, what do you have up your sleeve?"

"Please, can you just humor me? This once?"

I finally relent and hop in the shower before he does so I have time to dry my hair while he gets his turn. After drying off, and as Rory is in the shower, a lightbulb goes off in my head. I rummage through one of my suitcases.

As a parting gift, Pilar gave me a designer red camisole with matching robe. It's sexy in an elegant sort of way, and the feeling of the silk is divine. I put it on and wait for the shower to shut off. I give Rory a few minutes before walking into the bathroom with him. He is brushing his teeth and has a towel wrapped low on his hips. Water droplets roll down the rippled muscles of his abs, and I bite my lip at the beautiful sight. I lean on the doorframe and clear my throat. He turns to look at me, does a double-take stopping mid-brush, and when he eyes me up and down, rinses quickly.

"Valentina," he groans. "We're going out . . ." He says, but with less conviction now.

"You sure you want to go out? You wouldn't rather stay in bed our first night back?"

His eyes narrow as I approach him. I slide my index finger between him and the towel to unhook it, letting it slide down his body and pool at his feet. "Oops," I say, and he chuckles. "What's it going to be?" I ask, grabbing his hardening shaft and squeezing gently once, feeling as it stiffens further in my hand.

His green eyes darken under hooded lids. "It can wait," he says with a smirk, and I drop to my knees in front of him.

The silk clings to my skin with the steam from his shower, and the sensation forces my thighs to clench together. I pump him once more and bring him into my mouth. Rory has to lean back on the vanity as he loses balance, and I love what I can do to him. It's a power trip I haven't appreciated until him—like so many other things. I suck hard once, and he groans long and deep.

I suck and lick while I twist my grip around his shaft and then take him deep in my throat.

"Valentina, stop. I don't want to come in your mouth." I suck one last time before he draws away from my mouth. I stand and kiss him with an open mouth, our tongues dancing and playing.

Fucking Rory Dennis is so much fun.

He flips and lifts me until I'm sitting on the vanity, and he is between my legs. He feels the material of the chemise between his fingers. "This is nice," he says and nibbles my neck.

"You like it?"

"Mmm-hmmm. I insist you wear this to bed every night."

"You're very demanding, Doctor Dennis," I tease.

"I am," he agrees. "Lube?" he asks, and I hand him the small bottle I placed on the counter when I walked in. He pours it liberally onto his hand, warms it up, and my sex clenches at the sight of him sliding his hands up and down a now-shiny cock. Rory centers himself in front of me, and I wrap my legs around him.

He slides in slowly, slowly at first, until he bottoms out. I moan with pleasure, and he pulls out and slams deep and quick into me again. He kisses me, leading with his tongue, and comes back up for air as his thrusts quicken.

I forgot about the second mirror in the bathroom, and when I turn to the side briefly, an image of him thrusting into me as my legs quiver around him stops my gaze. It's so hot, seeing him —seeing *us*—like this. "Rory," I say. "Look." He turns in the direction of my gaze and stills deep inside me.

"Fuck, Valentina. You look so hot."

He fucks me harder, then, for the first time since we got back together. There is no hesitation, and I smile because I realize he couldn't stop himself from being a little rougher with me. We both look in the mirror now, watching how we fuck, and our eyes meet, catching the other doing the same. The corner of his mouth draws into a smirk.

My body shudders as I come, looking at Rory through the full-length mirror. He slides out, then slams in again, rolling my orgasm into two.

His hands wrap around me and grab onto my ass as he lifts me off the vanity and carries me to the bed, impaled on him. He lays me down gently and thrusts a few times before sliding out. I don't dwell in the absence of him too long before he flips me over, and grabbing onto my hip bones, pulls my ass up to face him. I smile, remembering his words from our first night together—this is his favorite part of my body. Rory Dennis is a booty-man, and he can't get enough of mine.

I look straight ahead to the empty wall, and before he is in me again, say, "We're getting a mirror right there—"

Rory slides in deep. "Agreed," he groans, and slams into me so roughly, my legs start to shake with my next orgasm. I'm afraid they'll give out soon, but Rory's growl breaks through the silence of the apartment, and he stills inside me.

I feel as he presses his forehead to my back and tries to catch his breath. Both his thumbs circle two spots on my lower back. "I love these dimples," he says, admiring my backside.

"They're all yours," I say.

We both collapse on the bed and stare at each other shyly. While it turned me on so much, somehow, looking at us through that mirror made me a bit bashful now that the deed is done.

I want to thank Rory for being rough and not treating me like a glass figurine, but I don't want to have another conversation like the one in Mexico, so instead, I trace the scar on his chest with my fingers. In turn, he traces my scars over my lower abdomen. We lie there, caressing each other's scarred and beautiful bodies without a word passing between us. His eyes search mine. "I love you," he says.

"I love you too."

CHAPTER 25

We are both sated but weak and tired, so it takes me by surprise when Rory starts getting dressed to go out. I don't understand his urgency to get to out the door until we arrive at our favorite bar, *La Oficina*.

The 'open' sign is off, and a flyer on the front door indicates the bar is closed for a special event, but the place is dark. Rory knocks, and Sofia opens up for us. As I step through, the lights come on, and a roar of "Welcome Home!" Blasts through me like heavy wind.

When my mind catches up to what just happened, I scan the room and see all the faces of everyone I met during my time in Kansas City. Dr. Ramirez, nurse Sara, Mandy, Tlali, and Izel all beam at me. They didn't forget me. I feel the tears coming on, and I try to sniffle them back in. All my friends are here—my new family.

Mandy nearly crashes onto me when she hugs me. "We missed you so much, girl. Wait until I catch you up with everything that's been going on." She loops her arm with mine, as she's done so many times before, and leads me to the bar to grab a glass of champagne.

When we get there, I realize Lisa and Tom, Rory's parents, are both here. I go over to them and give them both a hug.

"It's so good to see you, dear," says Lisa. "You're looking a lot better than the last time we saw you."

"Thank you. I'm feeling a lot better, and I'm in remission. Things are looking good."

"And you got some meat back on them bones," says Tom.

"Tom! Don't embarrass the girl—"

I laugh. "No. It's okay. You're absolutely right, Tom. I'm working on bulking up a bit again. Getting a little stronger."

"That's good," he says and winks at me. "The Dennis men like our women strong, with a little meat on the bone—"

"Tom!" Lisa scolds again.

"What? I didn't say anything wrong."

Luckily, Rory interjects before I laugh at his parents again. "I'm so sorry," Rory says. "Have they already gotten into trouble?"

"No, they're fine." I smile.

The surprise warms my heart. Rory had to have planned for this while he was in Mexico. I have no idea how he managed. I scan the room to see it's not only people I know. Neil, Rory's old roommate, who I remember from our one introduction, stands with a group of men at the other end of the bar. My mind flashes back to that moment at the bar when Rory told the group of men he was with he was bailing on them for someone else. I'm pretty sure it's that very table of men chatting it up with Neil.

It hits me, then, that Rory has invited all his friends and family, whether I know them or not. And this is a 'welcome home' surprise party? Something isn't quite adding up.

"Rory? What is this?" I ask.

Rory leads me to the bar and gestures for me to sit on one of the stools. With my back to the bar, I pin him with my eyes.

"What do you mean?" he asks.

"There are so many people here I don't know . . ." My thought trails off when Rory's mouth quirks into a playful smile.

He takes my hand in his and kisses it. He reaches behind me for something and then turns around to make his way to the center of the room. When he faces me again, I see a champagne glass in one hand and a spoon in the other. He clinks the spoon to the glass, and my heart rate quickens to the chime.

Oh god. What is he about to do? I want to run with the anticipation of his speech, but everyone is so silent and frozen to their spots, any movement from me will only draw attention. I curse Rory Dennis, and I curse barstools. There's something about a barstool and Dr. Dennis in the same room that always ends in disaster.

Then he speaks. "Thank you, everyone, for being here, and to those of you who helped me organize this, I am forever grateful. If you're in this room, you know the beautiful woman sitting at the bar." All eyes turn to me, and I sink in my seat a little. My face feels hot, and I want to run. But I can't. I'm going to kill him for this.

Rory goes on. "If you don't know Valentina Almonte personally, you know of her. You know of her because if you are here tonight, you're important to me, and if you're important to me, you know I can't shut up about her." Rory chuckles, and polite little laughs follow around the room. This isn't funny, Rory Dennis. I stew silently as he continues his speech.

"This year, I almost lost her. That experience only taught me to cherish her and have as much of her time as she'll allow me to have." Rory sets down the two items in his hands and holds my eyes. He fumbles a bit with his collar, then sticks his hand into his pants pocket, producing a familiar box.

Well-played, Rory. Well-played. The last time he tried to do this was in private. He won't give me a chance to say no; that's why he's doing this in front of everyone. If I hadn't already decided to marry him, this could be construed as manipulation.

Rory walks to where I'm sitting and gets down on one knee. I look down at the box in his hands, then back at him. His face is hopeful but strained, like he is holding his breath, and everyone around us quiets like they're holding their breath with him in solidarity.

I have my life back—a second chance. When I was diagnosed, all I wanted was to experience life, to see places, art, meet people, eat food I'd never dreamed of. Now I know that not only will I have the time to do all those things, but that Rory Dennis will be by my side for all of it. I know in my heart he is the man I will grow old with—now that I get to grow old.

"Valentina Almonte, will you do me the honor of being my wife?"

THIRTEEN YEARS LATER

EPILOGUE

THIRTEEN YEARS LATER

The gym closes early on Sundays—by lunchtime, the place is dead. This is the one day a week I'll allow Nayeli and Miles to train in the cage. I can focus all my attention on them.

At ten-years-old, Nayeli towers over her eight-year-old brother. I try not to smile at how cute they are with their child-size gloves as they paw at each other like puppies with little strength. Miles struggles to put on his kid knuckle wraps, and Nayeli groans and protests, but in the end, she always helps him wrap so they can spar.

She won't let Miles win, though. I think not until he outgrows her will he have so much as a shot at winning, and even then, I don't see it happening.

Miles takes after Rory. He idolizes him and proclaimed years ago he was going to be a doctor just like him. He follows through, too, and spends most of his time hitting the books, ever since Rory told him that's what it takes.

For her part, Nayeli has no clue what she wants to do when she grows up, but she is physically gifted. I've never hinted at a career in sports—it needs to come from her—but nothing would make me prouder.

I watch my foster children play on the mat with equal parts hope and dread. Rory and I have petitioned to adopt them, and we are awaiting our court date. I'm sure everything will work out okay, but there's a little part of me gnawing at my insides with doubt, as if something could go wrong. It's silly, though. Miles and Nayeli's biological mom already lost custody. There's no reason for the judge to rule against the adoption.

They are my children. Before them, we had temporary foster placements, all children who were successfully reunited with their families, and I hope, doing well now. But the moment Nayeli and Miles came home two years ago, Rory and I looked at each other, and we both knew. I told him, "These are our children," and all he said was, "I know."

"Mom! Mom!" Miles yells. "I tapped out. Make her stop!"

"Nayeli, you know the rules. If your brother taps out, you have to stop."

Nayeli loses her chokehold's grip around her brother and raises her arms in surrender as she stands. "Sorry," she whines. "Mom, I really need to fight with someone my own age. The twerp is too weak."

"I am not weak!" Miles snaps.

"Are too."

"Am not! You're bigger. That's all. Mom! Tell her."

"Stop teasing your brother, Nayeli. If you behave, we can look into getting you someone else to train with," I say.

I stifle a laugh when Miles sucker-punches his sister when she's distracted. *Serves her right*, I think, but I don't take sides with them.

The front doorbell rings as it opens, and I walk over to help my next customer. "Play nice, you two," I call after the brawling siblings.

The first one to enter the gym is a little boy I know and love.

"Tía!" my nephew yells and runs to me. I pick him up into my arms and embrace him as I carry him.

"What are you doing here, love?"

Pilar walks into the gym before he has a chance to answer me. "I'm so sorry, Tini," she says.

"For what?"

"For telling me where to find you," Dad's voice hits me like a ton of bricks as he enters my gym, the place he swore he'd never set foot in.

Mom and Dad didn't show up at my wedding. They sent a gift and claimed they were too busy with business and couldn't travel at the time. It was all horseshit, of course.

It was Tom, Rory's Dad, who walked me down the aisle that day. They've been a constant in our lives ever since. He and Lisa moved to Kansas City from Minnesota the minute they heard we would be fostering. They insisted they wanted to be a part of that with us. They are overjoyed at our adoption plans and already love Nayeli and Miles more than anything on this earth, dethroning even Rory from the number one spot. He is now third in their hearts—and okay with it.

My parents weren't quite so . . . graceful about it. When I told them over the phone, the roles reversed. Dad stayed quiet for the call, and Mom shouted. She couldn't believe I would adopt someone else's children. She yelled again at how stupid I was for not freezing my eggs so I could have a child of my blood. I hung up on them. I haven't spoken to them since.

"What are you doing here?" I ask Dad but then look at Pilar.

Pilar mouths, "I'm sorry," and I know she had little say in what happened.

"Can I talk to you, Valentina?" Dad asks.

"I don't see what we have to talk about," I say.

"Please. It's important."

It's then I notice the thick legal envelope in his hands. "Here."

I hand Pilar her son, and she takes him over to the mat to play with Nayeli and Miles.

"We can go into my office," I say to Dad and lead him there. He takes a seat in front of me. I clasp my hands and lean back in my chair. "Well? What did you want to talk about?"

"This." He lets the envelope fall with a thud onto my desk. I take it.

"What is it?" I say as I empty the contents.

"Your dowry."

"My what?"

"I am legally obligated to give you your dowry."

I scan the paperwork, at least the first couple of pages, and the pieces of paper confirm what he is saying, but nothing explains why I'm getting it now. I've been married over a decade.

"Why now?"

"Believe me, if it were up to me, you wouldn't be getting it."

"Thanks? I guess . . ."

"You can thank your great-grandma for that."

I shake my head. "I don't understand."

"I never told you girls, for obvious reasons, that there were two pathways to getting the trust fund."

"Trust fund?"

"Yeah. We called it a dowry to ensure you and Pilar made acceptable matches, but marriage wasn't the only way to get the money. If my grandfather had his way, and I had my way, it would be the only way, but my grandmother felt differently. Most of the family money came from her side of the family, so she had significant control over its destiny."

"I don't understand," I repeat. None of this makes sense.

"She felt that a woman could start a good life either in marriage or in business. My grandfather insisted that with the marriage clause, the father had to approve. Grandma only conceded that the clause could be overturned if the recipient of the funds started a business. She felt a woman should have success in either married life or business life and that the funds would ensure that either way."

"Oh," I say, realization hitting me. I opened up my gym this year. Rory and I saved for nearly a decade to start this business. He wanted my dreams to come true as well, and we've skimped but have finally gotten here. His salary as a doctor helped loads, and I coached during that time. "My gym," I say finally.

"Yes. Your gym made you eligible for the funds."

"Dad, we don't need anything. We're doing fine."

"I know," he says. "But it's not about that. Your grandmother protected you and any daughters you have and their daughters. I can't do anything about it. Legally, she left that to you."

"I guess I can finally pay Pilar what's left of my debt to her," I say.

"She won't care about that."

"I know."

"Have your lawyers look over the documents. You'll want to give them account information so that the money can be wired. There's also preliminary paperwork for your children's trust funds."

"What?"

"You adopted them, right?"

"We are in the process."

"Well, they're your children once adopted. That makes them eligible for family trust funds."

"Let me guess. Grandma protected an adoption classification for this?"

"It wasn't grandpa," Dad says and smiles. "Listen, I'm sorry about how your Mom reacted. She doesn't understand what you're doing here. With all this . . ." he trails off and whirls his hand in the air, motioning to the space around us. "I don't think I fully do either, but I know it's a good thing. I can't promise I'll see them as my grandchildren, but I want to try."

"You do?"

Dad's shoulders relax, and I see the walls he's put up between us start to crumble. "I do. You think I could meet them?"

"They'd love that," I say. "But not today. I have to speak with Rory first. You understand?"

"I do. I'm here until Tuesday. I would love to meet them before I leave."

"I'm sure I can make that happen."

We stand, and for a moment, neither of us knows what to do. I clear my throat and offer him my hand.

Dad laughs and pushes it away. He takes me into his arms. "I know I don't understand you. But I do love you."

This is probably the first hug he's offered since I was sick, and the only 'I love you' I've ever gotten from him that I can remember. I sniffle into his shirt. "Love you too, Dad."

PILAR AND DAD ARE GONE BY THE TIME RORY PICKS THE KIDS AND me up at the gym. Nayeli and Miles run up to him the second they see him.

"Dad! Dad!" Miles squeals. "I got Nayeli! Just the once. But it counts."

"Bet it does, buddy." He musses Miles's hair and hunches down to hug him.

"I was distracted," says Nayeli.

"Sure you were," Rory says, and Nayeli wraps her arms around his middle. "Anybody up for some ice cream? Maybe we can go to the park afterward?"

Both kids bounce with excitement, and both scream, "Yes!"

"Let me just lock up," I say. "Wait in the car."

WE GET OUR ICE CREAM, THEN HEAD OVER TO THE PARK. NAYELI and Miles go straight for the playground, and Rory and I sit on a bench where I fill him in on everything that happened that day.

When I'm done, he says, "Wish I could've been there."

I'm still dazed as I try to process everything Dad said. "Me too. Well?" I ask. "Are you okay with Dad getting to know the kids?"

He shifts in his seat and faces me. "Maybe," he says. "Only if he's serious. I don't want to introduce anyone into their lives who doesn't plan on being there for the long haul."

"I don't think Mom will ever get on board, but I have to say, Dad looked sincere. I get the sense he has some regrets in life."

"Let me talk to him. We can go from there. But if he is serious, I have no problem with the kids knowing their other grandpa."

I squeeze Rory's hand. "Thank you," I say.

Rory scoots over to wrap an arm around me. He still uses the same aftershave from when we first met, and I take in the comforting smell of sandalwood and suede. My husband hasn't changed much over the years. He started working out more when I opened the gym to spend time with me, and he has bulked up a little. The hints of wrinkles barely begin to play around his beautiful green eyes, and he is not allowed to shave his beard. He is as handsome as he has ever been.

And he is a fantastic father. Because he is involved with our local foster care agency, he understands how slim adoption chances get the longer a child stays in the system—that's why he wants Nayeli and Miles. The older they get, the fewer chances they have to be adopted. They took to calling him Dad fairly quickly, not that it was a contest. It would have been a contest if they'd called me Mom first, but they didn't. Rory doesn't let me forget that.

Our kids didn't laugh when they first got to us. It broke our hearts. We watch them now when they play, and all the laughter they can't help but let out, and I know both our hearts are soaring.

For our part, Rory and I have a wonderful, healthy marriage. We could live our lives afraid of Rory's heart patch giving out or of my cancer coming back, but instead, each morning we wake up and choose to cherish each other and our time together like the privilege the gift of time is.

"So," Rory says, breaking my thoughts. "You're a millionaire? And so are the kids?"

I burst out laughing, and he joins me with his own laughter. "Yeah. Guess we are. And so are you, Dr. Dennis."

The End

KEEP READING

You can read Sara and Ramiro's story in Sensation, a steamy, slow-burn, single dad, forced proximity romance. Keep reading for an excerpt.

If you're not ready to let go of the characters in the Heartland Metro Hospital series, join my reader club and get a free steamy romance novella at ofeliamartinez.com/freebooks.

ALSO BY OFELIA MARTINEZ

The Industrial November on Tour Series

Sofia & Bren's Story: Hiding in the Smoke

Lola & Karl's Story: Running from the Blaze

Erica & Friedrich's Story: Scorching to the Touch

The Heartland Metro Hospital Series

Carolina & Hector's Story: Remission

Valentina & Rory's Story: Contusion

Izel & Logan's Story: Incision (Novella)

Camila & Leonardo's Story: Palpitation (Novella as part of the *Heroes with Heat and Heart Vol.2* anthology)

Sara & Ramiro's Story: Sensation

Anthologies & Collections

Diagnosis Amor Vol. 1: Heartland Metro Hospital Collection

Camila & Leonardo's Story: Heroes with Heath and Heart Vol 2

ACKNOWLEDGMENTS

This book is dedicated to my partner and best friend, Robert. I would like to thank you for choosing me as your person and for loving me every day. You make me laugh on the best of days, but what I love most about you is that even in my dark moments, you find a way to make me smile.

As always, I owe much gratitude to my beta readers without whose feedback this book wouldn't exist: Claudia and Tamara. Big thanks also due to the editors at Midnight Owl Editors. Your team is amazing, and I couldn't do this without you.

And of course, a big thank you to you, my reader. Because of your support, I get to live my dream of making stories up and writing them down.

SENSATION

SENSATION EXCERPT: SPRING

CHAPTER ONE

I've been in love with Ramiro Jimenez since my junior year of college, and now his fiancée is dead.

I'm watching him, in love with him, and he's watching her, getting lowered into the ground in her beautiful white dress in her pretty mahogany casket, her engagement ring secure around her finger.

The tornado sirens that on any other day would send my heart rate through the roof stopped just in time for the service to conclude and allow the funeral procession to begin.

I've been terrified of that awful sound since I was a little girl, when I endured tornado warnings pretty much alone. Only, today, my heart is occupied with a grief so immense, the sirens are an afterthought.

I always thought the minute I graduated from college, I'd move as far away from the tornado valley as I could. Then I found my adoptive family when I was in college, and I couldn't imagine being away from them—every single person at this burial today—so I stayed.

Despite the love of all these people, spring is still the worst season of all in this place. It's rainy, gray, and those damned sirens go off at the worst times. Springtime in Kansas City always makes me think of Forrest Gump describing all the different types of rain. Today it was the sideways type for several hours. Now the raindrops are heavy, and the wind has died down a bit. They aren't pelting us sideways anymore, but the downpour is still heavy.

So heavy.

And despite all that, today, even the rain is an afterthought. I'm not cold, or scared, or annoyed at being wet. It's like none of us here care or can even feel the rain. We're all still numb, in shock.

This particular dreary spring day is the worst of them because today, I get to watch the love of my life bury his fiancée.

It's unrequited love. I'll make that clear now.

I met Ramiro when Carolina, my then-roommate and now best friend-slash-big sister, took pity on me and invited me to her home to spend the holiday break with her and her dad, Don Gustavo. Back then, Ramiro was the one deep in unrequited love for Carolina, whom he'd grown up with. So, in a way, he's already been through exactly what I'm experiencing with him.

But Carolina knew how he felt about her. And he has no idea about my feelings.

Nearly eight years is a long time to be in love with someone who will never love you back. I was only twenty when I met him, and I thought I'd outgrow it one day, but watching him today, with those big brown eyes, glassy as he holds back his sobs, hurts me more than anything ever has, and that's when I know—I'll never stop loving him. Even if he'll never see me as anything other than Carolina's annoying little sister—a gnat in his periphery.

After Carolina finally made it clear she'd never be in love with him, Ramiro had a whirlwind romance with a woman four years his senior, and they got engaged two months ago. He finally thought he'd found happiness.

They never made it to their wedding day.

Francisca Garcia died at thirty-four years old.

She hadn't been sick, and her sudden death at the peak of their love story crushed Ramiro way more than his heartbreak over Carolina ever had. It was an accident. A nighttime walk and an all-black workout outfit a driver couldn't see in the dark. She never saw her crossing the street, distracted as she was by texting on her phone, driving much faster than she should have been in a residential area. Francisca died on impact.

And I feel guilty.

Guilty, because more than anything, I wish I could allow myself to admire how handsome he looks today in his suit. I'm used to seeing Ramiro in what I swear is a uniform of jeans and a ribbed tank, all greasy from his work as a mechanic.

The only suit he had for today was the one he'd already bought for his wedding.

So here we are, Ramiro, dashing in his three-piece wedding suit, getting drenched in the rain as he buries his fiancée. I'd trade places with Francisca to save him this pain if I could.

Without thinking, I interlace my fingers with his, and on the other side of him, Carolina is also holding his hand. He doesn't flinch, or push me away, to my surprise. Today, we're the twin pillars propping him up, though Carolina and I are sobbing messes ourselves. We all do our best to keep it together.

We've known Francisca for years since she lived just down the street from Carolina's family home—and Ramiro's, who was Carolina's neighbor growing up. Though Carolina and I were never particularly close to her, this death still hits very close to home. Losing someone from our tight-knit community hurts more than I imagined, and not just because I feel this pain for Ramiro.

I'd gotten to know Francisca and her family over the years. We often invited them to our home—that is, Don Gustavo and Carolina's home. They also welcomed us as guests to their home when they had cookouts and birthday parties, and let's not forget invitations to watch the all-important soccer games.

Even when Ramiro fell in love with her, I didn't have it in me to hate her. Francisca was the embodiment of what Don Gustavo called de sangre livianita. During one of our Spanish lessons, he explained that when someone has light blood, it means they're easy to like, while someone with heavy blood, or sangre pesada, is a person who is hard to like. In reality, I saw how happy she made Ramiro—how he lit up when she walked into a room—and that made me happy, regardless of the weight of her blood.

Francisca must have had feather-light blood, though, because to know her was to like her. I understand why he fell in love with her so quickly once they started dating.

As they begin to lower the casket into the grave, Ramiro's grip on my hand tightens, and he croaks out, "Sara." I look up at him, blinking, surprised he called out my name. Not Francisca's. Not Carolina's. Mine. He said, "Sara."

I know what it's like to lose family and loved ones. Not to death but might as well be. That's probably why he said my name, knowing I understand what he's feeling with this loss. I squeeze his hand tighter and lean my head on his shoulder, hugging his bicep with my free arm.

"I know," I whisper. "I know."

A strangled sound leaves his throat, but he won't cry. I know he won't. Definitely not in public. Not even under cover of rain. In private? I'm not even sure he'll cry then, either.

Though only thirty years old, Ramiro Jimenez is a very proud, young Mexican-American man. Taught not to cry from his earliest memories by his father, who learned it from his father, and so on. At least that's my understanding of his upbringing.

I wish he would cry. He needs to. He can't bottle up all this pain.

This pain that is all around us. Pain reflected in Don Gustavo's eyes—who knows exactly what it's like to bury a loved one so young—and in Doña Pancha's tears at having to endure the pain of burying her child.

But the biggest pain in this tiny, wet patch of land today comes from the two little boys hugging their grandma, unable to stop crying because they'll never see their mom again.

On the day they bury their mother, René Garcia is ten years old, and Oscar Garcia only eight. Their father is still living, but he isn't here today and hasn't been for a single day of Oscar's life.

I don't think any of us can hear the priest's words any longer over Doña Pancha's wailing.

When the casket meets earth and the sound stops, Oscar finally looks up, and there's a wild look of panic in his eyes. He screams, "¡Mamá!" and lunges toward the opening in the grave as if intending to dive into it.

Ramiro's hands pull from Carolina and me, and he rushes forward to intercept Oscar. He barely grabs onto the back of Oscar's shirt in time and pulls him back before he reaches his goal.

"No!" Oscar screams. "Let me go!"

Ramiro's hand stays fisted firmly on Oscar's now drenched shirt, no longer under the cover of Doña Pancha's umbrella. Then Ramiro falls to his knees and spins Oscar around by his shoulders. He takes the little boy in his arms, and for a moment, Oscar fights it. Those tiny fists punch at Ramiro's sides, but Ramiro stays put in his embrace of the little guy.

All of us around them are stunned into silence because no one fucking deserves this kind of pain. Not Ramiro, and definitely not Oscar and René.

Eventually, Oscar stops fighting, and his cheek falls to Ramiro's shoulder, his sobs down to hiccups.

"I know, buddy," Ramiro says, rubbing his back. "I'm here,"

he says, just loud enough for me to hear over the rain. "I'll always be here." Ramiro lets his cheek fall to the top of Oscar's head. Fat raindrops roll down Ramiro's close-shaved head and onto Oscar's black, unruly waves.

If there's one thing I know to be true about Ramiro Jimenez, it's that he's a man of his word.

That promise he just made?

It transformed him into a single father of two little boys before my very eyes.

The velorio, or repast, takes place at Don Gustavo's, a choice that made both Carolina and me very nervous when we heard the plans. In the end, it was Doña Pancha's choice, which we decided to respect, but I won't lie and say we aren't walking on eggshells around Don Calixto, Ramiro's dad, and Don Gustavo.

"Ramiro looks a lot like his dad, doesn't he?" I ask Carolina as I watch father and son, standing tall—eyes completely dry despite the surrounding sniffles.

Carolina looks up from her barely touched plate of food and follows my stare. "Yeah. Both are very handsome, though I think Don Calixto is a little better looking. I like the gray in his beard."

I roll my eyes at my friend. "Why do you always go for the older guy? If you didn't have such an amazing dad, I'd think you have daddy issues."

Carolina shrugs. "It's just the look, I guess. I know objectively that Ramiro is handsome, but I've never been attracted physically to his type."

My jaw drops a little. Not attracted to his type? The perfect, muscular, handsome type? Maybe our friendship works so well because our taste in men is so different.

As we watch, it's hard to ignore how Don Gustavo avoids any room Don Calixto is in and vice versa.

I've never fully understood the rivalry between Don Calixto and Don Gustavo, but Carolina reassures me it runs deep.

The apple didn't fall far from the tree, and for his age, Don Calixto is a very handsome man. His brown skin has deepened further in his recent Floridian retirement, deep brown eyes framed by the same long lashes that grace Ramiro's beautiful eyes.

But there's a hardness to him, and not only because we've just attended his daughter-in-law's funeral. Not an ounce of feeling has crossed his stoic expression. I only really ever saw him at the various neighborhood events and family cookouts before they moved away, so I'd assumed his coolness was a permanent state of being. I realize now, of course, it deepens when Don Gustavo is around, and hardens into a distasteful glare.

As I watch him at the velorio today, it's hard to miss his back stiffening whenever Don Gustavo steps into a room, followed swiftly by Don Calixto exiting said room. They're cordial with each other, but it doesn't seem to extend beyond that.

Apart from the age difference and Ramiro's slightly taller frame, the only distinguishing factor between father and son is Don Calixto's dark waves, neatly combed back, contrasted to Ramiro's neatly trimmed head, giving him a near-bald look.

From my spot sitting on a bench near the dining room, I watch as Don Gustavo approaches the buffet table, making Don Calixto drop the serving spoon in his hand and walk away immediately before his plate is full.

I'm not usually nosey—okay, maybe I am, a little—but it's been hard to miss the animosity.

"What happened?" I ask Carolina, eyeing the plate on her lap full of asado rojo, rice, and a few tortillas.

"What?" she asks.

"Between Don Calixto and Don Gustavo. Why does Ramiro's dad look like he wants to murder your dad? I heard they were best friends when you were growing up. Isn't that why they used to joke around that you and Ramiro would marry when you grew up, to join the families?"

Carolina scoffs. "Don't remind me. And yes, when my mom was still alive, she and Doña Rocio were best friends, and Don Calixto and Dad were too. They were inseparable. But after Mom died, Ramiro spent a lot of time with Dad and me. Taking care of us, you know?"

I smile. Of course, young teenage Ramiro would have done something like that.

"It really connected him and Dad. Eventually, he ventured into Dad's garage and fell in love with working on cars. Don Calixto hasn't been able to forgive my dad, which is ridiculous because Dad didn't even do anything."

"Wow," I say and grab her plate from her to steal a few bites.

"Hey, that's mine," she whines, and we allow ourselves a small giggle. So absent from this day, the laughter is like coming up for fresh air after nearly drowning. My chest is so tight from the pain and the crying. It's a relief to have Carolina by my side. And a bigger relief our little community all showed up for Ramiro and Doña Pancha today.

Ileana, who lives a couple of blocks over, brought a big batch of asado rojo, my favorite dish of hers—pork in red sauce. And Don Gustavo made rice and handmade corn tortillas. Sofia, our best friend, brought several bottles of tequila and whiskey from her bar to spike our coffees with.

Few of Ramiro's friends showed up since most of them are in the military and couldn't find themselves in Kansas City for this. Leo Moreno, his best friend from childhood, is in the Army, and so are most of the guys they used to run with.

Ramiro isn't alone, though. His parents flew in from Florida, and he has Carolina, Don Gustavo, and me.

I hand the plate back to Carolina—with only half her food remaining—and she keeps nibbling at it. "That's too bad, for such a long friendship to end over something so silly."

"It's not silly to Don Calixto. He had grand plans for his son to take over his law practice when he retired."

I snort. "Can you imagine Ramiro as a lawyer? Wearing a suit every day of his life?" I shake my head. As dashing as he is today in a suit, his large physique, square jaw, and bald head are much better suited to his usual jeans and tee or ribbed tank.

"I know. He'd be miserable."

"He did the right thing," I say.

"Tell that to Don Calixto," Carolina deadpans. "But yeah, in Don Calixto's eyes, my dad stole his son from his predestined future—"

"You mean like the predestined future that you'd marry Ramiro one day?"

Carolina laughs. "I'm sure Don Calixto is relieved I didn't let that happen. We'd all be family then, and he'd never escape Dad."

That wouldn't be so bad, I think, for our families to come together like that. If Francisca hadn't died and everything had gone to plan, Ramiro would have joined her family and surely distanced himself from the Ramirez household. Even though this outcome is tragic, I can't help but feel a little guilty to be glad Ramiro isn't lost to us just yet. Though Carolina may not be in love with him, I know she loves him as she would a brother.

Rocio has her arm laced through her son's as they walk to Carolina and me.

"Caro, mi niña, I'm so glad you're here," Rocio says. Her eyes are red-rimmed and swollen as she pulls Carolina in for a kiss. "Thank you for being here for my boy."

Hard to believe that not two weeks ago, Doña Rocio was helping Francisca with her wedding preparations.

"Of course, Doña Rocio. Please let me know how I can help in the coming days," Caro says.

"Yes, thank you," Ramiro says, but his voice is sullen, hollow, and somehow robotic all at the same time. He kisses Carolina on the cheek, she returns it, then he turns to me, doing the same.

When his lips grace my skin, I feel all my blood rush to my cheeks. Then I hate myself a little for the inappropriate reaction. This is the worst time to blush from the chastest of kisses, but it's the first time since I've known Ramiro that I've felt his lips on me. Though a kiss on the cheek is the proper greeting of respect, somehow, Ramiro has managed to avoid it with me since I've known him—until now, when he's in the presence of his mother, who would undoubtedly say something about his rudeness if he didn't.

After years of dreaming about those full lips on my skin, my body was bound to react, but I feel like the shittiest human ever at my involuntary response, given the circumstances.

I'm such an asshole.

Thankfully, he notices nothing, and neither do Rocio and Carolina, it seems. I gulp my soda, resisting the urge to press the icy glass to my face to cool it down.

I've completely missed whatever the three of them are talking about when Doña Rocio turns to me. "Sara, could I have a moment with you?"

I look between her and Ramiro, taken aback by her request for a private conversation with me.

"You can go upstairs to my old room," Carolina offers.

Ramiro unlaces his mom's arm from his and pats the top of

her hand. He takes my seat next to Carolina as I walk away with Doña Rocio.

As we leave to go upstairs, I allow myself one glimpse back at them.

Ramiro and Carolina absolutely look perfect together—like they were made for each other. I understand why their parents wanted them together.

Carolina is nearly as tall as Ramiro. Her shade of beautiful brown skin is almost as dark as his, making her amber eyes pop. She's elegant, graceful, poised—everything I'm not. A parent's absolute dream. A driven doctor who looks like a bombshell. Even if Carolina won't entertain the idea of dating Ramiro, watching them together and knowing that their shared history runs deep forces my thoughts away from my dreams of one day being with him.

"Close the door, mija," Doña Rocio says.

"Sure."

She sits on the edge of Carolina's bed, and I flip around Carolina's old desk chair to take a seat in front of her.

"Sara, I need your help."

As much as Ramiro avoided me over the years, Doña Rocio always included me in her family plans. Just as Don Gustavo invited me into his home, Doña Rocio did the same. She's done so much for me and been there for me when I've needed a support system almost as much as Don Gustavo. Up until her move to Florida, we spent a lot of time together. I'd do pretty much anything for the only positive mother figure I've had in my life.

"Anything I can do, Doña Rocio—"

She cuts me off with a wave of her hand. "None of this 'Doña' business. It makes me feel old." She smiles a bit mischievously, like she's being sarcastic.

I smile back. "Rocio," I correct myself. It's a constant battle we've had since it goes against everything I've learned, to not use the respectful form of address for my elders. "Anything I can do to help."

"Calixto and I have flights to head back to Florida in a couple of days. I wanted to extend my stay, but Ramiro is as bullheaded as his father."

"He won't let you stay and help, will he?"

"Of course not! Have you met those men? And Calixto is no better. He's raised his son on tough love, and if it were up to him, we'd leave Ramiro to sort everything out by himself so he can adapt to his new situation."

"You mean Oscar and René?"

Rocio nods. "Yes."

"You think he'll become their guardian?"

"He'll do anything he can to make that happen. I know my son."

"Okay." I take a deep breath. "What can I do to help?"

"Ramiro won't grieve, not like he needs to, but he also doesn't have the first idea of how to raise two little boys on his own. He's going to need help, and I think a woman's hand, especially for the boys, could be very soothing to them all."

"Errr," I scratch my head nervously. "Shouldn't Carolina be the one to—"

"She'll help. Initially, I'm sure. But you know what her schedule as a doctor is like. And yes, I know a nurse's schedule is also hectic, but you could try, couldn't you? To spend some of that time here? Help with the boys?"

There's no way to say no to her in this situation, is there?

How could I sit here and say, ma'am, your son can hardly stand to be in the same room with me? He avoids me almost as much as your husband avoids Don Gustavo. I'd sound like an asshole, which we've established already that I am.

And yet, I can't bring myself to deny his mother this little comfort before she returns to her everyday life.

"Sure Doñ—" I clear my throat. "Rocio. I'm happy to help as

much as I can. I'll keep an eye on them, and you're right. I can ask for a more regular schedule or the night shift, at least for a while. I've been at Heartland Metro Hospital long enough to feel comfortable making that request. I'm due for some vacation days soon, so that will help."

"Thank you, Mija," she says, palming the side of my face.

We stand, and before I can stop myself, the question is flying out of my mouth, "Why me?"

That mischievous smile is back, tugging at the corner of her mouth. "Some things are just meant to be," she says.

I look after her as she walks out of Carolina's childhood room, leaving me to wonder what on earth that could possibly mean.

Keep reading Sara and Ramiro's story in *Sensation*, a steamy, slow-burn, single dad, forced proximity romance in the Heartland Metro world.

ABOUT THE AUTHOR

Ofelia Martinez is a Mexican-American author. Originally from the Texas border, Ofelia now resides in Missouri with her partner and their dog, Pixel.

This is Ofelia's second book after *Remission*.

She loves good books, tequila, and chocolate. She proudly shares a birthday with Usagi Tsukino. When not writing, you can find Ofelia making visual art.

Visit OfeliaMartinez.com to learn more.

facebook.com/OMartinezAuthor
twitter.com/OMartinezAuthor
instagram.com/omartinezauthor

9 781954 906037